CONSPIRACY UNVEILED

CONSPIRACY UNVEILED

Book Two in the Conspiracy Series

JOHN BERTUCCI

First Printing: April 2023

ISBN: 978-1-955541-10-7

Library of Congress Number: Pending

Cover and Interior Design: Ann Aubitz

Published by FuzionPress
1250 East 115th Street, Burnsville, MN 55337
612-781-2815

"If there was hope, it must lie in the proles, because only there in those swarming disregarded masses, 85 per cent of the population of Oceania, could the force to destroy the Party ever be generated."
~Orwell, author of *1984*

"The opposite of love is not hate, it's indifference. The opposite of art is not ugliness, it's indifference. The opposite of faith is not heresy, it's indifference. And the opposite of life is not death, it's indifference."
~Elie Wiesel, author and Holocaust survivor

"Our struggle is not easy. Those who oppose our cause are rich and powerful and they have many allies in high places. We are poor. Our allies are few. But we have something the rich do not own. We have our bodies and spirits and the justice of our cause as our weapons."
~Caesar Chavez, American labor leader and civil rights activist

*To LaVonne who has been on this
ride with me all these years.*

ACKNOWLEDGEMENTS

I would like to thank my publisher, Ann Aubitz, of Fuzion Press. Ann has worked closely with me on three books over the last several years, and she has been a huge help in bringing my works to life on the page. I would also like to thank Connie Anderson, my editor, who has been a wonderful partner in producing two novels. She is careful to allow my voice to come through my works and offers suggestions and asks questions that are so beneficial to the final document.

I am also grateful for all the teachers in my life, from St. John's School, St. Lawrence Seminary, Northern Michigan University, and the University of Minnesota-TC. They molded me into the writer I am today. There were no greater teachers though than my parents, grandparents, uncles and aunts, brothers and sisters, mothers and fathers-in-law, and cousins. Family is so integral to anyone's early and future nurturing. I would like to thank my wife, children, their spouses, and my grandchildren for making my life so rich and full of fun. Finally, a thank you to my colleagues everywhere, and to all those teachers who struggle daily to do one of the most important and difficult jobs in the world.

CHAPTER 1

The Upper Peninsula of Michigan

Majestic lakes, beautiful luscious green forests, wild trails that lead everywhere and nowhere, and animals like deer, coyotes, wolves, black bears, cougars, moose, maybe even a last wolverine, you name them, they are there. Rolling falls, the Pictured Rocks, pristine shorelines, and Brockway Mountain, highest above sea-level in the Midwest, with outstanding vistas of Lake Superior. This is the Upper Peninsula of Michigan—the U.P.

Those who are born there call themselves Yoopers, and even if they move away, they always remain Yoopers. Some who move there become honorary Yoopers. The Upper Peninsula is a wonderful place to live or to vacation. It's a land situated among three Great Lakes. Any season will do for those who love it there. Summer in the U.P. is grand, and it is perfect for most winter sports. But recently, it has become a haven for some people who would like very much to change, not only the Upper Peninsula, but the country. The U.P. just happens to be one of several spots where some very crafty and stealthy individuals are planning something sinister.

Since this is not occurring only in the U.P., where else might this be happening? It's everywhere, in every state, but there are seven hot spots, and one is hidden in the forests in the U.P. These sinister people have infiltrated every group, left and right, every political party, every level of government. They don't want to just change the country—they want to take over, and they have a huge event planned for the future, but no one knows what or when that will be.

Is that really possible? You bet it is.

Somewhere in the U.P., sometime in spring, 2021

Joe was terrified. His hands were bound, his feet tied, a cloth bag was over his head, a gag was stuffed in his mouth, and his head was still spinning from being knocked out. What the hell had just happened? He could hear someone talking, and now it all made sense. What had he gotten into this time? Ron was about four feet to his left. He was also tied up and gagged. Joe heard the men talking about a hole that had been dug right in front of him and Ron. Joe was sick to his stomach because he had gotten Ron into this mess. How in the world would they get out of here? Joe froze. He could not even think anymore—the barrel of a rifle had been placed at the back of his head.

CHAPTER 2

Michigan, February 16

The trip was almost over. The ride from Tampa, Florida, had taken them sixteen hours so far. It had been a couple of eventful years for the foursome sitting in the Chevy Suburban as it moved north on I-75 headed to a home in Michigan, north of the Detroit area. Their discovery—that a hidden conspiracy was developing in an attempt to divide citizens of the United States and to create such a division that it would take down the government—was driving them crazy. They had heard from one of the leaders that an event was to take place, but they did not know what or who was involved. They wanted to find out. They were returning to Michigan after trying to take down one of the leaders, so they could slow down the group.

The situation was such that they knew some rich oligarchs were spearheading the group, and they wanted to find out who the key individuals were, but it seemed to be beyond their capabilities. These very rich individuals were organizing the event and getting people to join by enticing them with tax-free dollars. Who was doing this?

Joe and Ron were now in the front seat, and their wives, Joette and Shanice, were asleep in the back. The two men had years of experience working in clandestine operations for the military and sometimes the FBI and CIA, but they were getting older now, and they were not as adept at their trade as they had been. They knew they had to get younger, more experienced people involved—and that was their next plan. They had a close call in Florida, and they never expected that their wives would have to help bail them out. Putting them in harm's way was not the plan. But, thanks to their wives, they were all saved from a near disastrous situation.

Ron and Joe had retired from their military involvement and both decided to go into the classroom and teach young students— *to make a difference.* They had both stayed in great shape and felt like they could go on forever, but they knew that wasn't the case.

"We're about an hour from my son's home. It'll be nice to be able to stretch our legs and get a good meal," Ron said as he left the interstate and headed there.

"It sure will be," Joe said. He was thinking about the event that they had heard about earlier. Joe was concerned and he said, "I wonder what will happen next?"

"Are you referring to the event?"

"Yes."

Ron was concerned too. "Good question."

Joe was sure that Ann, their FBI contact, should be their next stop. "We have a lot of questions to answer. Ann will be curious about our trip. I'm not sure how we will explain what happened. Maybe we should not even tell her about this trip, or maybe just give her a heads-up on that guy."

Joe and Ron had acted against Ann's warnings not to get involved. She was inflexible when it came to vigilante tactics. Even though she had worked with the two men many years ago when they were working with the military on some covert operations, she knew they were no longer a part of that, and she was concerned they might act on their own.

Joette awoke in the back seat. "What are you talking about? I wouldn't be too worried about anyone else right now. Let's find out how you both stand in Colewin." Joe had worked as a teacher in the U.P. in Colewin and had been accused of crimes by people who did not like him. "Are you still being sought after by the law? I wonder if I should call Cathy and find out." Cathy lived in Colewin, and she and her husband Wayne had been good friends of Joe and Joette, but they had not seen nor spoken with them for almost two years.

Joe agreed and said, "That might be a good idea. Who knows how many people will be looking for us? Surely this group is. What we have done should mess them up for a time, but it won't be forever." Earlier, Joe and Ron had been taken by the group of insurgents and had been designated for elimination for snooping around the group's hidden base in the U.P. They had been trying to find out what was going on—and had stumbled onto something much larger than they had ever anticipated.

Ron was concerned. "What's our plan now when we get back? Man, they have a lot of people involved, and they don't really care what they do."

Joette said, "We should start by finding out if the authorities in Colewin are still after you. We haven't heard anything from them since we left. We can't keep running and hope they don't catch up to us. We need to resolve this, so I think if we call Cathy and Wayne, we could get an update."

Shanice had also awakened and heard the discussion. She added, "That sounds good. Let's decide about our next steps when we're a bit more settled and can think clearly."

The ride proceeded quietly for a while. They had less than an hour before they arrived at Ron's son's home, and they were all tired. Ron's son lived between Detroit and Flint. The drive had been intense after what they had been through, and they were not sure if someone might be following them. They knew that once the story was out, if it wasn't already, they would be hunted by the group.

CHAPTER 3

Colewin, February 17

Charlie had been laying low for some time now. He wanted to get the few people he had left in his militia to begin training as soon as the weather cleared, but he had a quandary. His base, and especially his bunker, had been taken over by some over-zealous types who wanted to overthrow the government. He was not happy. Some of his own people had joined up with these insurgents for the money, and they now were no longer a part of his group. He wasn't sure where to turn. Even Sheriff Daryl had turned on him. How did that ever happen? They had been best of friends. Together, they even set up that teacher, Joe, and his friend. That was a mess. The two women that had accused him of sexual assault had been arrested and now the teacher was free. Damn! He had to call Sam to see what he was up to, and to figure out whether they could get their base back. "Hello, Sam?"

"Yeah, what you want, Charlie?"

"Wonderin' if we could get the old militia group together again. Maybe get some of the others who walked out of the last meetin' to join up too."

"What you plannin'?"

"Gonna take the base back."

"How the hell you gonna do that? We ain't got enough men or weapons. Those people have everything. I even saw some tanks the last time we were there. Tanks! What the hell!"

"I know, but we gotta do it. They ain't gonna throw this government out the window. We're gonna take over, and then we're gonna change the government."

"You got a plan?"

"Not yet, but it ain't gonna be purty. We're gonna kick their asses!"

1,500 miles away

The new interim boss who wanted the old boss's job was concerned for the event. The committee had built a huge network, and the assigned leader, the old boss that Joe and Ron had hurt, was in trouble and was recovering very slowly. This new boss who could and wanted to take his place permanently was aggressive and ruthless, and he wanted to be given the reins to move the event forward his way. He asked Randall, "What happened to the old boss? Where is he?"

"All I can tell you is we were outsmarted when we tried to get those two. We should have had a better plan. The boss thought that we could take care of it with the four of us and him. It didn't work out that way. I'm the only one not in the hospital right now, and we can't find Dominic. He was in the limo backing us up, and we were going to take out those two and their wives if we had to, but they outsmarted us. They took the limo, but we haven't found it yet."

"Why did the boss meet with them? He never does that, and how in the world did they pull that off? You are well-trained and some of the best we have."

"Not sure how it happened, but it did. Sergei and Stepan are still in the hospital too." Sergei has a broken ankle, and Stepan has a dislocated knee. I have a black eye, and I lost three teeth, but other than that, I'm all right."

"Will the boss survive?"

"Not sure yet. The doctors said he is in rough shape, but they are doing the best they can. Hopefully, he comes around."

"Well, keep looking for the limo! I'll let the committee members know what is going on, and that we have a problem. This will set us back a bit. We'll have to make some contingency plans for the event. We'll also have to contact all of our bases and make sure they are on hold."

"Sounds good. I'll keep you in the loop if anything changes."

"Right. Let me know right away if the boss comes around. I think we'll have to use some different tactics. The old boss was too soft with those two. It's time to just take them out. Go with our plan."

Randall nodded, yes. He knew what he had to do.

CHAPTER 4

Lower Michigan, Between Flint and Detroit

The Suburban came to a stop. The four people inside crawled out and stretched as they headed for Ron's son's house. Seventeen hours in a car with only a few stops for gas and other necessities was grueling.

"We should all take a long nap," Ron yawned.

"For sure. We need to get some rest before doing anything, especially talking to Ann. I wonder what she found out about the billionaire Adler." Adler was a member of the billionaire committee that was financing groups of men to overthrow the government.

"I'll give her a call after we rest."

Ron's son walked out to meet the group. He worked as a computer programmer, but recently, he had been helping to search for information to help his father and Joe. He was a sly one when it came to investigating individuals. He wasn't too happy to see these four retirees doing what should be left to the FBI, but he knew why they had to act. He was hoping that their adventures would come to a halt now. "How was your trip?"

"Long and stressful," Ron responded.

"I'm just glad you made it back safely. Not sure I agree with the four of you doing what you are doing, but I get it. Come on in and get something to eat and rest up a bit."

Shanice was very happy to see her son. "It's so great to see you. We've missed you. I hope we can stay here a while and just rest up and visit and get to play with our grandchildren."

"You can stay as long as you want. The kids will be delighted."

The Bunker, east of Colewin, February 18

Bates had been working for several hours, and he was getting tired. He was the tech expert and troop coordinator for a huge area at the secret base in the U.P., and he had been on the committee's payroll for several years. It had been a long week for him trying to organize everything in the bunker, and he was getting upset at all the people who kept coming in and bothering him while he was trying to get his work completed. They were a bunch of bullies who thought they were better than he was. They liked pushing him around and making him feel like he was nothing. He was contemplating what he had done to Charlie when he had told him the base no longer belonged to his militia. Charlie was pissed and said he would get the base back. Not any more with all the equipment and troops that were here now.

Just then the door opened and in walked three of the troops with assault rifles over their shoulders and wearing military gear. "Hey, you got any cold beer?"

"That fridge is my personal stuff. Go get your own if you want some." Bates had left the doors unlocked, and he decided that they would never be unlocked again.

"Yeah, well, we're here and we're thirsty, so what's yours is ours." The bully walked to the fridge and opened it and handed his two buddies a cold beer. "Here you go. Let's take the rest of these for the troops on the field." He and the other two took all the beer and some of the other beverages that Bates had in his fridge.

"It's twenty-five degrees out there. Why do you need a beer?"

"We're thirsty. Been running around this place all day."

"You're going to pay for those if you take them."

"Sure. Yeah. Come and collect." All three laughed as they left the bunker.

"Bastards. They don't care what they do, and they don't care about anything except playing war games. Idiots."

Bates was concerned because he had learned that the person that he thought was in charge of the event had been taken to the hospital. He heard some of the story, and he was certain that the people who put him there were the two that he sent away to be eliminated. At least the information he had, had indicated that. *How did they escape? How had that happened?* He was told that the event and the movement of troops would now be delayed, and that he should keep everything quiet until he heard from the boss, or whoever would take the boss's place.

He was fuming and said aloud, "That means these idiots are going to be here longer. They will make a mess of everything here. They are so rowdy. I'll have to get in touch with someone to find out what to do."

CHAPTER 5

Near Flint, February 18

Joe and Ron had spent some time debriefing the why and how of the operation they had just completed. It was really a rogue action on their part. After all, Ann, the FBI contact, had told them not to proceed with any freelance activity. They didn't listen, and now they knew they had to tell her, so the FBI could assist in taking down the organization.

"We need to contact Ann today and tell her what we did and what we learned," Joe said rather nonchalantly.

"I know we do. This won't be a lot of fun," Ron added.

"Nope. But that's all right. We had to do it. The government's hands are tied. Ours aren't."

"It would be great if we could visit with her face-to-face. I don't like phone calls. Too easy to get things messed up, and we won't be able to see her body language because I think she'll actually be happy with what we've learned." Ron half smiled as he spoke.

Joe sat up slowly and stretched. He was well rested now, as was Ron, and both were anxious to get this over with. "I guess we could call and set up a meeting. What do you think?"

"Let's do it."

Joe pulled out his phone and called Ann. She picked up on the second ring. "I've been waiting for a call from you. I hope this is about getting some protection because you have kept yourselves in hiding the last few weeks."

"Right," Joe said as he also cracked a big smile. "We were really hoping we could meet with you again soon. This time could it be inside? The last meeting was very cold and we ended up with two SUVs on our tail."

"Okay, now I know something is up. Your call is about what you have done, isn't it, not what you need?"

Joe again had a big smile. "Yep. You nailed it. Time and place?"

"Let me get back to you. I have a lot going on right now, and I'll have to make some adjustments to my schedule. I'll get back to you soon."

"All right. Talk to you then."

Ron looked at Joe and shook his head as if to say "no meeting." Joe looked up and nodded, then he said, "She'll call back."

CHAPTER 6

Colewin, Friday, February 19

The phone buzzed and Cathy picked it up. It was her lunch break and she had a few more minutes before she had to head back to her class. Without looking, she picked up her phone and answered, "Hello."

"Hello. Is this Cathy?"

"Yes, it is. Who's calling?"

"Cathy, it's me, Joette."

Cathy almost screamed into her phone. She had not seen or heard from Joette for almost two years. "Joette, how are you and where are you?"

"Ah, well, I'm fine, but I'd rather not say where I am in case the law is still after Joe, but I wanted to talk to you and explain what happened and also to find out if Joe is still being hunted by the authorities."

Joe had been wrongfully accused by a woman for attacking her sexually, and he was also unjustly accused of abusing one of his female students. He had been jailed, but when out on bail he had been taken by some devious people. Soon after, he was wanted for breaking bail.

"Joette, Joe has been cleared of any wrongdoing, and Ron has also been cleared for assisting Joe. We've been very upset and scared since you left. We've been harassed by some people. We think they had something to do with your disappearance. Wayne has had to keep a low profile because of this. He knows something is not right."

"Really? That sounds like this group. Thank God that Joe and Ron are cleared. These people are not very nice. In fact, they tried to eliminate us. We're trying to do something about it."

"Well, Wayne tells me that he and Tommy have kept an eye on the area that you said had something sinister going on—and was a bunker for military supplies and training. They say that the area has been built up and huge amounts of weapons and people are there. The place has been expanded, according to them."

"You'll need to keep your guard up because this movement is a big one, and there are a lot of rich people involved who will do anything to overthrow the government."

"Oh, my gosh. What next? You know that about ten months ago our capitol building in Lansing was stormed by people with assault rifles and who knows what else."

"I had heard something about that. I wonder if they're the same people?"

"Not sure of anything. We're just afraid for our lives. We lost contact with Tommy a few days ago, and now we fear for him."

"Oh, no. Maybe we can help. Hopefully he's all right. Cathy, I have to go, but I will keep in touch. Maybe we will be able to swing by there in the near future. Take care."

"You too. Hope to see you soon. Bye."

Saturday, February 20, 12:07 p.m.
"Ron, you're sure you want to stay? We could try to find a place to hide again. They'll surely be after us."

"I guess we just want to spend some time with our grandchildren. We'll keep in touch though."

Ann had called and set up a meeting with Ron and Joe. She suspected they had acted on their own, and she was not happy.

Joe said, "We'll have to meet with Ann first and see what she has to say. Then we'll head back and visit Colewin now that we're cleared. There are a few people that I'd like to check in on who were part of railroading us in Colewin."

"That I like. You'll have to let me know what some of them say. Not so sure it'll be a fun trip though. Bad memories."

"That's for sure."

"Let's head over to the meeting place and see what Ann has to say," Ron said.

The meeting with Ann was scheduled for 2:00 p.m. in Auburn Hills at a Marriott Hotel. They were not familiar with the place, but when Joe searched for driving directions, it indicated about an hour from where they were. Joe and Ron hopped in the car and left just after noon, giving them enough time to check out the place prior to the meeting and to allow for traffic.

Almost two hours later

Joe was glad they had arrived, but he was still not sure where this might lead, especially if Ann had been compromised, so he was cautious. He turned to Ron who had just parked the car and said, "This is the place. We need to walk around and check it out a little. Ann said someone will be in the lobby to direct us. We'll have to see if this is kosher. You never know what could be going on."

Ron thought they should split up until they were certain that everything was good. "You take the front entrance, and I'll wait a few minutes and see if I can enter through the side where those people are heading. If I can catch the door before it closes, I can enter from the side."

"That sounds like a plan. Let's go. Make sure your phone is on," Joe said.

"Got it."

Joe left first and walked to the front door. He entered and looked around. He saw only three people, plus two people at the desk. He walked slowly looking from left to right. A woman got up and walked close to him, but she just exited the building. Then a man stepped in front of him.

"You Joe?"

"Who wants to know?"

The man looked unshaven and was wearing a long-sleeved T-shirt. Not something he expected from the FBI.

"Ann. Follow me."

It wasn't long before Joe was standing in front of a door. The man knocked some kind of code and the door opened. A tall muscular guy answered the door. This was more of what Joe was expecting. He saw Ann sitting at a table with papers all over the place. He also noticed two other men who looked quite serious. Then Ron showed up behind him. He thought *why so many people? I thought this was going to be another one-on-one conversation.*

"Come on in, Mr. DeLuca."

"Hello, Ann. Good to see you. Why all the stealthy stuff?"

"You'll know soon enough." Then Ron peeked around the corner of the door. "And hello to you too, Ron. Why don't you both take a seat. This could take some time."

Ron and Joe said "Thank you" in unison.

"Let's get right to the point. Where have you been this past week?"

"Just relaxing and enjoying retirement," Joe said.

Ron agreed and added, "Yep, been great."

"Sure, you have. You realize that we are the FBI. We know you were in Florida, and we know it wasn't for a vacation. We just need to know what you were doing there."

"Vacationing. We took our wives on a long overdue trip. Right, Ron?"

"Right. It was a lot of fun."

"Okay, let me tell you what we know. First of all, this group is big and getting bigger by the day. They have billions of dollars, but we can't trace where all the money originates. We know a lot of it comes from overseas, and we think the headquarters is also overseas. Second, both of you are in big trouble. An informant of ours put both of you in Tampa where a person of interest that we were investigating ended up in the hospital. He has not recovered yet. We were making some real progress following him, but now the lead we had has gone dry. We think you had something to do with why one of the leaders we are investigating ended in the hospital in some kind of coma."

"Why would you think that?"

"Because it sounded like the two of you again. It's your MOS."

"We're not sure what you are talking about, but I hope it means that some rich SOB is out of commission," Joe said, half in anger.

"We're not sure what the situation is now because we no longer have him to follow and lead us to other people in the loop. Thanks to you guys."

Ron was sitting with his arms folded and said, "Sounds like he might have deserved what he got."

"We don't know what or if he deserved anything, but since this, we know you were involved in some way because there is an order to eliminate the two of you on sight—and your wives if they are with you."

That shook up Ron and Joe. They stayed long enough to give Ann the whole story and then left, knowing they probably would need to hide out again for a while.

CHAPTER 7

Colewin, February 20

Charlie had a plan. He figured if he could get enough of the old troops together, they could take a run at the bunker and drive everyone out of there, but first he needed to resupply his troops and get some weapons that could help them defeat those bastards. Where could he turn? He thought he should contact Bates again and tell him that he needed to collect all of his equipment that was still at the bunker, but last time he talked to Bates, he told him not to return or he would be eliminated. The one thing he had going for him was that he knew Bates was pissed at all the troops who were there now. He was especially tired of them calling him master. They were bullies and misfits who would just as soon shoot Bates as talk to him. They had little class. If Charlie could contact Bates, he might be able to convince him that the other guys were not good for him, and he should let Charlie help him some.

Charlie had Bates' old phone number, so he gave it a try. "Hello? This Bates?"

"Yeah, what you want, Charlie?"

"Well, I'm calling you 'cause I got a lot of equipment there yet, and I need it 'cause we're startin' up again."

"You know the answer to that, Charlie."

"I figured you might change your mind since you got all those guys buggin' you. I 'member the last time I was there and they kept harassin' you. They're no good, man. You want us to help you get rid of 'em?"

"Charlie, are you crazy? You know what would happen to you if you even got close to this place? They have twenty-four-hour sentries, cameras, machine guns, mines, night goggles, and anything else you can think of. You would need anti-tank guns, mortars, maybe even drones to get in here. How are you going to do that?"

"That's all good, but we know this territory better 'n anyone, and so thanks for the heads up. If you won't help, we'll find someone who will. Hope you survive."

"Yeah, good riddance!"

Colewin, Monday, February 22

Tommy was hiding in the old cabin on the ridge where Wyatt, the guy who shot his Uncle George and a cop a while back, used to live. His bear hunting season guiding Fudgies or Trolls (nicknames for those who live below the Mackinac Bridge in Lower Michigan) had been great, and he really wanted to just kick back for a couple of months, but he ran into some trouble. He was still angry about what happened to his Uncle George, so he was constantly investigating as best he could. He had made a couple of trips out to the bunker to see what he could find out, and that is when the trouble started. Now he was being hunted by this group. He shouldn't have been so open when he went to the bunker, but he didn't know about all the new people and equipment. Bates had to get him out of there, or he would have been killed.

Wendy, Tommy's girlfriend, was the only person who knew where he was. Wendy picked up her phone and called him. "Tommy, you need to stop hiding. Why are you out there?"

"You know why. I told you. That same group that killed Uncle George is now after me. I went out to the bunker to find out who might have been involved in my uncle's death, but I found out that the place had expanded big time, and those troops were belligerent, so I got out of there as quickly as I could."

"What do you mean? Someone is trying to kill you?"

"Exactly what I said! You need to keep safe too. Who knows what they could do? I'm sure that they don't know that we're together, so we need to keep it that way right now. Don't call anymore. You know where I am. Take the back road out here if you want to see me and make sure no one is following you."

"Oh, Tommy, I am so afraid."

"You should be okay. Just keep out of sight, and don't talk to any strangers or the law. You know we think that Sheriff Daryl is a part of this."

"All right. I won't use my phone. I'll meet you out there tomorrow after work."

"I've been working on cleaning the place out because the inside was torched, but the structure is in good shape. I have a lot of tools with me, but bring cleaning supplies if you can. I'm almost out. I've torn out all the burned cabinets, beds, couch, and a lot of other junk, so it's habitable now, but just."

"Okay, I'll get as much as I can. My mom and dad will help if you want."

"Sure. Just be sure they know the whole story. We can use all the help we can get. Oh, and can you tell Uncle George's wife Sherry that I am good?"

"Sure. See you tomorrow. Love you."

"Love you too."

CHAPTER 8

Near Flint, Monday, February 22

Ron and Joe had been pacing for hours, wondering what to do. After talking with Ann, they knew they had to do something quickly, and they had to inform their families. They were being hunted now. According to Ann, after their little trip to Florida, when the boss was taken out of commission, the leadership of the organization changed. Joe and Ron thought it would set the group back, but that organization was so large that they just moved on. This new boss, whoever he was, was ruthless.

Ann had offered protection, but they felt that would just make their lives more restrictive than they had been. They needed to be able to move and keep whoever was after them confused about where they were, and they didn't want anyone, since they suspected everyone, to know where they were. After being arrested by Sheriff Daryl in the Upper Peninsula, they were afraid to trust anyone they did not know well.

"What do you think, Joe?"

"I'm not sure, Ron, but, as I said earlier, one thing I need to do is get back to the U.P. and finish investigating. There are a few people there I would like to give a piece of my mind. What we went through was not necessary. I mean I was accused by two women and taken away by some vigilantes, and you were taken just because you helped me. Our wives were abducted and were sent to who knows what kind of fate."

Ron said, "I understand. I'm frustrated too, but I think I'm going to stay close to my family. We'll find a place to hide out until this calms down, but we need to keep in touch."

"That's a good idea. We should make it harder for them to find us. We can rendezvous later when we can get a bit more information. We should stay in contact daily in case anything occurs that we should both know."

"Agreed."

"It's been several days since we left Florida, so my guess is that they'll have a lead on us soon. They may already know where we are. Joette and I are going to head north tomorrow. We'll take the Corolla. You and Shanice have the Camaro, right?"

"Right. We aren't sure when we'll leave, but I think we all need to get away from here as soon as possible."

1,500 miles away

It had been a while since he had talked to the new boss, and he thought it was time to give him an update, so he pulled out his phone and called.

"Hello? Is this Ivan?"

"Why do you want to know? Who is calling?"

"This is your number one contact. We have information about those two that you requested. We now know that they did not fly anywhere. We found Dominic bound in the limo we sent. He told us that the last he knew, they were on their way to fly out, so we checked everything. We could not find any individuals who left around that time who fit the description."

"So, what is your lead?"

"We believe that they might have driven somewhere, so we are checking all the places that they had been prior to their trip to Tampa."

"And?"

"We guessed they might have gone to a place in Michigan where we encountered them last time when they took one of our men."

"Were they there?"

"No. We did get a follow-up on that though, so we traced them to a place near Flint, Michigan. We believe a relative lives there. We now have people there looking. It will not take long now if they are there."

"Good. But this better work. I have two assassins ready to go to work when they are found. They are the best. They are like, what is that show, you know with the cyborg that you can't really kill who keeps going after his prey?"

"*The Terminator?*"

"That's it. They are terminators. No one survives once I put them on a target. They never fail."

"This is a change from what we've been doing in the past. The boss rarely took out people like that."

"As I have told you, he was weak. Too soft. Now I am in charge, and everything will change. If you do not like the way I do things, then I will send them after you."

"No, No. Do it your way. I just need to adjust."

"Yes, you do. Keep me informed, and don't go soft on me, otherwise…. And do not call me Ivan. You are just a peon. I am to be called Baron."

"All right. I'll keep in touch, Baron."

"Very good."

When the phone went dark, the number one man shook his head. He wasn't ready for such an escalation, but he knew he had to follow along, even as uncertain as he was about it. He just didn't know what this man would do next.

CHAPTER 9

Near Flint, Tuesday, February 23, 7:00 a.m.

Joe and Joette had decided to leave early on February 23 and to drive north to the U.P., visit Colewin, later meet with their children, and then find a place to stay while they plotted what they were going to do next.

"You keep in touch," Ron yelled as they backed out of the driveway.

"We will," said Joe as he closed the window and turned onto the street.

They waved goodbye and then they turned away. Ron and Shanice returned to the house, and Joe and Joette drove away.

It was a quiet drive for a few hours. Both Joe and Joette were thinking about Colewin, and how they had left the place. It wasn't as if they just moved from there. They were both taken violently and luckily had survived, but it still bothered both of them, as it must Ron and Shanice. They had decided to go straight to Colewin and visit Cathy and Wayne. They also hoped to get some closure. However, Joe was not satisfied with just a little closure. He still wanted to find out how he could take down the bunker near Colewin.

They reached Gaylord and decided to stop for a quick bite. They had left quickly and told Ron and Shanice not to bother with breakfast. They were both hungry now and in need of a stop.

"How about we just stop at a fast-food place and get some hot coffee, hash browns, pancakes, and eggs?"

"Sounds good to me," Joe said.

They took the next exit and enjoyed a quick breakfast. Joette could tell that something was bothering Joe. "What's on your mind, Joe?"

"Not exactly sure. I do know that I want to find out more about that bunker. Why in the world did they try to get rid of us? Something major is going on. Ann said it was a big deal and that people were still out to get us, so what can we do to stop them?"

"I don't know, but I would like to take care of us first."

"We will, but I have some scores to settle in Colewin." They finished their breakfast and were on the road in no time.

"Here we are—back at the Mackinac Bridge," Joette said.

"Yes, every time I see it now, I just think of the time I was being transported somewhere in a wooden box. Never knew what the next day would bring."

"That's scary to think about. Let's try to forget that for now. We'll be in Colewin in no time. It'll be nice to see Cathy again. It has been a while."

They crossed the bridge into the U.P. Even in winter it was an impressive sight with Lake Huron and Mackinac Island on one side and Lake Michigan on the other, and the bridge rising hundreds of feet into the air. The ice on the lake and the snow-covered shores of the U.P. were unforgettable. Once across the bridge, it wasn't long before they were heading into Colewin and straight to Cathy and Wayne's place. It was just after 10:30 a.m. They exited the car and went right to the door and knocked, but no one answered.

"It's Tuesday and Cathy will probably be in school. I did not think of that, and who knows where Wayne might be?"

Joe was thinking the same thing. "I guess we can run into Colewin and see if we can find Wayne, or we can go to the school and find Cathy."

"Let's do that," Joette said.

As they backed down the driveway, two camouflaged individuals came out of the woods and watched them leave. The first guy swore and said, "That's not them. Not sure who it was, but we have got to take care of these people soon. I guess the new boss is not like the old one. He wants these people dead."

As Joe turned to go, he got a glimpse of something and someone lurking in the woods.

CHAPTER 10

Flint, Tuesday, February 23, 1:00 p.m.
Ron had been concerned since the meeting with Ann, so he wanted his family to take a brief break and find a good place to hide away until he could learn more. They had everything packed and his son had the Suburban filled with supplies and any equipment they might need. Ron and Shanice were going to take the Camaro and follow. They were only minutes away from their son's place when Shanice realized that she did not have her purse. She called her son, but his wife answered, and she said, "The last time I saw your purse, it was on the counter in the kitchen," so they returned for it.

"We'll catch up," Shanice said into the phone.

Ron turned around, and just as they were within a block of the house, there was a huge explosion. It rocked the car and threw debris all over the street.

"What in the world was that?" Shanice screamed.

"Not sure. Let's get out of here before something else happens."

As they backed around the debris, Shanice looked in the direction of the blast and saw her son's home had been leveled.

"Oh, my God! Our son's home!" Shanice shrieked as Ron pulled a U-turn and sped away for fear of another explosion. But that was it.

Ron backed into a driveway so he could see in the direction of the blast. He was looking for anyone who might be in the area. He wondered if the people who did this stuck around to see their handiwork. And sure enough, he saw a van all of a sudden pull away from the block and speed down the street past them as they sat quietly in a driveway.

"That might be the guys who did this. We can follow and see what we can find out. Call our son and tell him what has happened and not to turn around, but to continue to our destination. We might have to change plans."

"Are we the ones they were targeting?"

"I'm sure of it. Ann said that we are now on a hit-list of some kind. I guess the new boss is much more serious about moving forward faster and eliminating any problems."

Shanice called her son again, and again got his wife, and Shanice informed them of what happened. They both let out a scream, and Ron, Jr. hit the brakes. He immediately wanted to return, but she convinced him otherwise, and he continued to the destination that they had planned.

Ron kept a bead on the van and followed it to the highway where they took a wild left and headed toward Detroit. He moved fast and got a license number before they lost them in traffic. "Write this down. Florida license plate IXY G33. Unfortunately, it looks like an expired plate. They might have found it and put it on the van, or they just had an old one they used."

"Anything helps at this point. Let's turn around and meet up with our son."

"We will, but I better call Joe and let him know, and I have to give Ann the license number and let her know what happened." His call to Joe did not go through, and Ron was concerned.

Earlier in the day, Colewin, February 23, 11:37 a.m.
Joe and Joette pulled up to the school and were a bit pumped about seeing some of the people again. Some, because they were friends, but others because they were indirectly complicit in some way with

the incidents that had led to their capture and eventual near-death experience. Joette was excited to see Cathy, but Joe wanted to go directly to the principal's office and have a chat.

They opened the door and were met by a security guard who walked them to the main office. There they were given visitors' passes and the okay to visit some of the teachers and the principal. Joe went straight to the principal's office. Joette decided to visit Cathy first.

Joe walked slowly to the office. From his many years as a teacher, he seemed to be able to remember even the smell of the school building—that unforgettable scent of pencils, paper, bodies, cleaning supplies—and the sounds of banging lockers and feet plodding along the hallways. He saw it all: the busy hallways, student benches, the gym where he had refereed many games, and teachers congregating next to their doors. He turned a corner and walked into the main office.

Theresa was the first to welcome Joe. "Oh, my, Joe DeLuca! How are you, Joe? It has been such a long time. I am so glad to see you are all right." She jumped out of her chair and went straight to Joe and gave him a hug. "We hadn't heard anything about what happened to you or Joette. I knew you were innocent. I am so glad that you are all right! How is Joette?"

"She's fine."

"I'm so glad to hear that. We have missed you two!"

"Thank you, Theresa. It's great to see you too. I hope you and your family are doing well."

"We are. Thank you."

"Is Elizabeth in?"

"No. She's at a principal's meeting in Rudyard. She should be back by the end of the day."

"Okay, I'll come back another time."

"Would you like to leave a message?" Joe thought long and hard about what he might say in a note to Elizabeth, but he thought otherwise and finally came to the conclusion it might be best to say nothing. "I'm good. Guess I'll see you later. Have a good day."

"Bye, Joe. Don't forget about us. Stop by any time for a visit. We all miss you. Will you be coming back to teach here?"

"Doubt it, but thanks again. We'll be around." Joe turned and exited the office and headed to the other end of the building where his wife would be with Cathy.

It was strange being in a building that, at one time, had been a comfortable place to work. Now it just felt like something foreign. He walked past students that he did not know and some that he did, but few recognized him anymore. It was not the same place. When Joe arrived where he expected Joette and Cathy to be, he did not find them, so he walked to the teachers' lounge and there they were. Just the two of them huddled in a corner talking quietly.

"What are you two talking about so furtively? It looks like you have a secret you're trying to protect." Joette just glanced up with a serious look on her face. She did not say anything. Cathy looked like she had seen a ghost. They both just sat there staring.

"Wow, something is wrong. What is it?"

Joette finally spoke in a quiet voice. "Joe, Cathy and Wayne are being harassed, and so is Tommy. It's gotten so bad that Tommy is hiding out somewhere. They haven't spoken to him in several days."

Cathy finally spoke up. "Yes. We've been harassed for a while by the new people who stay at that bunker, but lately, especially the last two days, it has gotten so bad that we are thinking of moving."

"What exactly is going on?"

"First, it was just the local people in that militia. Those who joined with the new group, but it's not Charlie's people. Well, some are or were. Jim is one who joined the new people, and he has been a friend of Wayne's for a long time. He told us we better watch ourselves because the new word out is that Wayne and Tommy might be eliminated."

"What? Why? What did they do?" Joette asked.

"Whoever works out there said they identified them recently from a video they had taken a while back when they were looking for Joe. They had never been able to figure out who they were, but someone started asking around, and some of the local guys who are in their group finally recognized them on the video. I guess anyone who is not a part of their group, and who might know of the bunker, is fair game for them."

"My guess is that it's that Bates fellow who had the video. He's the one who had Ron and me sent downstate in wooden boxes. He's probably taking orders from the main man, and now they have a new boss who is a real vicious jerk. We thought we set them back last week, but this new boss, who's in charge now, will stop at nothing."

Cathy's voice gave away her fear. "Are we safe here in Colewin?"

"At this point, I'm not sure if any of us are safe anywhere. This group has a goal to take over the country, and anyone in their way is just fair game to be eliminated as you indicated."

"What can we do to be safe?" Cathy asked.

Joette suggested, "Can't we just hide out for a while until this whole thing blows over?"

Joe thought that was not even possible. "We could try, but I think this is something that will last quite a while, and if they get their way, we'll all be in trouble."

"Charlie has put a group together, and they are going to try to take back the bunker. At least that is what Wayne heard the other day. That could help."

"It might, but this is much bigger than just this place. They have multiple places like this, and they have a lot of money and people on the payroll."

Lower Peninsula, Thursday, February 23, 2:00 p.m.

Ron knew he had to call Ann. He was driving north again after tailing the white van that he thought might have something to do with the explosion they witnessed. They had not been able to follow it for very long, but he did have a license plate that might help. Ann had given Joe and Ron a private number where they could reach her. Ron pulled out his phone, found the number, and called. "Hello, Ann?"

"This is Ann."

"Ann, this is Ron. We've had a real development since talking to you. Joe headed north to find out what might be going on there. My family is now heading north to find a place to lay low for a while. Once we left my son's place, and we weren't far away, his place blew up. It was a very loud and very big explosion. I don't believe it was a gas leak or anything like that. We think someone found out where we were. You said it might get bad. I guess it just did."

"Yes, I've had a call from our agent in Flint who is already at the site of the explosion. Thank goodness you are all okay. We are sure this has something to do with this group. Let's call them revolutionaries. For sure they want to get rid of you, and so you absolutely need to hide. Don't tell me where you're going, but get there in a hurry. They have people all over so be careful. I thought you might have taken my warning and gotten out of here faster than you have, so now just keep moving. Keep me updated, but don't use a cell phone right now. You might want to get a burner somewhere and use that, and then trash it after you call."

"Right. First, I'm going to call Joe to let him know, and then I won't use it again."

1,500 miles away.

"We just got another ping on the phone of the Black guy who was in the lower. His partner, that Joe and his wife, are headed north as far as we can tell, but we're not sure. The one who just left Flint is for sure headed north."

The new boss was not happy. "What happened with our plan to get rid of them in that house you found? They were there, right?"

Randall was nervous. "They were. They must have left prior to the explosion. We're not sure if anyone was in the house. We thought we got all of them, but then we got the ping, and so we know someone survived."

The new boss said, "This is sloppy work. You will be replaced. I want these things accomplished now and finished the right way. Someone should have died. We need to eliminate anyone who is on to us."

"But we found the place and did what you said. Why are you replacing me? I've done everything you've asked."

"Not good enough. Don't call me anymore. I've already sent someone to replace you. It won't be long now."

Randall hung up, slipped his phone in his jacket pocket, grabbed his keys, ran to the door, and was on the road in no time. He knew that he was the one who would be hunted now. How in the heck could he get out of this place? He was now stuck in traffic, and he had little time to get away. Then he realized he should get rid of any electronics. He took out his phone and tossed it out of the window. He stopped his car on the side of the road, opened the back door, took out his computer, smashed it, and threw it into a ditch. He jumped back in his car and drove in the traffic until he reached the freeway where he hoped to hide in the afternoon rush hour. He would not make very good time.

Randall had risen through the ranks of this organization, but he knew little about it. He did know that the people in charge were ruthless, but he wanted in on the action. Taking down the government was the goal. He was always one to resist big government. He wanted freedom to do as he pleased. No more taxes, no more do this, don't do that. He liked to carry his AR-15 wherever and whenever he wanted. He thought he needed that in case the government tried to make him do anything he didn't want to do, but now he was mixed up. The organization wanted what he wanted, but they wanted even more. A war, I guess. A civil war. That's going too far. As he pondered these things, he kept increasing his speed as he finally got on the open road.

He knew he had a good start and could probably reach Cheboygan where he knew he could hide out for some time. Little did Randall know, though, that his car was bugged. No one gets away easily. Soon two men had a signal from his car and were on the way.

CHAPTER 11

Colewin, Tuesday, February 23, 2:00 p.m.

Joe, Joette, and Cathy had been talking for a while and decided that they needed to do something. They planned to get together after the school day. Cathy was already back in her classroom and would not be free until after 3:30. Joe and Joette had talked to Wayne on Cathy's cell phone. They decided they should not use their cell phones in case they were being tracked in some way.

Wayne said, "Let's all get together at my place when Cathy is free."

Joe thought about that for a second and then replied. "When I left your place, I saw some guys coming out of the woods. I'm not sure what they were doing, but they were heading toward your house. We should meet someplace secluded, and then you and I can go and scope out your place later."

"Good idea. If we are being hunted as you say, we need to be extra careful."

Then Joe's phone buzzed. He was planning to get rid of his and Joette's phones as soon as he could, so no one could track them. He had just turned it on after having it off for the better part of the day, so he hesitated to pick it up, but he saw that it was Ron. He knew he had to take it. "Hello."

"Joe. Are you in a safe place and can you talk? I've got some news for you."

"Yes. Go ahead."

"Today, a few minutes after we had left my son's place, the whole house was destroyed. Blown up. There is nothing left. If we had all been in there, none of us would have survived. As it is, we are all trying to find a place to hide right now, hoping to get away from whoever did that. I am sure it was no accident."

"What the hell. I guess Ann was right. We need to take some precautions right away. Where exactly are you headed? Wait, don't say. They could be listening."

"Yeah, for sure. We're trying to find someplace for tonight where we can be safe. We should end this phone call right now."

"Ron, come here. You know where. We can find a place to hide out while we plan what we should do to keep all of us safe."

"Not sure what we'll do, but I'll contact you soon. We better hang up."

"Get rid of your phones and get a burner when you can. I'm going to get rid of mine, so call Joette's number if you need to talk."

"Right. Talk to you later."

CHAPTER 12

Detroit, Michigan, 2:30 p.m.

"We got another contact with that guy who left the Flint area. It looks like he is on I-75 headed north."

"Let's get some troops on his tail right now, Stew. The committee has put me in charge, and I intend to do this the right way. Get the drones out—the small ones, and load them with explosives same as we have for Randall. We should have him in no time. Send a couple of our best out of Grayling. We have a small group there, but they are very active. They have all kinds of equipment. Hopefully, they have the drones that we've been shipping. Let me know."

"I'm sure they have all the equipment that we have here. They may have more. Drones they have. I'll meet them as soon as I can. We'll take a chopper up there and get this coordinated."

"Just get it done. Make sure they get Randall, too. These others. Just wipe them out. The event is coming quickly, and with me in charge, it could happen within the year."

The chopper was ready in no time, and the crew knew exactly what they had to do. Stew was sure that this was his chance for advancement in the organization. He really wanted to get an opportunity to show how good he was. "Let's get there pronto. Red-line this machine if you have to, but get us there as fast as you can."

Stew knew there was money in a job well-done. He also hoped to be a part of the event when it occurred. All of the bases were ready, and all they needed was more equipment and personnel.

Convincing people to be a part of this organization wasn't hard when the leadership could throw around the amounts of money that they do. On top of his initial pay, he had already made an extra sixty-five grand this year just doing what he was supposed to do, and there was always the chance for a lot more.

The helicopter was moving fast, and Stew could see I-75 clearly from where he sat. He wondered what type of car the guy had, and whether they could locate it in time. Hopefully he makes another call. They had a fairly good bead on the first one.

"Any contact with the vehicle yet?"

"Not yet. We might be able to spot it though. We were just given information that he is driving a Camaro. That should help."

"Sounds great. Let's fly lower and keep an eye on I-75 as we head north."

"Roger. Will do."

Midland, Michigan, Tuesday, February 23, 2:40 p.m.
Ron and Shanice were just past Midland. They had made good time. Their son was about forty-five minutes ahead of them. They wanted to keep as far apart as possible and not use any phones for fear of being spotted. Ron was on the lookout for anything in the air, and Shanice also had her eyes focused to the sky. Ron had enough experience to know that these people had the type of equipment that they needed to find him, so his obvious guess was either a small plane, a drone, or a helicopter. "If you see anything, yell. We'll have to dodge it and try to hide until whatever we see is gone."

"Ron, this is nerve wracking. I am so scared. What if they put a drone up there with some type of explosive?"

"Good question. Maybe we should just hide until evening."

"We should get out some of the weapons we have in the trunk, so we have a chance of shooting anything that might be a problem."

"Yes." Ron waited, then quickly took the next exit. They stopped at a truck stop and got out two assault rifles and a hand-grenade. They did not have much else to protect themselves.

"Let's stop here for a while and get something to eat. We might want to continue on a different road than I-75. It's too open to the sky."

"Good point. Let's head for Highway 33 and take the back roads as much as possible. We should get rid of any other tech we have. I'm sure they were tracking our cell phones. It was good we got rid of those. Let's hit some stores and see if we can buy a new one, just one."

Ron had smashed his cell phone and thrown it in a dumpster. Shanice's phone had been in her purse. He was sure that was destroyed. They drove around until they found a store where they purchased a new cell phone with a completely different number. They hoped they did not have to use it. At 4:15 p.m. they were back on the road, headed to their meeting place with their son.

Helicopter, Tuesday, February 23, 4:20 p.m.
"We have a lead on Randall, let's go after him first. My guess is he's headed for the old warehouse that we have near Cheboygan. Let's take a quick swing that way and see what we can find."

Randall had pulled off of I-75 and headed for Highway 23 north to the old warehouse. He was thinking out loud, "They'll never figure that I'd go there. I'll get some supplies and be ready for the long haul. I hope the road has been plowed, or I'll never get in there."

Randall had hoped that he would stay with the group until the event, but he had constantly screwed up. The old boss had given him several chances, but this new boss is a one-and-done kind of leader. You mess up and you're out. Randall began talking to himself, "Man, I'm going to miss the money, but I won't miss those bastards. They're more ruthless than I thought. I'm not sure I agree with the way they think, but then again, the money was good." As he was rambling on, he heard the thump of a helicopter. He knew what that probably meant. He pulled out and left the road and hid in a grove of trees.

The pilot in the helicopter contacted his boss, "I have the car in view. It's heading off the road. He doesn't know that we can follow him no matter where he goes. He'll probably try to hide. I'm glad he took that old road. Looks kind of desolate. We can let him have it here and then go on to find the others."

Randall was smart. He had been a part of many operations when they had to take people out, so he stopped his car and hid it under trees. Then he opened the door and ran as fast as he could. He made it to a drainage ditch just as the car was hit with a small device that blew it into a thousand pieces.

The helicopter circled around and made several passes before turning north and speeding off.

"There's no way he survived that. Let's get the hell out of here."

CHAPTER 13

The Bunker, Same Day

Bates had been extremely busy even before the change in command, but now, things were crazy. This new boss expected everything right now. He had poured more men into the base than his predecessor had for the last two years. Equipment was coming in faster than they could handle all of it. He was beginning to think that the event was about to happen. They always talked about a few years down the road, but now they seemed to have accelerated the timeline.

Bates took a look at the room he was in. It was so large now that he did not even recognize his old place. It was much better before the changes, and he did not have to deal with the troops constantly harassing him. He took a walk to the door to get some fresh air. It was cold. February in the U.P. has some bitter cold weather, and it has a lot of snow. He heard that some parts of the U.P. have gotten more than 200 inches of snow. He heard one place in the Keweenaw Peninsula had gotten almost 400 inches once. Trying to dig out of some of the snowstorms can be a chore. They finally got a huge snow-throwing machine. That helped Bates. The troops now took care of the snow. He figured there were more than 200 troops here now. He wondered how many they might have as they got closer to their goal.

He stepped outside and took a deep breath. He looked around and saw several barracks to his far right. They had been building them for some time now. Charlie would be shocked if he could see this place now. It's ten times bigger and more secure, and it has been camouflaged so no one would find this on the ground or even from the air. They kept most of the trees and built the barracks in the woods. Crazy.

He knew that before the event a couple of thousand troops would go through here. Almost 1,000 troops had already been trained and sent to other places where they would prepare and be ready for the event. The plan was fool-proof as far as he was concerned. Another delivery was to arrive today. He wasn't sure how many personnel he would be processing, but he knew that the numbers kept going up each time a group came in. As he turned toward the bunker, he heard some noise coming up the trail, and he knew this would be them.

Colewin, February 23, 5:00 p.m.

Joe and Joette met Wayne near their old home. They wanted to get a look at it one more time. When they arrived, they noticed that nothing had changed. No one was around, and the place seemed vacant, so Joe and Joette walked up to the front door. The place was empty. They walked around outside and decided they had better head to a place where no one would find them. Wayne said they should pick up Cathy and head to a secluded spot. He thought that Sherry might let them stay in the hunter's cabin where Tommy had been staying before they lost track of him.

Wayne picked up Cathy from the school. They had decided that they would not go to their place to get anything until Wayne and Joe had a chance to check it out. With Joe and Joette close behind, they pulled away headed for the hunting cabin next to where George's wife Sherry still lived.

Sherry was happy to see Wayne and Cathy. She was worried about Tommy. He had been through so much the last few years. He had been with her husband George when he was murdered by

Wyatt, who was part of the new militia; he had also gotten a bad case of Covid-19, and now he was being hunted.

"Sherry, this is Joe and Joette DeLuca. They are friends of Tommy's. They both used to teach at the school, but they were both abducted and sent away."

"I know who they are. Are you sure they are good people? I heard a lot of stuff from our neighbors about them. Tommy always talked about Mr. Joe, the teacher. I guess if you say they're good, then I'm good too. I know Tommy really liked him and his wife."

"They're good."

"Then they're welcome here."

Joe exited the vehicle and went right to Sherry and told her thanks for allowing them to be there. "We have had quite a rough couple of years. We spent a lot of time with Tommy, and we would like to help find and protect him."

"I'm really worried about him. I haven't heard from him in two days, and he always stops in to talk. He sometimes brings Wendy, but I haven't seen her much lately either."

"We know Wendy. She and Tommy helped my wife try to find Ron and me when we were abducted. I think that's why he thinks he's in trouble."

"I don't know. I just want to know that he's okay."

Wayne said, "That's why we're here. We all need to have a place to hide out, and we want to find Tommy, but we can't do it out in the open. That new militia is out of control, as far as we're concerned."

"Well, you're welcome to stay in the cabin. Tommy has been there for a while now, so his things are in there, although he never did bring much besides his hunting gear."

Joe was concerned and said, "From what we know, these guys who are after us and probably Tommy are professional assassins. We'll have to make a plan quickly because we can't stay here for long. It's just a matter of time before they find out where he was living. Sherry, you should be careful too. Are you here alone?"

"Since Tommy left, I'm the only one out here. He was living in the cabin."

"We're going to make a plan here today and hopefully figure out how we can find Tommy."

CHAPTER 14

The Cabin on the Ridge, February 23, 5:17 p.m.
When Wendy got to the cabin, she saw Tommy's snowmobile parked next to a dilapidated- looking building. It was a log cabin that had been burned two years earlier when his Uncle George had been killed, and it had charred black walls on the outside. The grounds looked like they had not been taken care of in a long time. A little tree or two had begun to grow in the path to the door. There were bottles and cans littering the ground on the left of the door, and a burned couch, bed, and an assortment of other household goods piled to the far left.

Wendy had never been here before, and she was glad when she found the cabin, but she was mortified by the outside condition. She mused aloud, "If this is the outside, what does the inside look like?"

Tommy heard the sound of a machine approach the cabin. His first instinct was to grab a rifle and point it out the smashed window where he had hung some muslin that he had purchased. He moved the muslin as he slid the rifle outside, and then he saw Wendy. He put his rifle away, went to the front door and greeted her, "Hey, thanks for coming. I haven't seen anyone in more than two days." He walked up to her and gave her a hug.

"Tommy, really, why are you out here?"

"Well, it's a long story, but the short part of it is that a few days ago, a couple of guys from the militia, old friends of mine who have joined the new militia, came and told me to get the heck out of here because the bunker people were after me and Wayne for helping Mr. Joe."

"That was a long time ago. How would they even know?"

"I guess they had a film of us that night that Mr. Joe was taken."

"Well, if they know this, why did they wait for so long?"

"They didn't have anyone local who knew who we were until Jim, remember him? He worked for the pipeline. Well, he identified us right away, and now I guess the leadership has changed and the new boss wants to clean house as much as he can. I hear he is the paranoid type, so he wants complete control and will eliminate anything or anyone he thinks is a problem."

"But why?"

"Don't know. All I know is that they are very powerful and have a plan to take over."

"Take over?"

"Yeah, to take over everything in the country. They want to change the government."

Then they heard another machine heading up the old trail toward the cabin. "Come on. Let's get inside and get some protection. We should have hidden the snowmobile. It's too late now. Come on. Head for the door."

They no sooner got inside and the machines pulled up alongside Wendy's. Tommy peeked out of the window and saw that it was Wendy's mom and dad. "Coast is clear. It's your parents."

"Thank goodness. I was really afraid."

"I know the feeling."

Wendy looked around the cabin and could see that it really was not habitable. The windows were broken or gone. Every wall was scorched. The kitchen was a total mess. All the cabinets were gone. Only the sink stood near the wall with all the pipes exposed and nothing really holding it up. The living room, if one could call it that, was completely charred, and there was no furniture. She could see that the bathroom door had been burned, but it still hung ajar from its hinges. The bathroom seemed to be intact and had somehow avoided the flames that had seared the rest of the cabin.

"Where have you been sleeping?"

"On the floor in the corner in my sleeping bag."

Wendy strode to the door and opened it as her parents were about to knock. When they entered, they both peered around the room with wide eyes and startled faces.

1,500 miles away, February 23, 6:00 p.m.

The helicopter pilot was on the phone with the head man. "Boss, we demolished the car, so I don't think he could have survived."

"Did you see the dead body?"

"Not exactly. We did see the car and anyone in or near it had to be dead."

"Did you see the dead body?"

"No. We did not."

"Then go back and find it. When you have taken a picture of the dead man, then I will know he is gone."

"But we're miles away from there now."

"Go back! Do it right—or do not do it at all. I will find someone else."

"Okay, we'll go back and we'll take a picture for you." Then the phone died.

"Imbeciles! That's why I send the right kind of people to do important jobs. These guys are lazy. My assassins will do the job right."

CHAPTER 15

Colewin, Charlie's Place, Wednesday, February 24, 6:00 p.m.
Charlie called a meeting for anyone interested in getting the old militia back together. He knew it was a long shot, but he had to try. He had some really faithful people that he knew wanted to get together again, and maybe even take a run at the bunker. He had eight people counting himself, not enough to make a difference, but it was a start.

Charlie was fishing for ideas. "Do ya think we kin get some of the others back with us? I mean the ones who left the group las' year. I mean some of those people were good troops, and we're gonna need a lot of 'em if we're gonna take that bunker back. We still have a lot of weapons and other supplies there that me and Sam couldn't take the las' time we were there. Now we can't get close to the place."

"Charlie, I think if we all got together and asked those other people, we could come up with ten or twelve more. Some of 'em just followed Betty. They like her and she's a leader," Robert said.

Sam said, "I kin get Betty back. I'm sure of it. She was angry back then, but she's really mad now that we lost the base. She thinks they're all crazy and will ruin the country. She's smart an' she could really help."

"If'n you could convince her that would be great. I know she won't listen to me. I mighta said some things that pissed her off."

"You did," came a voice that Charlie did not recognize. It was one of the Fisher boys from Poplar, a small community not far from Colewin. It was one of the new guys, Matt. "She's my cousin and I know she's upset that the old militia is out of action, but she hates yer guts, Charlie. Problem is we all kind of hate you for what ya did, but we're willing to join up with ya if we can get those people out of here, and I can guarantee that I can convince Betty and a few other friends to go along."

"You really hate my guts, but you'd be willin' to do that?"

"Yep, these outsiders don't belong here. We been keepin' a watch on 'em for some time. They have some good troops, but they don't know the area. We been spyin' on 'em regular like."

"Well, damn. How you been doin' that?"

"You know the old trail that winds in from the back of the grounds? Well, we jus' come up that road nice and quiet like, and we can watch those idiots, a lot of 'em are idiots. I'm not sure how they found them, but they're stupid."

"We're gonna need a lot more than ten or twenty people if we're gonna get the base back." Charlie's eyes turned up and he was thinking. "We'll need about a hundred is my guess. They got a lot of 'em there now, but from what that Bates tole me, they rotate 'em out all da time."

"We could do that. I mean we could get maybe fifty locals together. People around here are upset. Life just ain't the same anymore. Those troops make a lot of noise, and they're always at the Sportsman's Pizzeria and Bar. They've been chased out of town several times, but no one will follow through because they're all afraid. Even the cops stay away. Those girls that got in trouble last December, some say they were picked up by those imbeciles from the bunker."

Wayne's place, February 24, evening
In the woods near Wayne and Cathy's home, two troop members were talking. "We've been sitting here waiting now for two days.

I'm sick and tired of this shit. We need to find out where these people are. The boss wants this done pronto, so we need to do something. Taking them out will be easy, but we got to find them first. I think they might be onto us or something. Remember that car that was here the other day? Did someone see us and get them out of here?"

"I'm not sure what happened, but I know his wife is a school teacher. Maybe we can go to the school and follow her tomorrow. We'll probably have to take the two of them out though."

"No problem. We can make it look like an accident. We got the law behind us if we can do this right. If they don't return tonight, we can hit the school tomorrow."

"Let's do that then. We visit the school."

"We've got to be careful though. We can't give ourselves away to anyone right now."

CHAPTER 16

Colewin, Near Sherry's Place, February 24, Late Evening
Wayne and Joe had been in a long discussion about what to do when Joe's phone buzzed. He had destroyed his and taken Joette's just in case. He looked at the phone and did not recognize the number, so he just hung up. "Man, I don't want to pick up any stray numbers now. There's no telling who's looking for us." Just as he put his phone down, it rang again. "Same number. I sure don't want to give us away by answering this if it's some dudes hunting us." Again, he put the phone down. It wasn't long after that he received a text from Ron.

Joe, this is me, Ron. Hope all is well. Makes me nervous that you didn't answer Joette's phone right away. I have a new phone. Think the old one was being tracked. Call me if you get this.

Joe read the text and instantly said to Wayne, "It's Ron. He wants me to call." He pulled up the number and called right away. "Ron, is this you? Where are you? Are you okay?"

"Joe, yes, this is Ron and we're okay. We're in Colewin. We decided to drive all the way here. My son and his family are with us. We had to get the hell out of town. As I said earlier, my son's place was demolished. It was a huge blast. Luckily, we were all out. Shanice and I were on the way back to pick up her purse when we saw the explosion."

"Damn! You need to come here with us. We're staying in a cabin that Tommy was living in recently, but we can't find him. He and Wayne are being hunted too." Joe proceeded to give Ron the directions to the cabin—and he and his son's family were there in fifteen minutes.

Joe and Wayne went out to meet everyone. Joette and Cathy who had been asleep, awoke and got the bedroom ready for the children and Ron's son and his wife.

"Ron, glad you made it here safely. Come on in."

"Good to be here."

Wayne shook Ron's hand and gave him a pat on the back. "Come on, we have some food and drink in there."

Ron's son and his wife went to the bedroom with the kids and put them to bed. Shanice, Joette, and Cathy sat in the living room and tried to rest. Joe and Wayne got Ron caught up on what was going on. Their immediate plan was to take Wayne's truck to his house to investigate. They planned to drive over to the house, let the truck move down the long driveway with a dummy in it, and see what might happen. If nothing, then they would carefully search the area to see if they could find any signs of people.

Wayne and Cathy's place, outside Colewin, nighttime
The house lay on five acres of land, and Wayne had built a ranch-style home with a long driveway. The door, in the middle of the home, faced the road, and the garage was on the right. It was not a huge home, but it was perfect for the couple. There was shrubbery in front of the house and a few trees that Wayne had

planted that were placed strategically around the yard after the home was finished.

"Okay," Joe said, "Ron and I will get out about a quarter mile from your place, and then we'll walk down near your yard and cover you from both sides. Once we're hidden, you drive the truck to the driveway and just as you enter, pull up the dummy and jump out, let the truck move down the driveway slowly by itself." Wayne was worried that the truck might crash into the garage doors, and maybe into the garage, but they had to take the chance.

Wayne did as they said, and as soon as they were in place, he drove down the road, reached the driveway, turned in, jumped out, and let the car move slowly and quietly down the driveway. Just before the truck hit the garage door, a barrage of shots rang out and demolished the cab of the truck. There were so many bullets that it just about tore off the cab. The dummy must have fallen and hit the accelerator because then the truck slammed into the garage door, tore through, and blasted through the back wall before it stopped.

Joe and Ron were shocked, but at the same time, they were ready. Wayne was mesmerized by the number of bullets and was shaking violently as Joe moved toward him and handed him a .30-30. Ron and Joe both had M-16s. They waited.

CHAPTER 17

The Cabin on the Ridge, February 24, Late Evening

Wendy decided to stay with Tommy for the night. She wanted to continue to help clean and fix things. Her parents had helped clean up as much as they could, but it didn't seem to help a whole lot. They had covered the windows as best they could, and Wendy's dad had fixed the bathroom door. He had to repair it first, and then he rehung it. Her mother tried her best to clean the place, and it helped a lot, but the smoke smell still lingered, and there really was only one place to sit after they found an old wooden chair out in the yard and fixed it, but it wasn't very comfortable.

When they had done as much as they could, Wendy's parents left and told Wendy and Tommy to be careful.

"Tommy, we've got to find a better place for you to stay. It's winter, and it gets so cold out here. You still don't have the generator fixed either."

"I know, but I'm working on it. I've been able to cut enough wood to last a while, and I have this little fireplace that helps a bit."

"Why do you have to stay out here anyway?"

"I told you. The guys who told me about this new militia said they will not stop until I'm dead. The same goes for Wayne."

"Let's tell the police."

"That won't help. I told you what happened out in the woods when we tried to help Mr. Joe before he was abducted. The law was involved. Not all of the law, but we don't know which officers to trust. The ones we called for help last time are all gone. They were transferred or taken. What a mess."

"I know, but we have to do something."

Then Wendy's phone vibrated. She had it on silent mode. "This must be my parents. Hello, Mom. What did you say? Mr. Joe?"

"What's going on?"

"Sure. I'll tell him."

"So, what's up?"

"My mom said that when they got home, they heard that Mr. and Mrs. Joe were at the school the other day."

"What? That means they're alive. I thought for sure something bad had happened to them."

"We've got to find them, and see if Mr. Joe knows anything."

"I'm not sure. I don't think I should be seen anywhere."

"Why don't I find out where they're staying, and I'll have them set up a meeting somewhere safe."

"That sounds good. Let's do that."

Wayne's place, Wednesday, February 24, Late Evening

Joe, Ron, and Wayne all lay quietly on the ground. They had spread out so that Joe was on the left facing the house, Ron was on the far right in the woods, and Wayne was behind a rock to the right of the driveway. They had planned in advance that if anyone was here, they would try to draw them out, so they knew they were going to wait to see what the shooters would do next. Everything was really quiet. There wasn't a sound except for the truck, which was still running, but not moving.

No one said a word. Breathing became difficult for Wayne because he was so anxious about what had just happened. He was afraid that he might make a noise, so he buried his face in his hands. Nothing happened. They waited and waited. Everyone was getting a bit jumpy. Joe thought they might have too many people for them to handle, and he was worried that they might be surrounded. They waited. Nothing. Had they gone?

Joe could not see anyone. There was no moon, and in the woods, it was very dark. A bit of light was coming from the tail lights on the truck. The headlights were broken and out. His eyes had adjusted somewhat to the dark, and he thought they should have gotten some night goggles. He was sure the other guys had them, and maybe they could see their heat image.

Then a barrage of gun fire erupted from the far left. Joe could see tracer bullets hitting in the direction of where Ron was. Wayne was lying on the ground and had half-buried himself in the dirt. Now Joe was positive that the people who were shooting had night vision goggles. They had seen the image given off by Ron's body heat.

Ron was behind a small tree, but the bullets landed all around him. He knew he had to move, so he moved slowly backward until he had backed into a small gulley. He hoped it was enough to hide him.

Then a voice broke the silence. "If anyone is out there, you better just give up now."

Then another voice said, "I don't see anything anymore. It was probably just a deer or some other animal."

"Not so sure," said the other voice.

Then another round of shots was fired in that direction. Joe decided to move more to his left out of the field of vision for whoever was shooting. He thought he might even be able to get behind them, but in the dark and in the woods, it was too risky, so he just moved left and stopped.

They waited and waited. Then a voice could be heard saying, "There's nobody there. Who the hell would be out at this time of night anyway? Let's check him out and make sure he's dead. Hopefully his wife was with him, and we got her too."

"Okay, but move slowly and keep looking."

They broke into the open. "You cover me. I'll check him out."

"Gotcha."

The first guy walked slowly and carefully to the back of the truck, then he quickly moved back near the front door. When he got there, he yelled, "Get down. This is a trap. There's no one in the truck, but some kind of dummy."

It was then that Joe yelled, "Put your guns down and no one gets hurt."

That didn't work. It was followed by a stream of tracer bullets in every direction. They were spraying everything in front of them. Then Ron opened up and Joe did the same. The person in front of the house dropped to the ground and continued to shoot. The other one was gone. Where was he? The fire-fight went on for a while until the guy on the ground realized he was alone.

"Henry? Henry? Where are you?" No answer. He decided to get up and run for it, but that was a mistake. Joe, Ron, and Wayne all opened up on him, and he went down as soon as he jumped to his feet to run.

As the man fell to the ground, a snowmobile could be heard cranking and taking off. It did not come toward the house, but it took off through the woods. "Let's check on this guy." Joe rose slowly and carefully crawled toward the man. The man did not move. His weapon lay at his side and Joe saw that he could not have survived his wounds. He yelled to the others, "Ron, Wayne, he's down. Let's see if we can find the other one before he reports what happened."

The three of them carefully scoped out the area and found a lone snowmobile. They could not see much else in the dark behind the house, but it was clear that he knew where he wanted to go, and had escaped. They would have to wait until light to track him. They fired up the snowmobile and turned on the light, so they could see which direction he must have gone.

Wayne was sick when he got a good look at his house. The garage was totally destroyed and bullets had riddled the front of the house, but he was still thinking clearly. He turned off the truck, and then he realized that he could track the machine in the dark. He said, "I know these woods and I know the area. I can follow the trail and maybe catch up."

"Not alone, you won't," Joe said. Ron agreed. They decided that Joe would ride along with Wayne, and Ron would call Shanice to bring a snowmobile and get him. Joe and Wayne were gone in a flash.

CHAPTER 18

Lower Michigan, February 24, Late Evening
Randall was not sure if he had lost them. He had been in hiding since his car was demolished. He had walked several miles when he found a home. It had a detached garage, and he figured he could stay there for the evening. It was cold, and he needed some shelter. He tried the garage door, but it was locked. The garage had a side door, and so he tried it, and it was unlocked. He entered, found a car, got in, and fell asleep in the back seat.

The men in the chopper had been looking for Randall for hours, and had gone back to the site of the destroyed car. They landed nearby, and two of them got out and followed his footprints as far as they could, but then they lost them. The chopper had left, but the two men kept in contact with the pilot and copilot. They had found a place to rest. It was late, but the only thing they saw was a lone house in a sprawling open area. They had a popup tent and sleeping bags, so they decided to bed down for the night and pick up the trail at first light. They hid in a group of trees and set up the tent. One stayed up and kept watch while the other got some sleep. Then they switched.

Randall knew he had to keep moving, and so in the morning he was up before sunrise and decided to try to steal the car he had found. He got up, opened the garage door, got the vehicle started, and drove down the driveway.

The guy who was on watch heard the noise from the garage and woke up his buddy. As the car approached, they flagged it down. Randall saw them and knew what was up. He punched the accelerator and tried to speed away, but both men opened fire at the same time. The car veered off the road and slammed into a ditch on the other side of the road.

Both men hustled to the car. When they got there. Randall was trying to get out, but he was stuck. He knew this was the end. Both men put several bullets into his skull. Then they took a picture, called the chopper, and left.

The cabin on the ridge, Thursday, February 25, 8:00 a.m.
Wendy spent the night in the cabin on the ridge, and had a meager breakfast with Tommy. He had food, but she did not want to eat up the little her parents had brought. There was no telling how long Tommy might have to stay at the cabin. She finished her breakfast and said goodbye to Tommy and promised she would be back soon to let him know what she had found out.

"Don't get yourself in any trouble over this. I don't want you getting hurt because of me."

"I'll be careful. You stay safe out here, and you be careful."

"I will."

And Wendy was off. Her first thought was to go to the school and talk to Cathy. She jumped on her snowmobile, cranked the machine, and left the cabin. She decided to go home first and clean up a bit. She knew that Cathy would be getting ready for class, and she did not want to interrupt her right then. She took some time and by 9:15 a.m. she was ready to go. She arrived at the school at 9:40.

Wendy went straight to the front desk and got a visitor's pass, but when she told the secretary who she wanted to see, she was told that Cathy had a sub that day. "Do you know why?" Wendy asked.

"Not sure. She just called in and said she would not be in today."

"All right. Thank you." And she was off. She figured that Cathy would be home, so she headed for her place. By 10:00 a.m. she arrived only to find a mess. Wendy stopped at the driveway and could not believe what she was seeing. The garage was destroyed. It looked like Wayne's truck had driven through the garage. She moved slowly up the driveway, cautious because of all that was going on with Tommy and Wayne. She got closer and could see holes in the front of the house. "Are those bullet holes?" she gasped. She looked around, but she could tell no one was there. She saw that something had made a mess in the snow near the front door. She drove closer to look and thought she saw something red. "Is that blood?" she screamed, and she immediately turned her snowmachine around and bolted out of there.

Wendy could not even think. Were Wayne and Cathy hurt? Now she really believed what Tommy had said about being hunted. She felt ill and confused all at the same time. Her head was spinning, and all she could think to do was drive quickly away from there.

Earlier that morning, Thursday, February 25, 5:08 a.m.
Joe and Wayne had followed the trail made by the snowmobile as well as they could, and it led them right where they thought it would. When they reached the bottom of a hill, they knew they were not far from the bunker, and that the person they were pursuing had gone there. They did not want to get involved with anyone, and so they turned around and drove back to Wayne's house.

When they arrived, everything was as they had left it. Ron was gone and the truck was still stuck in the back wall of the garage. They knew they had to get the truck out of the wall and get rid of the body and clean up as much as they could. The truck was in really bad shape. The cab was almost torn off, but after freeing it, they were able to get it running. They retrieved the body from where they had hidden it and loaded it in the back, cleaned up as much of the garage as they could, shoveled most of the snow that had blood pooled on it, and then took the truck and snowmobile and headed to Sherry's cabin.

Ron was worried. He and his son, Ron, Jr. were preparing to go and find Joe and Wayne. They felt that in the daylight, they could navigate the territory even though both had little experience with the terrain. They were not quite ready when a noisy truck and a snowmobile came roaring into the yard. Ron was relieved. "Man, am I glad to see those two." After Wayne parked the truck and Joe cut the engine on the snowmobile, Ron said, "How did it go? Did you find him?"

Joe responded, "No luck finding him, but we know where he is. We followed him to the hill below the bunker, so we're sure that's where he went. I still have awful memories of that place as I'm sure you do too, Ron."

"Can't get that place out of my mind. I'd like to find out what's driving all this military preparedness up here. Ann said it is happening all over the country, but this place is crazy."

Wayne agreed, "Ever since we found out that Tommy and I might be targets, we have been looking over our shoulders and wondering what really is going on. Why are we a threat? We tried to help you a while back, but that was a long time ago."

Joe was concerned. He said, "I think this is a lot bigger than we originally thought. Ann, an FBI agent that we know, told us that it is going on all over the place, but I have a hunch that this place is a key hub in their plans. Whatever those plans are, Ann said that the FBI doesn't have the personnel to help out up here because they are spread so thin, so I think we need to do something to protect all of us and to defend this area against these people."

"What exactly can we do though? We're a small minority against this group, and now with this new boss in charge, we've got to be extremely careful. I don't know if Joe told you, Wayne, but they have two assassins after us. I'm not sure if the two we saw last night were the ones. They didn't seem very well trained."

"I'm sure they're not," Joe said. "They would have been much more effective and wouldn't have walked out into the open like they did. My guess is they were two of the troops from the bunker."

Wayne was quiet and looked angry when he said, "Well, enough is enough. I could have been killed last night, and Cathy too, if she had been with me. I'm ready to do something drastic. First, I've got to find Tommy and get him involved. We know this area better than anyone—and we need to take it back and make it the quiet place it used to be."

Ron was angry too. "That sounds great, but how will we do that? They have so much equipment and men. We'll need to build an army to defeat them or drive them out, and they are vicious— and have money."

"We'll figure something out, but I think Wayne is right. Let's find Tommy and then get a plan together. Maybe we can round up some help from people around here."

"I'm sure we can," Wayne said. "Their troops have been carousing around town, ransacking the bar, and just being unruly. There are a lot of people who want them out of here, but they just don't want to get involved."

Joe knew what he meant. "Yeah, a lot of indifference. All right. Let's get to work."

CHAPTER 19

Colewin, Thursday, February 25, 5:00 p.m.
Charlie had big plans for getting his bunker back, but he also had bigger plans for settling the score with people like Bates, and whoever that boss is that kicked him out of the place. Charlie had already been plotting and making plans for how they should approach the place. He knew the back side was very hilly, and that gave him an advantage if they took the high ground, but he also knew that the bunker people had a much larger group that was growing daily. He was still confident.

"How you gonna get this place back? They got so many people, and they don't give a care what they do or who they kill." Sam was very dubious.

"Just leave the plannin' to me. If we can get fifty troops like that Fisher boy promised, then we'll be close to havin' enough, 'specially since we know the area."

"Yeah, but you ain't got a tank and helicopters. You don't even have enough firepower. They'll have all kinds of weapons. Shit, I ain't gonna put myself in a situation like that."

"You calm down now, Sam. We'll be jus' fine."

Then Charlie's phone lit up. "Now who's this? Hello. Yeah. You sure? She will if'n I'm not involved. That ain't gonna happen! I'm in charge. We don't need her."

Matt Fisher was a very genial guy, but this did not sit well with him. "Listen Charlie, we need everyone we kin get. Let someone else lead, so we kin get her on board."

"Don't need her."

"But you need me and my people."

"Don't need you. You're either with me or you're not."

Now Matt knew that Charlie was the one person who knew the bunker and the people in it. "Okay, let me see what I can do. I do have another thought. There's Tommy who lives in Colewin—'member his Uncle George was kill't by the militia."

"Yep. I remember."

"Well, my brother knows him well, and he said he knows the area better'n anyone. I wonder if we should get him involved?"

"I know him. His people live over there, not far from where George used to live. I guess Sherry's there now."

"You want my brother to get ahold of 'em? We could use everyone we kin get."

"Sure. Why not? Although I remember he was close to that schoolteacher that got in trouble a while back, and I ain't too fond of that."

"Whatever you think. Jus' let me know, and I'll have my brother contact him."

"We'll let you know."

"Sounds good."

CHAPTER 20

The Bunker, Thursday, February 25, Early Evening

Bates was on the computer for several hours with some of the key players, and he was getting bored. It was the same old stuff. Then he heard that two assassins were on the way—and would be there soon. He was finally able to sign off and take a break. He stretched and stood up. He was stiff and sore. Since his buddy Wyatt had been killed, he hadn't had anyone to talk to, so he thought he would take one of the snowmobiles and head for his truck and maybe see if he could drive to St. Ignace and find a bar to have a drink.

As if his computer monitor was alive, he talked to the main screen as he shut it off. At the same time, making sure he kept the security cameras on. "Damn boring place. I've got to get out of here for a while."

He heard noise from his outside speakers and saw a helicopter enter the grounds. He opened the door and looked out. He figured that it must be the assassins that the boss was sending. This was unsettling for him and he mouthed, "Why he has to send them here is crazy." He watched as three men jumped out of the chopper, and then it took off and was lost in the sky. The three men walked toward the bunker. They looked at Bates, but did not say a word.

"Who the hell are you?" Bates barked.

"One man answered, "What's it to you? We're here to do a job. The boss should have contacted you by now."

"He did. I was just wondering if you had names." Bates was irritated because these troops always treated him like he was a nobody.

The one who was doing all the talking said, "I'm Vince." He pointed to the other two and mumbled something in a foreign language.

The one who walked in first said, "Adrik."

The other said, "Borya." And that was it.

"What do you want? Where did you come from?"

"Chopper. Didn't you see?" The main man just pulled out some pictures and showed them to Bates. "Doesn't matter where we came from. By the way these two don't speak much English, so if you have any questions, just ask me."

Bates realized these were definitely the assassins that the boss had said would be there soon. He did not know there would be three, and that the assassins would not speak English. When the two assassins said their names, they looked like normal troops. They were all in camoflauge and carried sidearms and one had an AK-47, the other, a peculiar rifle. Bates thought it was a sniper's rifle. Is he a sniper? Why in the hell would he send a sniper?

Then Bates took a good look. The two seemed normal until he looked into their eyes. There was nothing there. Just darkness and firm jaws that probably never cracked a smile. Bates shook a little and turned away. He was glad they were not out to get him. "Okay, you know who you want to take out. Do you know where they are?"

Vince again responded, "Well, we hope to find out. We have two marks that the boss needs eliminated and quickly. He also mentioned that you would give me two more targets."

Bates realized he had better tell them what had happened before they arrived. "Regrettably, we had two guys try to hit one of the subjects. One of ours was lost and the other came back and told us that they had been tricked, and he was lucky to get away. He thought they might have followed him, but we did not hear or see anyone, so be careful."

"So, they botched a hit."

"Yep."

"That means they'll be alert to this type of ambush. We'll have to be smarter."

"For sure. Okay, I'll show you where you can bunk for the night."

"No. We get to work right now. You have a map of the place? Just show us the area, and we can find them." The other two grunted like they knew what was going on.

"All right. The boss told me to identify them for you. I can only tell you where two of them live in Colewin." Bates pointed to a spot on a map. "Those other two older guys are here somewhere, but no one knows where they are staying, but the boss assured me that they are back. We tried to take them out last year, but we weren't successful. Here you go. You can have this map. I marked where the two younger ones live, and this is where the older one might be staying. The other one isn't from here, so he usually stays with this older guy. The two towns are here and here. One is quite small, called Poplar. If you head down the hill, take a right at the first road. Right here." Bates pointed at the map. "See? Then follow this trail. We've mapped it out clearly for the troops so they don't get lost. Any questions?"

Vince turned to Adrik and Borya and said, "Take a good look and memorize this map, and, yes, we'll need a few vehicles. What do you have?"

So, they do understand English, Bates thought. He let the sentry on duty know that the three would be leaving the base shortly, so he unlocked the gate and waited. Bates told them to follow him as he walked out to a spot near the training grounds where a new building stood. Inside were all kinds of vehicles: snowmobiles, ATVs, dirt buggies, and jeeps. "Take what you need, keys are in them, but I have only two available snowmobiles. This one is the one I use to get in and out of here."

Vince looked at Bates and laughed. He said something in a foreign language, and his two partners each started a machine, flipped their weapons over their shoulders, and drove out of the building. They had a head start on Vince as he argued with Bates before he finally started the other machine and drove it out as Bates yelled at him. "You need helmets and warmer clothes, you idiots." But they were gone. "Good enough for you, you jerks! I hope you freeze to death."

Vince drove off without even looking back. It was already quite dark, and Bates wondered if they were going to get lost, but he didn't much care. "Assholes!"

Colewin, Thursday, February 25, evening

"Ron, the first thing we have to do is find a safe place for our families. We also have to have some plan for the guys who are hunting us. Ann said they were professionals. She guessed they would try to take us out from a distance, so we have to prepare for everything. Last night was kind of an amateurish hit. That won't happen again."

"Absolutely right, Joe. Do we need to send our families to your brother's cabin? My son has been there, so he knows where it is."

"We do need to send them somewhere, but this time I think we'll check with my younger brother, James. We need a different spot. I'm sure they'll be able to stay at his cabin in the woods. Let me check with him right away."

"If you think that's best. I'm good with that."

"Let's get everyone going right away. We don't have any time to waste."

"Ron's son and his wife packed, and so did Joette and Shanice. Cathy decided to go with them, and so she took a leave of absence from her job. Ron's son decided to stay, but Ron said, "No. You need to go along and help everyone. We'll be fine. You can return when everyone is settled and safe.""

Everyone was packed quickly, and left right away. Joette and Shanice were in the lead car so Ron's son could follow them to the cabin deep in the woods in Ishpeming, a city in the central U.P. known for its iron ore mining. It's the home of the National Ski Hall of Fame, and is known for its statue of "Old Ish," an Anishinaabe native who stands tall in the center of downtown. The name means "high" or "above" and some locals interpret this to mean heaven.

When they were out of sight, Joe, Wayne, and Ron decided that they had to get rid of the body in the truck. There was no bringing the law into this one since it would just end in trouble for them, so they took the body to a secluded spot in the woods and buried it. They thought they might be able to identify him, but he had no ID. Sad. Some family would be missing someone—and there was no way to let anyone know.

Shortly after that, Joe, Ron, and Wayne began a search to find Tommy. Their first stop was Wendy's parents' place. The men now had three snowmobiles. One, thanks to the person who ambushed them, one that Sherry gave them, and Wayne's that he had brought in his truck. This would be their main mode of travel until spring. They were armed, but they knew they would be outgunned by anyone who was after them. They were hoping that they could find some help and protection, like Kevlar vests.

When they pulled into Wendy's parents' place, Wayne decided to do all the talking. He walked to the front door and knocked.

Everything was quiet. No one answered. He knocked again. No answer. Then he yelled. "Paul, are you home?" Nothing.

Wayne turned around and headed to the snowmobiles. He spoke to Joe, "This makes me worried. Somebody should be home. Could be Wendy and Paul are working, but Paul's wife, Sarah, has been off for months."

Ron was looking at the house as they talked, and he noticed a movement in one of the windows. He said, "I think someone's in there. I saw some movement."

As Ron spoke, the door opened and Wendy leaned out and said, "I was so glad to see it was someone I knew. Oh, my gosh, Mr. Joe. I heard you were in the area. Come in."

Before they did anything else, they moved their machines to a less obvious place before going into the house.

"Wayne, I am so glad you're all right. Is Cathy okay? I saw your house, and it was a mess. Do you know what happened?"

"Cathy's fine. Yes, I know what happened to our house, and that is partly why we're here. We know it was troops from the bunker out east of here. They attacked us at night, but luckily, we were ready."

Wayne introduced Ron to Wendy's parents who were hiding out at home. He told everyone why they were there. "We're trying to find Tommy. We want to get after the people who tried to take us out."

Paul said, "We were hiding because of what Wendy had found. We were afraid it had something to do with Tommy, and that someone might be after Wendy."

Wayne was convinced. "I'm sure you're right. Someone is trying to get at us as we saw the other night, so we all need to take shelter somewhere."

"But more importantly," Joe said, "I think we need to get to the bottom of what is going on. We know that most government agencies are not going to be able to help because they have so much on their plates right now, so in a way, we're on our own."

Wayne said, "You can't stay here. I'm sure if they can't find Tommy, they'll be looking for Wendy to see what she knows. Cathy is already on her way to safety. You should do the same."

Paul had fire in his eyes as he announced, "We're not going anywhere. We can find a safe place for Wendy and my wife until this blows over, and I'm going to help you do what has to be done."

Ron added, "Then let's begin by getting some protection as we mentioned earlier. Let's get on it."

Wayne asked, "Do you know where Tommy is?"

Wendy immediately said, "NO! We don't."

Wayne was not convinced. "Wendy, you need to know that we're not going to do anything that will hurt Tommy. We just need to find him. He could help a lot because he knows the area better than anyone."

CHAPTER 21

Woods Near Colewin, Thursday, February 25, Late Evening
Adrik and Borya had taken off as fast as they could. They seemed to be enjoying the wild ride. They hit the road to the right and took the turn at a speed that was too fast. They went sliding sideways, but they were able to recover and continue on to Colewin.

Vince was behind them, and did not see them when he hit the hill. He sped down and then went as fast as he could to catch up, but he was going so fast that he missed the right turn.

Adrik was in front as they sped to a split in the road. He could not remember right or left. He waited for Borya to catch up. When Borya arrived, they thought they should wait until Vince showed up, but after fifteen minutes in the dark and cold, they decided they better head back. They would have to find Vince before they could continue.

Vince knew that he had to take a right turn, and since he did not see a road, he realized he must have missed it, so he turned around and headed back to the hill. When he arrived, he was stopped by the sentry that had let him through the gate earlier. At first, he didn't let him enter, but then he recognized Vince and let him in. Bates saw him drive back to the bunker after the sentry opened the gate, so he went to meet Vince. "What's up? I thought you were going to check things out."

"I did, but I missed the trail and headed back. I was hoping that my companions had done the same." Shortly, two machines came roaring up the hill. They stopped by the gate. Vince saw them and told the sentry to let them in. Bates agreed.

"Sorry. I got lost. I'm glad you headed back."

Bates said, "It's probably for the best because I just had some information delivered that might narrow your search. Come on into the bunker and I'll show you."

All three accompanied Bates into the bunker where he had a map on the wall. He explained that someone had sent information about one of the men they were hunting, and he showed them where they should go to find him. Vince was happy to have a definite place to hit right away.

"So, we head to town and then take a road out before Colewin and head for the ridge?"

"Right. You should find a cabin there. The word is that this Tommy is the only one there."

"Let's go right now," Vince said.

"This time take some helmets, heavy gloves, and warmer clothes. Go to the shed. You will find everything you need."

Near the cabin on the ridge, Friday, February 26, early morning 4:00 a.m.

The noise of the machines woke Tommy out of a deep sleep. He had been alone since Wendy had left, and he was worried about her. He thought that this might be her and her parents because he heard more than one machine. It was still dark, and he looked out into the trees and he could see three or four lights. This must be them, but he could not be sure, so he retrieved his .30-30 and sat on the floor near a window. When he looked out, he could see four people on sleds.

Then he heard someone yell, "Tommy! It's me, Wayne."

Tommy was instantly relieved, but he was still cautious. He was not sure who else was with Wayne, so he did not answer for fear that he might be tricked into something.

Wayne yelled again. "Tommy, it's me Wayne." He waited, but there was no answer. Joe decided that Wayne should move carefully to the cabin while the other three covered him. Wayne crouched low and crawled quietly and went straight to the door. "Tommy, you there?"

Tommy finally grunted, "Yeah. Who is that with you?"

"It's Wendy's father, Mr. Joe, and his friend, Ron. May I come in?"

"Sure."

"Can the others come in too?"

"I guess. Why did Wendy's dad give my hiding place away?"

"Why don't I let Mr. Joe do all the explaining. We are all being hunted and need to stick together for safety."

"Wouldn't it be best if we kept apart to make it more difficult to find us?"

Joe entered the cabin as Tommy was speaking. He was followed by Ron and Wendy's father, Paul.

"Tommy, good to see you."

"You too, Mr. Joe. I'm so glad you are all right. We didn't know where you had gone or what had happened to you. Wayne and I saw a lot of stuff back then that shook us up. We thought that you were gone until that phone call to Cathy."

"Yes, a lot happened, and we have been through a lot, but I understand that now we're all being hunted, so I have a plan for us to find out what's going on—and to mess up this group's plans out at the bunker. We were wondering if you wanted in, because of all the people around here, you're the most knowledgeable of the area and could guide us through the woods around the bunker."

"Yeah, I could, but I am afraid of them. They want me and Wayne dead."

"Same with us. We have some assassins after us, so we'll have to be careful."

Ron added, "Tommy, if we stick together, we can beat them. Joe and I have been through a lot over the years, and we've learned how to deal with these types of situations. If we can get a good plan together, we can drive them out."

"Tommy, we have got to stick together. My home was attacked on Wednesday, and I might have been killed if it weren't for Joe and Ron. They saved me and Cathy from these guys. We have to do something because they're not going to leave here or leave us alone until we're dead."

"I hear you. I guess it would be best to have help. I can't hide out my whole life. Besides, I still really want some revenge for my Uncle George. If they had never come here, he would still be alive."

Paul spoke up next. "Just want to remind you that we need to keep an eye out for anyone and everything. Our machines are in the open out there if someone were to find this cabin. We either have to leave here and plan somewhere else, or we need to hide the machines and keep a lookout on both sides of the cabin. I doubt if outsiders would find our trail through the woods, but the road in front of the cabin is well known and anyone could come from that direction."

"Good point," Joe agreed. "Let's hide the machines and set up a watch. It'll be light in a few hours, but we'll need several hours to plan this out."

Paul volunteered and said, "As you plan, I can watch the road for a while if someone watches the woods in back."

"Sounds good. Wayne, why don't you watch the back of the cabin and Ron and I will fill Tommy in on the plan."

"Will do."

CHAPTER 22

Earlier, the Bunker, Friday, February 26, 3:00 a.m.

It took a while to get ready, but by early morning, the three were ready to move out. Vince thought it best to operate at night, even though they did not know the area well. He had good knowledge that this guy they were going to take out first, was alone.

"We'll follow the route that we were given. It follows a road out to this ridge. The cabin is somewhere between here and here." He pointed to the spot so both men could see. "Let's proceed quickly so we have darkness to keep us covered. I'll lead the way."

Both men nodded, and all three prepared to leave. Bates told the sentry to open the gate now—and to let them in later when they return. The men left, and this time they stayed together so they would not make any mistakes.

They drove for about half an hour and Vince came to a stop. He decided to take a look at the map so they didn't mess up.

The two men following Vince stopped and watched as he got off of his machine, took a flashlight out of his coat, pulled out the map, and pointing to it, he said, "It looks like we're not far from the ridge. We'll take this road, but when we get here where the river bends, we'll stop and hide the machines. We'll walk the rest of the way."

They agreed and all three continued to the spot. When they arrived, Vince decided that he would walk the road because it was plowed, and he sent Borya higher on the ridge in the woods. Adrik, he thought should stay low in the woods near the road. "Remember, we're looking for a cabin which is supposed to be on the ridge, so if you see anything like that, stop and let us know before proceeding."

They knew that since there were no leaves on the trees, the cabin should stand out. Because the snow was deeper in the woods, Borya moved slowly, but he plowed ahead. He knew the cabin had to be on high ground. They had walked for about ten minutes when Borya stopped, spotted the cabin, and walked down to meet Adrik. They both found Vince and made their plan based on where the cabin was situated. All three had their night vision goggles ready and were now scanning the ridge.

Paul saw something. He thought it might just be an animal, but something definitely moved. He was hidden, not far from the cabin, and he thought he should let the others know, but he wanted to be sure he saw something...so he waited.

The men were in the woods now. They could see the cabin, but they were not getting any signs of any warm bodies. They decided to move slowly forward while keeping each other informed. Then Vince got a hit. He saw something that looked suspicious. He motioned for the others to check out the spot. Their goggles gave them the same image. They had to make sure they weren't just seeing a deer or some other animal, so they decided to have Adrik move toward the spot. He was an expert at this—knowing how to sneak up to find out what they were seeing. As he moved closer, he also moved higher and there he realized that what he was looking at was probably a human body.

Adrik aimed his rifle, but, in the thick woods, he did not have a great shot. He also realized that out here there wasn't a sound, and even though he had a silencer, he knew if there was a sentry that there would be more people in the cabin. He decided to move back to Borya and Vince and reevaluate the situation.

Vince agreed. There were probably more people here than they had planned. He was supposed to be alone, so why a sentry out front? Vince thought that they had to work silently and perhaps take the sentry out quietly. Then they heard voices.

Ron had come out to relieve Paul.

Vince focused on the area and saw that now there were two people. One left and the other took his place. This made Vince think they had been played. He motioned to Borya and Adrik and asked, "Do you think this is a trap? Did Bates get the right information?" Both men agreed that something was up. They did not know what type of fire power they might have, so they decided to wait until light to see if they could ascertain what might be going on.

Paul mentioned to Ron that he thought he had seen some movement, so Ron went back inside to see if Joe still had his night vision goggles. He did.

Vince saw the first man leave, and then the second man. He wondered what was going on. Then someone came back.

Ron went right to the spot where Paul had been. It was a spot that provided protection since there was a small hole in the ground where they sat. He put on the goggles and looked out. He did not see much. He kept scanning the area—then he got a hit. Something was out there. It looked like a huge blotch of green. It must be more than one animal or person. Ron knew from his army experience that this was not a good sign. He knew they were all being hunted, and maybe this was the beginning. He decided to stay put to see what would happen.

Vince was now sure that something was up. He thought, *what if they can see us?* He quickly decided to leave the area and figure out what he could do next.

Ron saw whoever it was back away from the road. It looked like they were running. Now he was sure it was someone after them. He pulled out his rifle and fired several rounds in the direction of the runners.

Vince was behind the other two men who were complaining about his methods. They kept saying that they do not work like this. They usually wait quietly and let the target get comfortable, and when the person thinks he's safe, that's when they hit. Vince was not happy.

Joe, Tommy, and Paul heard the shots. Wayne came in from the back door, and they told him to stay put while they find out what was going on. They went out and saw Ron shooting in the direction of the road. Joe asked, "What's up?"

Ron yelled, "I saw a lot of movement near the road. I think someone was stalking us, so I let them have it, but they're running away."

"Let's follow," Joe said.

All four of them began pursuing the three men. They could not see that well since it was still dark, but they fired in the direction that Ron said. They followed for several minutes before they heard machines fire up, and they watched taillights move rapidly away. They fired in the direction of the lights, but they did not have any luck.

The cabin on the ridge, February 26, morning
Tommy was the first to speak, "I guess my cover is blown."

"We knew that would happen, but this is a little faster than we thought," Paul added.

Joe said, "We have a plan if you are interested. It involves a lot of risk, but we could get to the bottom of this."

Tommy was confused. He did not know what to do, but he knew he could not stay in the cabin. "All right. What's the plan?"

Joe and Ron began to give the others the rest of their plan. It took some time, but everyone was in agreement that something must be done to end this. "That's it. Tommy, if you want in, we can begin building a larger group. We've all talked before and decided that we'll need a lot more than we have now. We've sent some of our family to a hiding place, so if you need anyone to be safe for a while, they can join them. Our sons are returning to help, and I think I can get a few more, but we're going to need a lot of firepower and equipment."

Wayne was listening, and he turned to Joe and said, "I had heard that the old militia is planning the same thing that you just told me. I tried to stay out of it, but I know they've had meetings."

"Would that be Charlie's old outfit?" Joe asked.

"He's always been in charge."

Joe was horrified. "If he's in charge, then I can't join his group. You know he helped send us out of the area to be eliminated. Ron and I are lucky to be alive."

Wayne knew the whole story, and he was not sure he could go along with Charlie's group either, but he was also afraid that if they did not join forces that they would just have to leave the area and get a new life—and he wasn't ready for that. "I know that Charlie was part of that plan to get rid of you and Ron, but I think he was somehow forced into it. I don't know how, but I know he has that side of him."

Ron spoke up. "I can't even begin to tell you what I think of him. He did not like me from day one, and people don't change overnight."

Paul added what he knew. "Well, I know for a fact that Charlie no longer has the same people in his group now. They are almost all new because his group broke up a while ago. Some of the people who are involved are good people who just want them out of here. They're taking over the entire town."

Joe was still unsure whether they should continue this line of thought. He knew that they had to get more information and somehow avoid the people out to hurt them. "We need to create a base where we can hide, and we'll need munitions. We do need help, but first we have to understand just what is going on at the bunker, and we should set up a camp somewhere near their base so we can investigate."

Morning, February 26

Bates was tired of all the crap that had been going on at the bunker. Now he had to deal with these three who were sent by the new boss. They had come back from their supposed elimination of some people in town. How in the world did they hope to get away with that? Two botched attempts on the life of some guys the boss wanted eliminated immediately. Now they were sitting in the bunker planning what to do next. Bates liked it when he was alone and could do what he wanted, but this past six months had been crazy.

Vince told Bates their new idea. "So, we're planning to take up a position somewhere near town, and just wait until we have a shot. Enough of this running-around stuff. Let us know if you get any new information that'll help."

Both Adrik and Borya agreed, and in broken English said, "Time to be like the soldiers we are." All three men approved of the new plan, looked over the map, and told Bates they would not return until the jobs were completed.

Bates had to hold back a smile.

CHAPTER 23

Afternoon of the Same Day

Wayne and Tommy decided to take a chance and set up a meeting with Charlie. They knew that convincing Joe and Ron would be almost impossible, and maybe even difficult to convince Charlie of their plan. They knew their lives were on the line—and that time was important. The event was on the horizon, according to Joe, and they were not even sure what that was, but they needed help and they needed it quickly.

Wayne picked up his phone and made the call, "Yo, Charlie. Wayne here. How are you doing?"

"Not bad. How've ya been?"

"Good. Say I have a question for you."

"Shoot."

"We have a problem."

"We. Who's that?"

"Right now, me and Tommy."

"That so. What you want?"

"Could we meet somewhere so we don't have to be on these phones? Never know who might be listening."

"Sure. Been wantin' to talk to Tommy. Had some people sayin' he's good in the woods out there to the east—you know, where the bunker is."

"Yes, he is. His Uncle George took him all over there when he was learning the trade."

"You're kinda in the hip pocket of that teacher though, aren't you? 'Cause he caused all kinds of trouble before, so if it has to do with him, I'm out."

"Well, let's meet and talk it out. You know where that road is that leads to the old dump, just outside of Colewin? Just past that old farm house. We can meet you there in thirty minutes."

"I know where that is. Okay, I'll see ya there in 'bout thirty minutes then." Charlie hung up and called Matt.

"Hello."

"This Matt?"

"Yep. This you, Charlie?"

"Hey, Matt, no worry about gettin' ahold of Tommy. I'm meetin' with him in thirty minutes."

"Great. I hope it goes well."

And Charlie hung up.

Thirty minutes later

Tommy and Wayne pulled up to the designated spot, and Tommy shut down the truck. They decided it would be best if Tommy and Wayne went alone, but the others would be close for backup if needed. Tommy took a big deep breath and blew it out loudly.

Wayne said, "I feel the same way."

They both were nervous—and at the same time, angry. Charlie had been on the other end of the situation that had gotten them in trouble with these people they did not even know. Tommy felt like his heart would jump out of his chest. It beat fast, and he could not calm down. "How does Charlie get away with what he's done? It isn't right. We have to hide out because someone wants to kill us, and it was Charlie and Sam who were on their side. I haven't spoken to either of them since Mr. Joe disappeared that night, and now we have to agree to some kind of alliance with these creeps."

"I agree," Wayne said. "My stomach is flipping, and I can't stop thinking that we should get rid of these bunker people to start, but Charlie is the only one who has any real knowledge about the bunker area, and if we're going to get rid of them, we have to trust him for a bit."

"Trust!" barked Tommy.

"Well, we may never trust him, but we'll need to work with him until we can come up with some plan or find out what we can do."

Then they heard a vehicle and saw Charlie coming from a direction they did not think was possible. It must be a road, and sure enough there he was. He had two other people with him.

Tommy was nervous. "Who the hell is with him? I thought we were meeting with him. We better be prepared for anything." Tommy did not move, but he pulled his rifle from behind his seat. Wayne had only brought his .45 that his father had given him, and he wrapped his fingers around it as Charlie got out of his truck. Charlie did not have a weapon.

Wayne opened his door and got out slowly, looking in all directions to make sure this was not a trap. He wasn't sure if Charlie might still have ties to the people who were after him and Tommy. After he had surveyed the area, he yelled to Charlie. "Who's in the truck?"

"Just Sam and a buddy of mine. He's from over near Poplar. You know the Fisher boys."

"I know them."

"Well, let's get down to business."

Wayne said, "Yeah, Charlie we were wondering what you were planning to do about the bunker. We know you're planning something, and we would like to help."

Wayne was standing in the open in line with Charlie's truck— and just as Wayne spoke, he moved toward Charlie. The Fisher boy got out of the truck and moved between Charlie and Wayne. Bad timing, because at the same time a bullet tore through his head and slammed into Wayne. Charlie saw what happened and ran to the Fisher boy on the ground. Everyone took cover. They looked around. The Fisher boy was dead for sure. Wayne lay on the ground with a wound to his upper torso. They all pulled out their weapons, but they could not see or hear anything.

A short distance from the road
"Got two," Borya mumbled. He did not have another shot.

Vince whispered, "We should move. This is too close for comfort." This was a difficult shot in the woods. They did not have the clearing they liked for this type of hit. Vince was looking through his binoculars and could see they all had weapons out, so he made the decision to move. It looked like they got at least two down. They quietly moved toward their machines and tore out of there.

Tommy and Charlie heard the snowmobiles, but they did not move for fear of another shot. After a few minutes they could hear the machines fade in the distance, and they moved slowly out of their defensive positions. Then they decided to get help for Wayne. The Fisher boy could no longer be helped. They planned to meet later.

Tommy was shaken. He knew they were after him and Wayne, but he could not believe that it would happen as it did. They called for an ambulance while Tommy and Charlie attempted to stop the bleeding. Then they loaded Wayne into the back of the truck, and Tommy drove him to Colewin to await the EMTs.

The bunker, about an hour later
Bates had heard from the new boss. The new boss's first concern was whether the executions had taken place. He had four on his

mind that he wanted completed now. He had sent his best people—and he wanted results. Bates told him they were on it right now, and he would report as soon as they were back. Bates also learned that the new leader wanted the event to take place in the near future.

The new boss was impatient. "Enough of this waiting around. Get your people prepared. We'll send out the last groups that we will need to be in place. We are almost ready at the other bases. We can surprise everyone and take over before anyone knows what is happening."

Bates was a bit doubtful about moving so fast. He had worked with the original leader, and he knew his plan was about a year or two away, but he did not want to raise the ire of this man. He could read him and he knew he was no one to underestimate. "Whatever you say. We'll work on it and let you know how it goes. If you can get the troops to us soon, I'm sure we can get them ready. The people who train them are good, and they can speed up the process."

"Good."

"I'll keep you informed," Bates said, but the line was dead. Bates was worried and wondered. *This new boss is moving too fast! Why doesn't he wait to hear if the boss recovers? If not, this could go sideways if he hurries into it. Whatever, I better once again prepare myself and be ready to hide if need be.* Just as he turned back to his screens, he saw Vince and his two comrades roar up to the gate. The sentry opened the gate and let them in. Vince headed right for the bunker door.

CHAPTER 24

Colewin, February 27, a.m.

Wayne had been sent to the Newberry Hospital where they patched him as best they could before he was transported via helicopter to Marquette. He had gone through extensive surgery, but they thought he might pull through. It would be touch and go for several days. Joe had called Cathy at his brother's place, and now she was at the hospital with Wayne.

Joe was fuming. "Okay, this is getting too close. They killed a young kid for no reason, and they were able to get Wayne. They must have somehow known about the meeting. We didn't tell anyone else. Tommy, what do you know?"

"All I can tell you is that Wayne and I contacted Charlie to set up the meeting. He showed up with two other people. That was not supposed to be part of the plan. One of them might have said something to someone."

Ron had been listening. "Whatever the plan is. We know they want to get rid of the four of us, and they're willing to take out anyone else who's in the way. Wayne was lucky his injury wasn't fatal, but who knows how he's going to do, or if he will recover. We need to figure out a place to hide—and we need a plan to find out what they're going to do next as far as the event is concerned."

Joe said, "I agree Ron. We need to update and improve the plan. What did Charlie say? Is he really on our side?"

Tommy spoke up. "I think Charlie is as upset by all this as we are. Besides, that guy that was killed was one of the Fisher family, and they want the bunker destroyed and those people chased out. Now they are going to be enraged. I know Charlie wants to do something, but he doesn't feel safe with you two since he participated two years ago in getting the two of you out of here and almost killed."

"He should be concerned. I can't even look at the guy."

Ron agreed. "I can't either."

"But we do need help. We might have to work with him for a bit, but then we're out of here. First, we need a plan to keep the three of us safe. Let's brainstorm today and find a place to hide out where they won't look. Somewhere that will give us time and also allow us to investigate the bunker some way."

Tommy was listening and finally spoke up. "I think I have an idea that might work. It could keep us safe and away from these bounty hunters or whatever they are."

Joe was interested. "All right. Let's hear what you have. You know this area better than anyone."

Tommy was concerned and nervous, but he knew that he could help. He just didn't have all the answers that he needed, and he realized that they *could not trust just anyone.* "I know we shouldn't involve law enforcement because we don't know if they're working for the bunker people. Even after that Fisher kid was killed, not much happened. Sheriff Daryl came and investigated, but I don't think anything will come of it, so we can't depend on any other help, but what we might be able to pull together."

Joe was interested in what Tommy had to say. "What are you thinking?"

"You know that the bunker was built into the side of that big hill. There are two roads in. One from the west that seems to be traveled the most out of Colewin. The other one, also from the west, is more north and is not used. It is overgrown with brush and small trees that have sprung up in places. There's a road that goes south to U.S. 2 where the bunker people haul stuff in and out. The north side has nothing but thick woods. We could establish a place there and keep tabs on them from behind. I know how to get within a few feet of their barracks—and they would never know we were there. If we could somehow establish this as our base, maybe we could get someone to tap into their command center and find out what the plan is. They would never suspect that we would be that close to them."

Joe looked at Tommy and said, "That's an interesting plan, but do we want to be that close?"

Ron wasn't sure exactly what he meant, but he thought that they needed to come up with something to observe what was going on. "Let's talk some about what we might do if we can pull off something like this."

"Would we need Charlie at all to do this?" Joe questioned.

Tommy answered, "We'll need him and some others because we need assistance to get this done."

Ron agreed, but he knew they did not have to be close for electronic surveillance. "We can have my son try to get into their computer system. He would not have to be close to do that. He can investigate from anywhere, so for that, we don't need to be that close."

Joe agreed and said, "However, we do need to set up some type of physical surveillance to see who is going in and coming out. If we are going to take this base down, we'll need that."

Charlie's house, February 28

Matt was furious. "Charlie, what the hell happened? My cousin is dead. How did these people find out about your meeting? I thought you said that you and two others were the only people meeting. How could they have found out? They aren't even from around here. This is on you!"

"They couldn't have known. They just could not have. I only tole your cousin and Sam. They wouldn't have said anything."

"My cousin went only because you asked him."

"I wanted you to get the information from someone you trusted. That's all."

"Did you tell anyone else? I've got to know, Charlie."

"No. Jus' Sam like I said."

"We need to talk to Sam," Matt shouted.

"He'll be here anytime now."

It wasn't long before Sam's truck pulled into Charlie's driveway. Matt walked to the truck, yanked the door open, and pulled Sam out. "Who'd ya tell?"

"What are ya talkin' about? Who'd I tell?"

"About the meetin' where my cousin was killed and Wayne shot."

"I didn't tell no one. Just tole my wife I was meetin' with Charlie. That's it."

Charlie was pissed. "What? You told that old busy body wife o' yours! Geez, Sam, I told you not to say anything."

"She never told no one."

Matt didn't know what to think. He just said, "Well, find out if anyone knows anything. I've got to get back home and help with the funeral. You son of …. I should shoot ya right here. Charlie, that goes to show—we can't trust anyone, and now we're gonna take these people down. You have my word!"

At the bunker

Vince went to tell Bates of the successful kills. He had to report to the boss who and how many of the four had been put away. "Bates, report to the boss that two are down. That's one of the four he wanted out of action."

"Do you have a way to verify your kill? You know he is going to want that."

"We have a long-distance photo of the two where you can't really see the faces, but they're dead."

"You know that is not enough. I'm not calling him with that. You need verification that they're dead or he will not be happy."

"I know. We can wait until the word is out that they were killed, and we'll send an obituary or something."

"Are you serious? He doesn't operate that way—and you know it. He always wants absolute proof. If you have a picture of the man with a hole in his head, then you might be all right. You need to prove it!"

"Got it."

CHAPTER 25

Colewin, March 1

After much brainstorming and hours of negotiating, Joe, Ron, and Tommy came to the conclusion that they would need the help of Charlie and his people if they were going to succeed. They knew they needed some physical presence in the area around the bunker. Individuals that they could trust to keep an eye on the comings and goings of personnel. They especially knew they had to keep an eye on the people who were after the three of them. They needed to find out who they were and eliminate the threat, or at least know where they were at all times.

Ron had recruited his son to try and break into the database at the bunker. If he could keep constant surveillance on these people, they might figure out exactly what their plan was. Joe's son was going to assist him, and together they had as much electronic equipment as they needed to do a thorough search.

Joe was still not sure about a real alliance with Charlie, however. "I know what you told me about Charlie's plan, and I know if we're going to shut this place down, we're going to need more people, but I can't even think about seeing Charlie after his involvement almost got us killed."

Ron agreed. "I'm with you there."

Tommy was concerned because he knew that with Charlie, they could have a much larger force. "I have an idea. Why don't you work directly with Matt Fisher instead of Charlie? He can be the go-between. After all, Charlie wants to actually get into the bunker and get his equipment back. As we discussed earlier, he has a plan to set up a base camp less than a quarter mile behind the bunker on the highest point and have his people dig a tunnel into the bunker. He thinks he could actually break in from behind, where we discussed setting up a camp, and they would never know."

"That sounds a bit risky," Joe said. "If he can do that, I'm guessing that we could get most of the weapons that we need to run these people out of here, but it makes me nervous."

"But if he can succeed, that would really be helpful," Ron added.

"All right. Tommy, you get ahold of this Matt Fisher and tell him we want to meet right away so we can get a plan together."

"Will do."

Poplar, March 2

Joe and Ron needed to meet with Matt early in March. There was a lot to discuss, but first they had to feel each other out about what had to be accomplished. Then they could make a real plan. Tommy was to set up the time and place.

Matt was all for the plan that Tommy described. He could understand Joe's and Ron's hesitation to meet with Charlie, but he also knew he needed Charlie. He had knowledge of the bunker that they needed in order to get in and rescue the equipment.

But to understand Matt, one had to understand where and how he lived. Matt was a good guy. He lived in a home that had been his parents until they had passed a few years back. He was a hard worker and very friendly. He believed that people should work hard and pay for what they get. He did not believe in things like credit cards, borrowing money, or cheating to get ahead. He made about thirty-seven thousand dollars a year—and he was happy.

Matt did not understand though how he and so many of his friends and family lived week-to-week, paycheck-to-paycheck, even though they worked fifty to sixty hours a week. To him it wasn't fair how some people were paid huge amounts of money for doing very little. It just wasn't fair, but he did not complain to anyone. He just kept to himself, worked each day, and didn't feel he had to hate anyone just because they made more money. Yet, he knew the system was rigged against him and many others.

It bothered Matt that some people would do anything for a buck, especially those people who joined up with the bunker, and he could not grasp why so many people were indifferent to the threat to the area. Either they didn't care—or were too afraid to do anything.

Matt said, "I will do what I can to help make this work. I'll need to meet with Charlie. We have already talked about diggin' a tunnel to the back of the bunker and makin' it big enough to get what we need. We have sentries posted in many places to keep track of people in and out. One team is situated not far from the gate, so we can relay information to you and Charlie's team. Maybe together we can figur' out who these guys are who killed my cousin and shot Wayne."

"That sounds good. It is exactly what Joe and Ron were thinking. They need to meet with you as soon as you are able to get our plans synchronized, so we're not duplicating or getting in each other's way."

"Okay, let's set up a meetin' for tomorrow to plan the next moves. Somewhere out-of-the-way. Don't let anyone else know. It'll just be the four of us. I'll have my lookouts let me know if anyone leaves the base so we can keep an eye on those snipers or anyone else who might be out ta hurt us. Damn, we have to be careful."

Tommy agreed, "All right. I'll let them know."

The bunker, March 3

The word was out that a group was going to try to take down the bunker. Bates was involved in the discussion when some news came to him. There were several individuals in Colewin who were kept undercover so they could find out whether anyone had plans against the bunker. Bates knew that Charlie was upset about what had transpired, and Bates knew he had to keep these people in town so they could report to him. One of them had given him a tip earlier that he passed along to Vince, and now this info about several people organizing some type of revolt against the bunker. Bates informed the leader, who was not happy.

The leader responded, "Just take out as many as you need to eliminate threats. We need to have chaos anyway before we pull off the event, so just do it."

Bates was not really shocked at this request. He knew it was coming. "Okay, I'll get the guys on it. Anyone we suspect, that's who we're taking out."

"Perfect!" was the leader's response.

Bates called Vince to the bunker, and they decided that they would start right away. Anyone in their way, or anyone suspected of working against them, would be taken out. What would it matter? Soon, the event would occur and a lot of others would also go down.

Vince was happy for the tip. He was tired of having to be careful and work around people. Now, he had carte blanche—freedom to do what had to be done. Who cares anyway? These jerks don't know their asses from a hole in the ground. Best to take them out so they don't get in the way.

CHAPTER 26

The Cabin, March 3, Early Afternoon

The plan had been changed several times. Joe and Ron had met with Matt on a few occasions. They included Tommy when they could. Charlie was included once, and his ideas were considered, but before any of this could begin, they would have to wait until the ground thawed a bit more and all the snow was out of the woods. They did not want to leave any trails that could give away their plan.

Each day at the cabin, they had decided to keep one person on watch. Today, Tommy was outside in the woods. He knew no one would just come right to the cabin on the road. Having lived through one nightmare when his Uncle George was killed, he was always on guard. Today was no different. His guard was up, and he knew he had to be sharp at all times.

Earlier in the day Ron had gotten word from his and Joe's sons about some information that they had been able to glean from their electronic surveillance. One of the ideas hinted to what might be coming as part of the event. They had Ron's son on speaker phone.

Ron, Jr. said, "We found some interesting and alarming information about the event. They are going to be quietly sending a lot more troops to the U.P. to be trained for the final push. They'll be sent to various places in the country before it begins. One piece of information, which we lucked out finding, sounded like they are planning a siege similar to the one on January 6, except that they have a much larger force, and they included training on how to hold individuals for ransom or execute political figures."

Ron, Sr. was astounded, "What?"

Joe said, "Sounds like what happened back in 2020. Wasn't there also a plan to take down the Michigan Governor?"

Ron, Jr. had lived near Lansing and knew the story. "There really was no proof that something like that would take place, but the fact that they even thought about doing that makes me wonder."

Joe was thinking out loud. "So, we know that there will be many more troops sent here."

"Yes. It also sounds like they will be getting several more shipments of armaments. We did not learn about what type, but if they are sending more troops, they will need more rifles, ammunition, gear…no one knows for sure what."

Joe thought that the situation called for them to move faster, but he was not sure what they could do to hasten what they had planned. "We have our hands full right now just planning and staying safe. We can't move around much for fear of getting shot."

When they ended the call with Ron, Jr., Joe and Ron wondered if they might have gotten in too deep, but they knew they had to continue since they had little help from any government agency. Joe had talked to Ann, the FBI agent, and she said the agency was extended beyond their scope and still could not give any help.

Joe was thinking about the situation with the Michigan Governor, and he wondered if they were planning to take some politicians for ransom. They could hold these people hostage. How would the federal government react to this? Could they somehow save the hostages? What if these people had another run on the Senate and the House with all these troops? "If we're going to do anything, we need more help, but who? We have only a handful right now that we can trust."

As shots rang out, Joe and Ron ran for their weapons and for cover. They could not see Tommy, but they knew it must be him. After scouring the area, they could just make him out in the woods outside lying on the ground with his rifle aimed at something deep in the woods. It *had been* Tommy who had fired. He took another shot and then stormed into the cabin. "Joe, get your gear. I think we're being watched. I saw two people moving through the woods, and a third not far away scoping out this area. It must be those same ones who hit Wayne and that Fisher boy, and who tried to attack me at the old cabin on the ridge."

"Are they still there?" Ron asked.

"I think I might have scared them off for now, but we need to find a new place, and we need to get more help."

Joe knew he was right. "We'll pack up tonight and leave in the dark, but first we're going to inspect the area."

Tommy, Ron, and Joe slid out of the cabin's back door and each searched the area that Tommy identified as the hot spot. They did not find anything, but they did locate some snowmobile tracks off to the north of the cabin. "This must be where they came in," Tommy said.

"No sense following them. We know where they go when they have to hide. They'll be at the bunker in twenty minutes. Let's contact the sentry out there to find out if they've seen anyone leave or return."

Tommy got on his phone and called Matt. He told him what had happened and who they thought had been near the cabin. "Could you check with your sentry to see if anyone left or returned?"

"Sure. Give me a few minutes. I'll get back to you."

It wasn't long and Matt returned the call. Three guys left about two hours ago. They're going to let me know if they return."

"Thanks, Matt," Tommy replied. "We need to get better ways to quickly communicate their movements or someone else is going to get hurt."

"I agree."

March 4

Joe, Tommy, and Ron met with Matt the next day. They came up with a plan to track the three they suspected of hunting them down. They were going to set a trap at the cabin for the next day. Matt would bring some of his relatives to help, and they would surround the area. The plan was to wait until the three left the base and then follow them. If they did not go to the cabin, they would check where they were planning to hit someone next and set the trap there.

The bunker, March 4

Bates was trying to get control of the situation the new boss had concocted. He knew he had a lot of troops heading his way, and he needed to have everyone ready to get them trained and sent to their spots. His only problem was that Vince and his friends were keeping him focused on the wrong things. They had not eliminated all of the targets, and Bates was concerned. As he contemplated this situation, he saw Vince pull up, so he unlocked the door. Vince opened it and walked in.

"Had a near-miss yesterday."

"What do you mean?"

"We had the three of them in one spot. We had some of your people check out the area, and they gave us these guys. Sitting ducks. But someone spotted us before we were set up. He must have eagle eyes."

"It must be that kid. He knows this area and these woods. He can probably pick you out a mile away. You mean you aren't good enough to outfox a Yooper."

"It's not that. We thought this would be easy pickings, but they're smart. They post sentries and know how to hide. We'll be better prepared now that we know what we are up against."

CHAPTER 27

April 1

Most of the snow had melted around Colewin and Poplar and near the bunker. The ground was mostly thawed, thanks to some rain and warmer-than-normal temperatures. The plan that had been decided upon was a combination of what Charlie wanted—and what Joe and Ron hoped to accomplish. They had all decided a frontal attack of some kind was out of the question since so many troops were in and out constantly. Ron and Joe had a plan to follow some of the troops that were leaving to see where they were sending them, but that plan was on hold right now.

Charlie was determined to dig a tunnel to the bunker and retrieve his equipment. Joe and Ron wanted to capture Bates so they could learn all that they needed to impede the event. Matt had somehow gotten the three men to work together. He had also managed to speak to some of the men from Colewin who had joined the bunker. He found out that their sole reason for joining was the money they could make to help support their families. They were tired of the poor pay and lack of benefits in the area.

Bill was one of them. He and Matt had been friends since high school, and they trusted each other, but Matt was confused why Bill would hang with these people. He could understand why, but he knew they did not realize what the ultimate plan was, so he confronted Bill. "You know what they're up to, right? They been harassin' our town and our women and men for the better part of the las' year. How can you stay with 'em?"

"I really need the money."

"I can understand that, but how do you think this will end?"

"Well, I'm not happy with how the country is going, so I guess I don't really mind. How can you not join in? We need people like you."

"Sorry, Bill, that ain't for me, but, if they plan on hurtin' any of us, you'll let us know, right? I mean they already killed my cousin."

"You can't be sure of that. Sheriff Daryl says it was a hunting accident."

"It was no accident. It was an assassination, and I'm still pissed and upset! Like I said, how can you be a part o' that?"

"Well, I am. I'll let you know if there is any plan to hurt anyone in town, but I think you're wrong about that. They aren't into that."

"They're not? Then who attacked the three girls the other night? They were high school girls. It has to be those troops from the bunker."

Matt and Bill talked for a long time, and Matt finally gave up trying to convince his friend to quit. He hoped now that he had someone on the inside if he needed information, but he was cautious because Bill was so connected to these people.

Later that day

Charlie knew the exact spot to start the digging. It was about a quarter mile from the bunker. He knew he needed a lot of help since he could not bring in noisy equipment. He also knew he had to bring in logs for supporting the tunnel, but at the same time, not make a noticeable trail that anyone could follow. He wondered if his eight-foot-long logs would give them enough clearance for the trucks they would need to haul supplies out. He could get one of those little backhoes that are fairly quiet to help dig, but most of the digging would be done by hand. He had recruited several individuals who could help, both male and female. They would dig using number two round point shovels and pails, once they had the hole started.

Charlie had brought in several eight-foot-long logs to use as the first supports. He had dragged them in while the snow was still on the ground, a few at a time. He and Sam had quietly brought them in using their snowmobiles. Now that the snow was gone, there was no trail to follow. He and Sam had used different entrances to the spot so as not to get any one trail developed enough for anyone to follow.

Matt told Charlie that he had access to a small excavator, so Charlie's backhoe was not necessary. He brought in a small excavator that he realized would work great in this area. It would be quiet enough and could get the digging started without a lot of workers. This would help get them started sooner and might help in rough spots. He would still need his people, however.

Ron and Joe went to the site early one afternoon to see if there had been any progress. The excavator was there, and Charlie had already begun the digging. They had all they could do to face him. They still had not forgiven him for his part in what had happened to them, but right now they had a plan—and they needed to tolerate him. Joe noticed that Charlie had four other people working there, and he was concerned about the digging.

"Is this going to work? Won't someone hear you?" Joe asked.

"They won't hear us, 'specially once we get the excavator inside the tunnel. It don't make much noise."

"What about the mosquitoes? How is that working? It's going to get hot out here, and you'll have to have everyone covered when they're out in full force or you'll all get eaten alive."

"It don't get really hot out here in the deep woods, and we've sprayed the heck out of the area to kill any skeeters that might be out here. We got mosquito nets too, just in case. We should be all right."

"Who are these people?" Ron asked.

Joe knew right away. "These were students of mine that I had before we were sent away. That is Charlie's nephew and those are his friends."

"Can you trust them?" Ron asked.

Charlie was quick to respond. "These people are going to be all right. This here is my nephew and his friends. We can trust 'em. You see my nephew and his friends are really afraid of what these crazy people at the bunker might do next. I can trust 'em more'n anyone else, and they're good workers. They don't complain, and they'll do whatever I say. I also have three others in the woods around here. One is Sam and two of 'em are young friends of Matt Fisher."

"Where in the world are they? I can't see a thing beyond this opening you made," Joe said.

"That's the idea. If anyone comes near here, they'll be our defense. They have silencers on their guns, so if they take anyone out, it shouldn't alert the base."

"Great idea," Ron and Joe both said.

Joe and Ron looked around and had trouble finding them. The area was very dense. He could not tell how Charlie and Sam had gotten in here as easily as they had. Joe looked at the spot and noticed the thick foliage and the sloping hill that dropped quickly right where the digging was going on. Charlie had figured the height they needed in order to be at the level of the bunker, and if they dug straight ahead, they would run right into it.

The sloping hill had to be cleared of some small tree growth, but it was nothing the small excavator could not handle. It looked like they had gotten a good start on the tunnel. Most of the dirt they hauled out was sand. It would be fairly easy to dig if they did not run into anything, but it presented some problems when it came to caving in, so there would have to be a lot more of the supporting beams. He could see the people hauling buckets and pushing wheelbarrows taking the sand quite a distance from the tunnel. He thought they did this so they would not create any noticeable piles. They were also filling in a valley to Joe's left as he faced the tunnel. This would take some time, but if they could get in and take over the place, then they could find out what they needed and take some hostages.

Joe's only fear was that this was only a quarter mile from the bunker, and he knew that they always patrolled around the place. "Hopefully, they don't get this far into these woods."

Charlie agreed. "We're ready."

Ron turned to Joe and said, "We need to get out of here and plan for the next steps."

Joe agreed and they hopped on their four-wheelers and headed out.

Later that same day

Joe was very cautious as they left the area. They knew they were still being hunted—and he and Ron were taking as many precautions as they could. Their current plan involved the troops that were stationed at the bunker. They knew that they were moving in and out, and they wanted to know exactly where and how many they were sending to various places. He and Ron thought they should follow a group out of the area as soon as some troops were sent out. That would get them out of the crosshairs of the guys who were after them, and it might give them some information to feed to Ann so she could know that these troops from the U.P. were being sent all over. They were also concerned about the digging going on in the woods. "What do you think, Ron? Is what Charlie's doing going to work?"

"I believe if they can get in and out quietly, they have a chance. If anyone gives them away, then we will have a huge problem."

"Hopefully, they send out some troops soon so we can follow. I'd like to get out of the area for a while and take a little heat off of us. We'll have to do it on the sly so no one picks up on it though."

"We just won't let anyone know. If we get the word that they are moving, we'll just quietly head out after them."

"Yes. If our sentries are good and keep us informed promptly, then we'll have a chance. Let's take a different route back to our hiding place and make some plans."

"Sounds great. I'll follow."

The bunker, April 2

Bates was not surprised when another group of troops came in, but he was concerned that they could not house many more without problems. He already had some of them go into town and cause all kinds of trouble. He wanted to tell the new boss to slow down, but he knew that this new boss was different and violent when he did not get his way, so he just thought that he would have his leaders hurry the training and get rid of a number of them. He was involved in some contacts on the web when he noticed on his monitor one of the troops knocking on the bunker door. "What the hell is that?" Bates said aloud. He checked again on his monitor to see if he knew who it was. He did not know him, and he could not figure out why he was knocking so furiously. Bates finally went to the door. He opened it a bit and yelled, "What in the world do you want anyway? You don't have to pound the door in. I can't hear pounding in here."

"I got something to tell you and it's important."

"Important? What's it about?" Bates asked.

"I think you got some trouble in town with some of these locals."

"And how do you know?"

"Cause I'm one of 'em. Lived here most of my life."

"Yeah, big deal. So what?"

"This is about them trying to take over the base."

"I heard something like this earlier, but had no real information to work on, so what do you mean? This base would be tough to take down. We have all kinds of troops and weapons. Who would try that?"

"You know someone named Charlie? He used to run this place."

"I know him, and he isn't anyone to worry about. He's crazy."

"He might be, but I heard he has a plan to take this place down. Now I don't know what it is, but you better make sure you have people posted all over this place to watch for them. They're serious."

"You sure about this?"

"Got it from a friend of mine who doesn't like what we're doing here."

"Should we take him out?"

"No, I don't think that would be necessary. You just have to build up your security, so you can be prepared if anything happens."

"All right. I'll take your warning and pass it on to the leaders. They'll take care of it."

"Great. Don't want this place to go down. We like having this income. Don't want to jeopardize that," the man said.

"Fine. Who are you anyway, so I can let them know who to talk to if they need more information?"

"Bill. Just Bill will do." And with that Bill turned and left and went back to his training with the troops.

Bates realized this was the guy who had given him information about some of the local troops. He just stood at the door and watched him walk away as he figured out what he should do. He knew he had to talk to his training leaders as soon as possible, just in case. Bates knew they had gotten a bit lax about security at the base and more concerned with getting troops trained and prepared for the event. They were all too focused on the event since the new boss took over, and they had developed tunnel vision. He shut the door, turned back to his computers, and sent out a message to his leaders to connect with him as soon as possible.

Bates was mumbling while he typed, "How did this Bill find out that we need more security? He's from here, so could he be part of a plan to get us focused on something that isn't important? What's his deal?" He knew he would have to have Bill investigated too to make sure that he wasn't working with anyone outside of the bunker. Bates was nervous. Will he have to get Vince and his partners on this? They haven't been able to even get the people they need to take out, let alone anyone else. They botched the last one and the sheriff had to cover it up, but now this is a second warning about a takeover.

CHAPTER 28

Hideaway, April 2

Matt and Tommy were the only people who knew where Joe and Ron were staying. The earlier plan to set a trap and catch the ones who were hunting them did not work, so they went into hiding. They kept it that way because there were few people they could trust. Matt was waiting for them when they arrived.

"Hey, how ya doing?"

"Good. How are you? We were just out at the digging where Charlie has set up his camp. Hope he's successful."

"I do too. We need what he can get there. The trouble is we've got fewer and fewer people to help us. They've started joinin' up with the people at the bunker. It's got to do with money. Most of the people around here lost their jobs durin' the pandemic, and it hasn't come back yet. I'm worried we're gonna lose most of the people I could trust. I just spoke with an old friend, Bill, and he's on their payroll. He doesn't much care what they're gonna do— but they give him an income, and he's content with that."

"That doesn't sound good. They have so much money to throw around that we cannot compete. We might not be able to turn the tide on them unless we have help."

Ron agreed. "Could we look elsewhere for help?"

While they discussed the issue, Matt received a call from one of the sentries at the bunker. The sentry was well hidden and had been on duty for several weeks. He knew what had been happening, and that some vehicles brought in more troops this past few weeks, and he knew that it would only be a matter of time until some troops had to leave. He had been in contact with the other sentries—one covering each direction, and one near U.S. 2 who had just called to tell him two large semi-trailers had arrived. He put two and two together and figured this is how they would get the troops out.

Matt answered, "Hey, what's up?"

"Got some news." He explained the situation and then signed off.

Matt turned to Joe and Ron and explained what was happening. They looked at each other and knew what they had to do. Joe said, "This might be our chance to see where they're sending these people and to get some idea about what they might be doing with all these troops. We could clue in the FBI once we know. Hopefully, they could get a jump on them if we can give them enough information."

Joe asked Ron and Tommy, "You ready for some traveling? It'll do two things. It'll take some heat off of the three of us, and it'll get us some information to pass along."

Tommy was excited to get involved again. He had been hiding for too long, and he was still upset about Wayne and wanted some revenge.

Ron also agreed that they had to do something, and this sounded like a chance to make a difference. "Let's do it. We'll need two vehicles, and each car can follow one of the trucks if they split up and go in different directions. Two in each vehicle will work."

Matt wasn't so sure he could pull it off. "I have to stay here and direct everything, but my cousin David can ride along with Tommy. You know him, Tommy, right?" David was a young man who had graduated a few years ahead of Tommy. He was a very friendly and dependable person. Matt could not have chosen a better partner.

"Yes. I know him. We get along, and we could work together. I guess we better plan this operation so we know what exactly we need to do. I think Wendy will want to come along too, so there could be three of us. She's a big help and very good with technology, which we may need."

Joe was all right with whatever they planned, but he told Tommy that they should not take any chances, and that they were only trying to find out where the troops were going, not engaging them.

They spent some time discussing just exactly what they should do. Matt was also concerned that they did not take any chances. He was determined to stay near Colewin to assist with the tunnel and help direct Charlie, so he would have assistance with any situation that might arise.

Before leaving, Matt and Joe had a conversation about the tunnel and decided that they needed some expert advice on digging. Joe said he had contacted his brother, Frank, who had years of experience with mines and tunnels. He told Matt to lay off the digging until his brother got there. Frank was retired and was happy to help, and he said he would leave as soon as he could, and he could be there sometime the next day. Matt agreed to wait. He would discuss the decision with Charlie right away.

After his talk with Matt, Joe knew he had to move quickly if they were to follow the semis. Ron and Joe planned to ride together. Just in case, the two cars would be positioned near U.S. 2, one on the east near where the semis were parked, and one on the west to wait for the trucks. If the trucks went in the same direction, they would both follow. If not, they would split up so they could each follow one. Otherwise, they would continue to follow together and back up each other in case there was any trouble.

The bunker, April 2, evening

Bates decided to get troops on the lookout around the base just in case. He sent three men to the south to follow the road to U.S. 2, but they were to stay in the woods and walk to the highway looking for any suspicious activity. He sent three to the east with the task to check out the woods for about a half-mile for anything or anyone who might be there, He also sent four to the west since it was filled with trails and a lot of heavy woods.

Bates kept Vince and his buddies for the north side. It was the most difficult, and it had the densest woods. It would be slow going since it was uphill at the beginning, and then downhill for over a quarter-mile. The terrain was rugged, and he knew that these three were in the best shape and the most knowledgeable about how to handle a problem if there was one. Bates suspected that if Bill was right with his suggestions that the north would be the most difficult direction to plan an attack on the base, but it was also the most difficult for them to protect.

Bates had all thirteen men in the bunker as he laid out the plan. "All right, here's what we're going to do. You're looking for any activity. If you see anyone who might be checking up on the base or moving against us, you are to shoot them on the spot. If you run into too many to handle, then you call back for as many reinforcements as you need. Be quiet and be stealthy the entire time. No stupid stuff. Be smart and report back with whatever you find. I'll relay any message to our troops if you need assistance. Check in every fifteen minutes by texting the word '*Clear,*' if you do not find anything. You will all move in a straight line for a half-mile. After that, if you do not find anything, move back carefully looking for anything you might have missed. Got it? Any questions?"

One of the troops spoke up, "So we have the okay to shoot whoever is out there on the spot?"

"Right!" Bates answered. "Anyone. If someone is out there, they are not on our side, so just take them out and ask questions later."

"Sounds good," Vince said.

Near the bunker in the woods to the east, April 3

Matt's sentry was growing tired. His watch was almost over and his replacement had not arrived. As he was yawning for the nth time, he heard noises coming from the bunker. It had been a trying day, because three troops came poking around his hiding place a few minutes ago, and he had to keep hidden most of the time they were there. They moved past him and kept going, but he now had to keep an eye out in all directions in case they came back his way. He had informed Matt as quietly as he could and as soon as he was able—and now this.

Suddenly, he heard a loud noise. He picked up his M22 binoculars and focused on the bunker and saw the large door going up. He watched as it lifted and opened all the way. This was the first time he had seen anything like that at the base. He had never heard or seen any activity in the bunker itself. Soon he heard vehicles roaring, and out came several troop trucks. All military vehicles that he knew usually carried men with weapons. He figured about twenty to twenty-five men per truck if that is what they were carrying. He saw four trucks move out and park near the barracks to the west.

The sentry jumped on the phone and called Matt. Matt was out near the tunnel, and he and Charlie had to stop work because they too had people snooping around. They had the digging stop and had everyone hiding near the tunnel for protection. The three sentries around the tunnel were on high-alert and no one was making a sound. When Matt's phone vibrated, he picked it up as quickly as he could. He knew it must be important since the sentries were given the word to call only if there was danger or something of major importance. He moved near the tunnel and said, "Hello. This is Matt. What's up?"

"They're moving, Matt. Not right now, but they have four troop trucks parked near the barracks, and there is a lot of activity."

Matt said, "Okay. Keep safe. We'll relay the message." As he ended the call, he heard someone moving through the brush coming from the direction of the bunker.

CHAPTER 29

U.S. 2, a mile from the road where the semis had entered the woods, April 3, evening

Joe and Ron were parked on the west or Naubinway side. Tommy, Wendy, and David were on the east, or St. Ignace side. It was getting dark and Joe wondered if there would be any movement today. There had been little change at the bunker, according to the sentry who was stationed there. Maybe they had the wrong day, and the troops were not going to move until later. Yet, they had to stay and wait it out. Joe called Matt, but there was no answer. He relayed a message to Tommy to give Matt a call, but he did not have any luck either. All they could do now was wait until they got word that there was some movement at the base, or else they had to call it a night—and Joe did not want to do that. Joe turned to Ron and said, "We need to contact one of the sentries to see if anything is happening."

"I wouldn't do that, Joe. We can't risk giving away their positions if they make noise or have to move around."

"Good point, Ron. I guess we'll just have to wait it out."

"For sure. We have nowhere to be anyway."

It was a long wait before it paid off. Both Joe and Ron had fallen asleep. They had been up for many hours and must have dozed off without knowing it. When Joe's phone buzzed, it was Tommy. "Joe, are you there?"

"Hey, Tommy. What's up?"

"Just received a message from the sentry near the bunker. He said that about fifteen minutes ago trucks started rolling. They should be near U.S. 2 by now. I'm waiting to hear from the sentry who is watching the semis to see if the trucks are headed there."

"Good. Keep us posted."

Ron was disappointed that they had both fallen asleep—it wasn't like them. They had not planned who would stay up. They just figured they would be all right, but the weeks leading up to this night had been stressful and very long. They had not gotten the sleep they should have, and they knew it. Hopefully they had not missed their chance to find out where these troops were going.

It wasn't long before they received another message from Tommy. "The sentry posted near U.S. 2 said that some trucks started rolling in, and troops were leaving the trucks and headed to the semis. He said it looks like the semis were set up to hold a number of men. There are benches on each side of the trailer and some down the middle. They'll hold a lot of people."

Joe wondered how many vehicles were dropping off troops. "We'll have to be ready to move out. It shouldn't take long to get them all loaded. Although we're not sure if the trucks have to return to get more people. How many trucks are there now?"

"The sentry saw only five trucks dropping off troops."

Joe was sure that they would have to return for more troops. He thought each truck would hold a maximum of twenty-four individuals, so if they had five trucks, that would be more than one hundred. Maybe that is all that will be going. "Let us know what's happening. We have to be ready to move quickly if they fill one and then the other. We're not sure where they're headed, so if one leaves, one of us will have to follow. The other will have to wait until the second leaves."

"Right."

"Just got word the trucks are returning to the bunker, and all the troops are milling around, not getting into any semis yet. Looks like someone is in charge and is separating them into two groups."

"All right. Good work by those sentries," Joe said.

Tommy was excited. "As soon as they start moving, he's going to let us know, and we'll let you know"

"Okay."

Joe and Ron waited for what seemed like forever, but they did not get another call for over an hour. Then it happened.

After more men arrived from the bunker, the sentry reported, "The semis are rolling. All the troops were separated into two groups. They filled the trailers, and it looks like just under one hundred men in each."

Joe was surprised. One hundred troops? Is that possible? How in the world are they fitting that many troops in there?"

"As I mentioned, the way they have set up inside the trailer. I guess they have four rows of benches, so yes, they could get about one hundred in each. They're rolling. Be ready to move."

"Okay Tommy. Keep us posted on what you see, and where you're going if we get separated."

"One semi is on the highway and is turning east. We'll follow. The other is right behind. Looks like it's going west. We're on the highway keeping a safe distance from the semi. You will have to follow the other."

"We're waiting. Nothing yet. We'll let you know when we see it." It took several minutes before Joe and Ron saw the truck. It was the only vehicle headed west. There wasn't much traffic on the road at this time of the night. Now it was a matter of following at a distance so they did not know that they were being followed. Joe let the semi move ahead quite a distance.

They looked for any signs that might give them something to identify the semi if they got separated. They checked the license plate number and also noticed on the back that there was a huge scratch near the bottom of the big back door. That would have to do for now. They kept their distance and would lose the truck sometimes on big curves. When they moved through Manistique, they got mixed up in some traffic and lost them for some time. They caught up near Big Bay de Noc, but they could not verify the truck until Rapid River when they got close enough to see the license plate and the scratch on the back door. They were relieved that they had not lost it.

They were headed south now. They realized that they might be leaving Michigan. Maybe this truck is headed for Wisconsin. They passed Escanaba about ninety minutes into the journey. It was almost 5:30 a.m. It would be light around 7:00 or 7:30, so they would have to be very careful after this, although the traffic was picking up speed.

Tommy called at 5:35 a.m. "We've crossed the Mackinac Bridge, and we are south of Cheboygan by the looks of it. Not sure where they're going."

"Be careful and keep your distance. We don't want to get caught. We just need to know their destination."

"We'll be careful and keep in touch."

Joe and Ron were concerned for Tommy since they had been through so much near the Cheboygan area over a year ago. That was where they were taken and almost killed, but now they had to focus on where they were headed, and they had to be careful themselves.

Now they knew for sure that they were headed out of the U.P. They were on M-35 headed toward the Menominee-Marinette area—the border between Michigan and Wisconsin. They had been on the road for about two and one-half hours. They both needed a quick stop. They were hoping the semi might stop soon too. That did not happen for a while. They merged onto U.S. 41 and were headed south.

At 7:00 a.m. the semi headed off the main road near Oconto, Wisconsin. Both Joe and Ron were now confused. "Where are they going?" Ron asked. They did not want to make the quick turn for fear they would be seen, so they slowed and pulled over, giving the truck time to move ahead a bit. Then they followed. The semi took a left off the regular road, and Joe and Ron realized this was a planned stop since the road was in good shape, and they could see the semi come to a stop.

They moved ahead and pulled over where their car would be hidden by some trees. Joe and Ron were happy for the stop they needed, but they were also wary. Joe stayed with the car and kept it running. Ron moved through the woods to see if this was the destination for the troops.

When he got there, he could tell they were just given a chance to stretch their legs and use the latrine, or whatever they had to do. Ron kept watch until they started to load again. He could see that the semi driver had a good spot to maneuver and get back on the road, so he quickly headed back to the car. As he entered the vehicle, Joe's phone buzzed.

Meanwhile, lower Michigan, 5:45 a.m.
Tommy, Wendy, and David had been following the semi in Tommy's truck since it turned east on U.S. 2. It had been an uneventful trip to St. Ignace and then across the Mackinac Bridge. They were now on Highway 23, and Tommy had been able to mix with the traffic, but now it would be difficult to follow closely on the roads that the semi was taking. The roads were in good shape, but they were more rural than he liked, so Tommy kept back quite a distance and hoped he would not lose them. They wound around

several small towns before the semi left the road a little less than two hours into the journey.

Wendy was the first to bring it up. "Remember what Mr. Joe and Ron told us about their capture and trip downstate? They said they were held someplace near here. I never really understood just where, but they talked about a warehouse where they were kept and almost killed. Could they be heading there?"

Tommy was thinking the same thing, but he wasn't sure exactly where the place was that Mr. Joe had mentioned. "I agree. This must be very close to that place. We had better be careful. If he pulls off the main roads, we may have to change our plans about following."

David was not aware of any of what they were referring to, but he could tell they were getting farther and farther from any city or town. He was getting nervous. "Should we keep following if they head deeper into the woods?"

"No. I'm not sure what to do. Mr. Joe said not to get ourselves into any trouble, but just to get an idea of where they're going." The semi turned left on a side road. Tommy stopped the truck, and found a spot where he could pull off the road. He said, "This is getting us close to Lake Michigan. They must have a stop nearby. Let's hide the car, and I'll walk down the road to see if I can find anything. If I run into them, I'll move into the woods. You stay hidden until I get back."

Tommy walked for some time and came to a curve in the road. He ducked into the woods and moved ahead. He could see the semi, and it was opened, and all the men were standing around. Behind the semi was a warehouse. It was similar to the one that Mr. Joe had told him about where he and Ron had been taken. He was sure this was it. Tommy watched for a while and then moved back to the vehicle. It took him some time to get back. When he returned, he told Wendy and David about the warehouse, and he decided to call Mr. Joe, but he waited for a while to see what might happen. They waited for a little over an hour and nothing changed, so Tommy decided to call.

"Hello."

"Hello. This is Tommy."

CHAPTER 30

The Tunnel, Morning of the Same Day

Matt told everyone to hide and to get ready for trouble, but he saw that it was the sentry from the bunker side—and he went right to Matt.

"Matt, I have word that several of the sentries on the west and east of the bunker have seen troops from the bunker searching the woods. It's not going to take long before the same is going to happen here. I decided to come straight here and not call because we need to set up a better perimeter and let everyone know what's going on. We have only three of us here protecting you, so I suggest you get armed and ready just in case. We need to call others to come and help."

Matt said, "I know. I already heard from one of the sentries. We have all the people we can trust already either workin' here or hidden as sentries, so there's really no one else to call. Paul is not around right now, but he's the only one I can think of who could help. Some of Charlie's people that we had hoped to enlist already had joined up with these people because they offered 'em an income. These guys have gotten to our people in Colewin and Poplar. They're offering a lot of cash and people are buyin' in. They're takin' advantage of us. Most of the people don't even know what they're in for—and neither do we, but our life here is in jeopardy if we can't fix this."

"I agree. Most of my friends have joined those guys. All because they have promised them more money than they could ever get working. Makes me mad. What is going to happen when they're finished with their recruits, and they don't need them anymore? They'll just throw them away, but I get it. The money helps right now."

Matt said, "Let's make sure everyone here is on high alert. We'll be as quiet as possible. You stay hidden like we practiced and shoot anything that moves. You have silencers. We don't. If we shoot, we'll have a whole bunch of trouble—and we'll have to abandon this project."

"Good point, Matt. I'll inform the boys on each side of you and I'll take my spot. Hope we don't see anyone, but if we do, we'll be ready. One thing we have going is that this area is thick with trees and shrubbery. Whoever comes this way will have a lot of trouble." The sentry turned to go back to his post.

"A'right, be careful," Matt said. He let Charlie know what was up, and he and Charlie warned the workers to keep on the lookout as they continued to dig and haul the dirt away. They had given each one a weapon when they had begun the dig, and the weapons were placed outside of the tunnel near the entrance and were covered to keep them clean. Each worker had been trained to use them, but while digging they did not usually think much about that, but now they were ready.

Charlie had been inside the tunnel helping to put another set of beams in place. The process was slow and difficult since they had only five people to move the eight-foot-long poles in place to shore up the wall and ceilings. Matt was the lookout while they were all busy. Now, he felt a lot of pressure to keep everyone safe. He hoped that Joe and Ron and the other young people who were following the semis could get back as fast as possible. They needed every body.

In the woods near the tunnel, April 3, fifteen minutes later
Vince and the two assassins were moving in the direction of the tunnel. They were spread out and were moving very slowly looking for anything that might be suspicious. Vince felt they would not find anything, and he was a bit bored and pissed they had to move north in the thick woods. He could not see more than a few feet in front of him. How were they going to find anything? Adrik and Borya, on the other hand were taking this quite seriously and were hoping for some action. It had been a boring month for them hanging around the bunker or sitting around patiently waiting for their marks. They were ready for anything that might change things—they had not come all this way for nothing.

Vince knew his two comrades were getting bored, and he wanted to make sure they did not do anything stupid. He had worked with them for a while now, and he knew they were good at what they did, but they were also ruthless and annoyed that they had to come to the U.P. and do the same thing day after day. They were ready for action.

They had been moving through the woods at a very slow pace. The trees and foliage were as thick here as anywhere, and the going was slow. How were they to find anyone? He had to keep pushing branches out of his way, and he fought to move in a straight line. Had anyone been through this place in the past? Vince could not see a foot in front of him. How would he see anyone who might be hiding here? He could not see Borya or Adrik. They were about one hundred meters apart, but he could occasionally hear movement. Was it them or someone else?

The three men moved slowly when Borya thought he heard some movement in front of him. He crouched low and sent a quick message to his partners. "Stop. I hear something."

Vince got the message and dropped to his knees. Adrik who was on the left flank facing the movement was ready to shoot anything that moved. All three had their rifles facing the tunnel. Vince usually did not do any shooting, but he was ready just the same. All three had silencers and knew they could hit someone and get away without anyone knowing. That is, if this was only one person. Vince knew if anyone was out here that they had a reason, and he figured that Bates must think that something must be going on in this direction. Unfortunately, he really did not believe that anything was, so he stood up and tried to see if anything or anyone was moving. His heart was pounding. That's when he saw something move. He lifted his rifle, and noticed it was a squirrel. Is that what Adrik saw? "Shit!" he said quietly.

The sentry did not move. He could see the man right in front of him. Even though he was well hidden, he did not know if he would walk right into him. It was very dense here and it would be difficult to get off a clear shot. He hoped he did not have to do that.

Vince kept moving ahead, straight for the sentry. Then he stopped and said, "Shit!" again. "This is ridiculous. There is no one here, and who would try to approach the bunker from this direction? The woods are too thick, and it would not make any sense to try an assault from the north. We're stopping here." As Vince took a few more steps, he saw a little opening in the woods. He thought for a second about continuing to check it out, but he also saw that the woods were very thick just beyond the opening.

Everyone at the tunnel was already on high alert. All the digging had stopped, and they all had their weapons and assigned spots. No one moved. All was quiet.

Vince tripped on a branch and fell to the ground. This time he yelled, "Damn it!" Everyone heard him. No one moved. Vince tried to stand, but he hit his head on a broken branch that stuck out just far enough. He swore again and half crawled and half walked until he could stand straight up. Then Vince turned and began walking back to the bunker. He hoped he could make it back without any more trouble, and he sent a text to his friends.

> Head back. We're done.

He left Borya and Adrik to fend for themselves and find their way out. "Shit!" he yelled at the top of his lungs as he fell to the ground with a thud.

Everyone at the tunnel smiled, but they kept focused on the direction of the sound—and they waited.

The sentry saw the movement backward by Vince, and he breathed a huge sigh of relief. He sent a message to Matt.

CHAPTER 31

Near Oconto, Wisconsin, April 3

Tommy told Joe what he had found so far. It sounded to Joe like the same place he and Ron had been taken.

Joe spoke quietly into the phone. "Tommy, this might just be a quick stop to give the men a break. Don't get too close, and keep following until you see the final destination, but be careful."

Tommy thought that was good advice. "We'll do exactly that. Once we see what they are up to, we'll head back as we planned."

"Sounds good, Tommy. Keep safe."

"For sure. Talk to you later."

Joe hung up, and as he did, the semi began to move. Ron was buckled in, and they were ready to move out. They gave the semi as much room as they felt they could, and then once they moved again, he began to follow. Ron pulled out a couple of sandwiches and two bottles of water that he had packed, and they ate as they moved ahead. They had no idea where they were going. They had really thought that both semis would be headed for the east coast, but that was not what was happening. Where were they going? How soon would they be put into action—the event?

Joe and Ron were off after the semi. The truck rolled down Highway 41. In no time they were near Green Bay. Joe thought about when he was a young man and his father had given him tickets to go to a Packers-Dallas game in Green Bay in 1967. His father was supposed to go, but he became ill at the last moment, and he gave Joe the tickets. Joe quickly dressed and left with his father's friends. Big mistake. He did not dress warm enough, and consequently, he did not enjoy the game. He froze. It was a very cold ride home from the Ice Bowl. He put that memory aside.

Joe noticed that the semi kept moving forward on 41. Where were they going and why through Wisconsin?

Ron was tired so Joe kept the wheel. He told Ron to get some sleep while he could. They were both tired, but they had to keep following. By 8:00 a.m. they were on the west side of Lake Winnebago. They took Exit 113 and moved onto Highway 26. This put them on a route for central Wisconsin. At 8:30 a.m. they were about to leave 26 and head onto Highway 151 when traffic slowed to a crawl.

Joe was not sure what was happening. All he could think of was that there was some construction up ahead. They were moving slowly, and he could see the semi just about ten vehicles ahead. They were on a divided highway now, yet traffic was slow. Then Joe saw the lights. It must be an accident. As he drove closer, he noticed the police were letting a few cars through at a time. As they drew closer, he could see several cars and a jackknifed semi. Not the semi they were following, thank goodness. The police let several vehicles through, and one was the semi. Joe had to sit back and wait, now four cars behind.

Joe wasn't concerned until a wrecker pulled up behind him on the shoulder and moved to the front of the cars. It took long enough to get into place that Joe lost sight of the semi. He woke Ron to help him spot it. They were both concerned. By the time they were let through, the semi was gone. They kept following 151 for some time, but they never caught up. Ron spoke, "Did it take a turn off the road somewhere?"

Joe was mystified. "We'll probably never know. We could keep traveling down 151 for a while to see if we can spot it. No sense pulling off the road at any of the exits. It would just be a guess. Joe continued for a while, but by 10:00 a.m., they realized they had lost it.

"Might as well head back," Ron said.

"Maybe we should call Ann and let her know. Maybe the FBI can give us some information about them. Last time she wasn't sure about much."

Ron said. "True. We could tell her what we know, and it might help them."

"Right. At any rate, she'll have this information. When I hit the next exit, I'll pull over and give her a call." Soon Joe pulled off the freeway, and he called Ann at the number she had given them if they needed her. He wasn't too sure if what he would tell her would help. "Hello, Ann?"

"This is Ann. Is this Joe?"

"Yep. Got some new information for you."

"Go ahead."

"We had two semis load up with troops from the bunker. We decided to follow them."

"Joe, I told you to stay out of this and be safe."

"I know, but Ron and I have a vested interest in this since they almost killed us."

"Sure. I get it, but you should find a safe place to hide and stay there. Anyway, you might as well go ahead and fill me in."

"When the semis left the U.P., we thought they would both head to lower Michigan and then to the east coast, but only one went to lower Michigan, and the other went to Wisconsin. We followed the one that went to Wisconsin, and thought we might be able to tell you where they were headed, but we lost them. One of our friends, Tommy, is still following the one in Michigan. They last spoke to us past Cheboygan, not far from where we were taken a few years ago."

"Hmm. They are all probably headed to the D.C. area. We noticed a large contingent of these types of troops headed near there. We have a few people who infiltrated them, and we believe they are planning another siege of the capitol building."

"Really? Then why would they go through Wisconsin? Seems a little out of the way."

"They are probably trying to keep us from figuring out this event. My guess is that they are all just diversions to keep us guessing. Our informants say they are headed to the D.C. area, like I said."

"All right. Well, there are two more semis on the way."

"We'll keep a lookout for them. Thanks for the update and stay safe."

"Will do. We'll let you know if anything else happens. Take care." Joe hung up and turned to Ron. "I guess we'll head back and keep abreast of Tommy's situation. He might be able to figure out where they're going. Ann says they are all headed to D.C. I'm not so sure. Maybe Tommy will find out if that is a fact."

They had tried to follow the semi for more than an hour since the wrecker had gotten in their way. They were just past Milwaukee when they decided to turn around. Ron told Joe that he would take over and drive for a while until they could stop for some lunch and gas, and so he drove while Joe tried to sleep. It was getting past lunch time when Ron pulled over and woke Joe.

Lower Michigan, April 3, noon
Tommy, David, and Wendy were parked safely out of the way. Tommy decided that they should wait it out and see if they could follow the semi again and determine where it was going. An hour later, they heard a noise, and they knew it was the semi heading out. They got ready to go, and as soon as it passed the spot where they were hiding, they followed.

An hour and twenty minutes later

Ron and Joe took their time eating at a fast-food place not far from DePere. They decided to return and help out at the tunnel. They knew they had to keep out of sight, and find a new place in Colewin to keep hidden. They would do whatever they had to so that they could get into the bunker and take Bates as a prisoner. They would not be able to trade him for anything. Their guess was that he was as expendable as any of the people that this group hired. They knew working close to Charlie would be tough, but if it got them what they were looking for, no problem.

Joe was pensive. "I guess we should get on the road. This has been a nice stop, but I'm disappointed that we couldn't find out where they were headed."

Ron agreed. "We could be a lot of help at the tunnel. Now that you've contacted your brother, there will be more help with building the tunnel the right way."

Joe agreed. His brother had been a miner in Ishpeming for many years. Years ago, he had been involved in some of the underground mines, and he had worked on shoring up the tunnels. Nowadays there was none of that. Most mining around Ishpeming and Negaunee was open pit mining. It was a huge hole in the ground and open to the air. His brother had also worked on some gold mines in the U.P. Joe was not sure where, but they had similar tunnels, and Joe knew that his brother would be a great help. "Yes. I think he may already be there. I spoke with him on the phone, and he was happy to help. He's older, but he's in great shape and will be a great assist."

CHAPTER 32

The Tunnel

Charlie was frantic. He was supposed to wait for Frank, Joe's brother, to arrive to get some advice on building the tunnel, but he thought they were all right, so they had continued digging. The four young people had kept it going as much as they could, but now two of the helpers were trapped in the tunnel. They had been digging and making really great progress when all of a sudden, the ceiling gave way. Charlie thought they were almost thirty feet in when the tunnel had caved just inside the opening—then Charlie panicked.

Matt was there too, and he wasn't sure what to do, but he knew they had to dig them out. Hopefully, they were all right. Charlie decided first to reinforce the ceiling. He added several pillars and cross beams. Once this was completed, they began digging again. The young people were nervous to go back into the tunnel, but they were afraid for their friends and knew they had to dig.

Charlie and Matt were helping now. They were hoping that Paul and Sarah would also get there soon. They needed the help, and Matt knew that they wanted to help because they felt they had to clear the area of these people at the bunker, and the sooner they could get this tunnel dug, the faster they could get rid of them. They had poisoned the area with these people who were trying to take over everything—and a lot of people in Colewin were upset, but they were afraid to do anything—or just didn't care.

Paul and Sarah showed up and began digging. It was great to get the help. It had been twenty minutes since the cave-in, and they were getting worried. Charlie was beside himself because he had ordered the digging to continue even though he had earlier agreed with Matt and Joe to halt the digging until they had some expert help, and then he heard another crash…

The bunker

Bates was ready to send out more troops. They were going to receive another group late today, and they had nowhere to put them. He called his trainers and told them to get ready to send out over one hundred more troops when the new ones arrived. They would use the next semi that arrived to send the others to their destination.

The trainers were not happy. "These troops are not ready yet," one of them protested.

"Too bad. They have to go. We can't keep this many people here or we're going to have trouble. They already are restless and are causing trouble in the community. Why do you even let them leave the base? The boss will not like it if they cause too much trouble and the cops have to come again and settle things. The sheriff, Daryl, has about had it with them. He can't keep coming up with ideas of how to cover up their messes. Get this done now!"

The trainers agreed to select the best troops. They would be ready by late afternoon.

Bates went back to his work, but he was not pleased. How am I going to get the boss to slow this thing down? Everything is moving too fast, and we are going to end up with a mess. We need the old boss back. He moved at the right pace for this event. As Bates was pondering the situation and as the trainers were leaving, in walked Vince. He was bleeding from his head and looked like crap. "What the hell happened to you?"

"That escapade you sent us on in the woods to the north here was crazy. Those woods are so thick no one is going to get through there. It's insane! Keep your troops checking in other directions, but that one is out of the question. You have to fight each step of the way uphill just to move one foot, and then you fight to stand going downhill."

"Where are your buddies?"

"They're heading back. We decided to keep about one hundred meters apart in the woods, and I could not see them. I'm full of sap from trees, and I cut my head and my cheek on branches, and I'm miserable, and I hurt my ankle too! Can you imagine what that will be like when the mosquitoes are out in full force, and it gets hotter?"

"Oh, quit the bitching. Forget that direction. We'll post a few guards on the hill to keep watch."

An hour later

Joe and Ron had reached Marinette, Wisconsin, just on the other side of the state line separating Upper Michigan. They were making good time and wanted to get back to make sure Joe's brother had arrived and given Charlie the information he would need to proceed. Then Joe's phone buzzed.

"Hello."

"This Joe?"

"Yes, it is. Is this Matt?"

"Ah, yes, Joe. I got some bad news."

"What? What happened?"

"It's the tunnel, Joe. It collapsed and two of the young people are in there. Your brother just arrived and is helpin' us. He said we didn't have the walls and ceilin' braced like they should be."

"So, you were digging again. Was my brother there when you started?"

"Nope. Charlie decided to go ahead. We're only about thirty feet in, and the roof collapsed just inside the opening of the tunnel, so the kids are trapped in there. We're doing the best we can. Your brother has us bracin' the walls and ceilin' as we go. We shoulda waited."

"Damn! We just entered the U.P. We're still in Menominee. It'll take us over two hours from here. Keep us posted and get those kids out of there!"

"We'll do our best. I'll call if anything changes."

"Okay. Hope all works out. Put my brother on."

"He's in the tunnel right now. I'll have him call ya when he's free."

"All right. Talk to you then."

The bunker

When Vince left, Bates wondered if he should increase the number of men searching the woods around the bunker. He knew that Charlie was after his cache, and he knew Charlie was hard-headed when it came to getting the bunker back. He had also learned from Bill and some of the local recruits that they had knowledge of a possible attempt. He called his trainers and had them recruit ten more men to help with the security of the base. He decided to send three more troops east and west and four to the south. He already had assigned some to the north, so he felt comfortable with that. He thought that should keep the bunker safe from any infiltration. He told them to secure the area around the bunker night and day. He also put more men around the inside of the perimeter just in case. Bates had fenced most of the perimeter, and now he decided to fence the north hill.

"We think this might be overkill, Bates. We also need to get these troops trained and ready to go."

"You let me worry about that. Just get back to work and get the rest of the troops ready." Bates did not care for the head trainer's attitude. He was trying to take Bates' job—and Bates did not like it. He was aggressive and he knew the new boss, so that was a problem. "And I'll need ten troops to help with the fencing."

The trainer fumed. "You aren't the boss, you know. I can have you in deep shit if you keep this kind of stuff up."

"What kind of stuff?"

"You know. Like you're the head man or something."

"I'm not the head man, but I take care of the bunker, and you work for me."

"I damn well don't work for you, you ass."

"If you're here, you work for me. Now get back to work." Bates was a little afraid that he might have overstepped here, but he was tired of the guy. Bates had been here longer than anyone, so he knew what had to be done.

The trainer walked away, but he was upset. He complained all the way to the training area. "Who does he think he is anyway? We could do away with him and no one would know. All he does is sit at that damned screen all day and play games. We need to do something about him. Why in the hell do we need so many securing the base in this remote area? He's nuts, and now he wants to take ten men to fence the north hill. He's crazy."

CHAPTER 33

April 3

The chase was on. Tommy was following the semi as closely as he could. It returned to Highway 23. They continued to follow for quite some time, keeping their distance. They knew that they would have to stop every several hours to give the guys a chance to stretch and use the facilities, unless they were headed someplace close. If they had planned to go to D.C. and hide near there, then the trip was going to be a lot longer. Tommy kept wondering what they were really up to.

They followed for another hour. They had left 23 and were soon on Highway 33 heading south, and then past West Branch, they jumped onto I-75. Tommy muttered to Wendy and David. "Now what? I thought they would stay on the back roads, but here we are on I-75. What is the next move? It's going to be tough to stay with them if the traffic gets thick down here."

David was concerned. "Man, I hope we don't have to go a long way with this truck. Who knows where they're headed?"

"Good point," Wendy added. "How long do we have to keep following?"

Tommy knew they were concerned. "Mr. Joe said to follow them and try to figure out where they are going. That's what we'll do, but we won't take any chances. If they stop, we'll keep our distance like we did and just watch and report."

David was reassured. "That sounds like a good plan."

They kept following until they hit Highway 10, then the semi left the main road and headed to a more remote area. It looked like a road that had just been created. It was in good shape. They could not follow right behind for fear of being identified, so they pulled over and watched as the truck disappeared into the dense woods. Once again Tommy thought it might be good to get out on foot and follow the road until he could see what was going on. Wendy did not agree.

Tommy slipped out of the car and followed the road, making sure no one could see him. He stayed close to the side of the road. It wasn't long before he noticed that this was again just a stop to let the troops rest and stretch. He watched for a while as most were just hanging around, some were smoking, and some just enjoying the sunlight.

As he watched, two of them came into view, and he realized that they were a couple of his old classmates. He knew they had joined—and had spoken with them about it. He wondered if he could make contact with them right now to see if they knew what was up, but he knew it would be risky, so he just turned around and quickly jogged back to the vehicle. Once there, he said, "It's just a quick break. I think they'll be on the road again soon. It looks like they must have planned the stop and made a spot where they could hide for a short time. This is really organized."

"Well, I'm glad you're back and safe," Wendy said.

"Guess what!" He turned to David and said, "Remember those two that joined up from my class? Willie and Ed, they always hung together. Remember they started that gun club? They would go out each weekend and shoot at the range for hours."

"Yep, I remember them. They were a couple of years behind me, and I didn't hang much with them, but I did shoot with them on several weekends. They were very gun crazy. They were always trying to get military-style weapons. They did get some guns somehow, a long time ago. Not sure how. I'm not surprised they're here."

"I'm going to move back farther from this road, so we can keep an eye on them, and yet not be as close as we are."

"All right."

The tunnel

Work was progressing slowly with Joe's brother keeping everyone on task, but at the same time making sure that the tunnel was properly supported. He had Matt purchase some materials. He had him go to the Engadine Hardware, about twenty minutes away to the west, to keep people from figuring out what they were doing. He wanted a better job overall, so he had him buy several bags of cement. They would have to mix everything by hand. They had plenty of sand, but they would need water.

Frank told Charlie that his plan was too aggressive. The shaft was too large, and it would not be safe to continue the way he was doing it. He told Charlie, "Once we dig to rescue those kids, we're going to reinforce everything and then cut the tunnel down in size. Eight by eight is just too big for what you're planning."

"But I want to be able to drive my trucks out of there. They have kept both my best vehicles as well as all my weapons that we have collected over the years."

"I'm telling you that you can't do that in these conditions. It's mostly sand here. You've got to cut it down in size and reinforce properly. You'll be able to get a small vehicle through, but that's it. If you want my advice, you'll need some other materials besides what I told Matt to get. You need to cut timbers to the dimensions I have on this sheet here, and we'll need a lot of them. You have an angle square? You'll need one to cut the angles we need. They're all on this paper. Get to work as soon as you can and then get the timbers here. I'll keep these people digging, and I'll make sure we're braced enough to keep everyone safe. Now get going!"

"Okay, I'll get on this. Jus' so you know, this is gonna take some time. I only have Sam and another guy I can trust to help, but I got a good place to do 'er. I'll head out right now and get 'er started."

"Make sure you get the lagging we'll need too. We need a lot of it right away just to shore up what you have completed so far."

"I'll get on it right away, but like I said this is gonna take some time." Charlie left to begin the work that Frank had ordered. He wasn't happy, but he thought even if he could get most of his stuff out of the bunker, that would be a good start. Then he would have a chance to get the bunker back.

Frank barked orders to the few people he had working. They needed to get more help. He asked, "Is there anyone else around because time is important? They said there were three sentries here. Maybe two of them could help us until Matt returns. He's going to bring one of his cousins."

"Sounds good. Let's get them on it." Soon they had seven people digging as fast as they could. It had been some time, and they were getting nervous that those in the tunnel might run out of air if they weren't dead already.

On the road

Joe and Ron had just passed Escanaba, and Joe had not heard anything from his brother. He did not want to call him, but he was getting nervous. Ron was driving now and he was going as fast as he could on U.S. 2. He thought he could get away with five miles over, and that is what he held.

Joe asked, "What do you think Ron? This seems very bad for us if we lose those kids. They have been a great help. Hopefully, they can get them out."

"I agree, Joe. What a mess. We should have been there to help."

"Right. I think we'll have to send other people to follow these troop transports. We need to be close to keep Charlie from doing things that aren't safe."

"Yeah, he's really anxious to get his equipment back. I'm not sure why he wants it to happen so quickly."

"I want to get to the bunker to see if we can take that Bates guy hostage. We could get some real good information about what is going on, and that could help Ann in her job, too. Not sure if any of this will help for sure, but it could break everything wide open if we can get enough information."

"For sure."

Joe was very nervous and was hoping to get news from his brother, and he did. His phone buzzed and he quickly picked it up. "Hello. This is Joe."

"Joe. This is Frank. We were able to get a hole through the top of the cave-in and put a pipe in. We're hoping to get some air into the area behind the cave-in. If these kids are okay, this will give them enough air to keep them alive. We haven't heard anything. No sounds or noise from them. They may be passed out, knocked out, or worse, dead and buried. Hoping for the former. It should not be long now if we can keep digging. Matt and his cousin are back, and Charlie sent Sam and another guy to help until we get them out, so we have a lot of help."

"That sounds good. Hopefully, you can get to them ASAP."

"We'll keep working. Talk to you soon."

"It'll take more than an hour before we get there. Hope all is well when we do."

"Take care."

"You too."

The tunnel

It was dark and hot behind the sand that had fallen, but the two who were trapped were lying together on the ground. They could not see anything, and they were struggling to breathe. When the pipe slid through, they did not even see it, but it brought in more air, giving them some relief. They knew that the others must be trying to get them out, but they could not move. They were sitting under a beam that they had put in just before the cave-in. It was the pounding on the top cross piece trying to get it in place that probably caused the dirt to give way. They were weak and frightened.

CHAPTER 34

Lower Michigan

Tommy backed away and hid farther down the road. When the truck with the troops came out, it went right back to the route that they had been on before getting on Highway 10. They followed toward I-75, but before they hit the exit, three other semis that looked exactly the same pulled into view alongside the one they were following.

All four got to the exit about the same time and then headed south on I-75. Tommy followed and kept his eye on the one they had followed to this point. As they moved south toward Saginaw, the traffic got a lot heavier, and as they got closer to Flint, more and more vehicles got between them and the truck they needed to follow until they finally got confused.

"I think our truck just passed that Amazon truck," Wendy said.

"No, I'm sure it was the one right in front of that white SUV. See the markings on the back. Keep your eyes open for the license plates to see if they're the same."

"No. I'm sure of it," Wendy yelled.

David wasn't sure himself. "I'm not sure any more. The trucks keep switching lanes and passing each other. I think they are doing this on purpose."

That had not dawned on Tommy, but now he was certain of it. "They're doing this on purpose—trying to confuse us, or trying to keep anyone from following the truck."

They kept following, but it was getting impossible to even keep their eyes on any one of the trucks because of the traffic. Then they noticed that the semi they thought it was, began to leave the highway.

"Tommy was completely confused now. Which one do we follow? Is it the one leaving the highway? Where is it? They thought the semi was heading south, but with so many trucks on the road now, it was impossible to know.

"Well, I think we're screwed," David said.

"That's for sure." Tommy was dismayed.

"We got this far, so we know that they're heading south in Michigan. The question is—are they going on to D.C. like Joe thought?"

They decided to follow one of the trucks that they thought was it. It took an exit and they followed it as it turned onto a road heading west. They followed for a while and then the truck took a left and pulled into a Walmart Supercenter. They watched as it pulled around to the back of the store and backed into one of the loading docks. Tommy pulled nearby, but he stayed hidden. "I'm going to jump out and check if this is the truck we were following. I'm really doubtful now, but you never know with these people."

Wendy said, "Be careful! Check the plates!"

David jumped out of the truck and followed behind Tommy. "I'll go with you just in case."

"All right, but be careful."

It took some time before anything happened, but finally someone came and opened the back doors. A fork lift pulled up and started unloading large boxes. Tommy turned to David and said, "This is not our truck. We have really lost them. Damn."

David agreed, "Yeah, it looks like they are a lot smarter than we gave them credit for. Those truck drivers really knew what they were doing to lose us. They don't want to be followed, so they had a plan in case anyone was on their tail. See the plates? They're not the same."

"Yup. We've been fooled. They really don't want anyone to know where they're going. Mr. Joe says that Ann, his FBI friend, believes they're headed for D.C. I'm not sure if they are or not, but they could be. It's too bad we couldn't have followed them for a little longer. We would have known for sure which direction they were headed."

"Bad luck. We didn't expect to have this happen, so I guess we were just outsmarted," David added.

They headed back to the truck and explained to Wendy what they had seen, but she was sure this had to be the truck. "Maybe they are just trying to trick us by hauling out some boxes. Maybe the troops are in there!"

"No way, Wendy. We had a pretty good view and the plates were different. There were no people in that trailer. Let's head back. I'll call Mr. Joe and let him know."

The tunnel

Joe and Ron arrived near Colewin sometime before 5:00 p.m. They wanted to get to the tunnel as soon as they could to help out, but they also knew that it was daylight, and they had to keep away from anyone or anyplace that might give them away—and give the people who were after them a chance to take them out.

"Ron, we need to find a spot to hide until it gets dark or we need to hit the back roads and keep out of sight. We could head to the ridge cabin for a short time and take the back road to the tunnel. We shouldn't run into anyone that way. We could hide the car and walk in. It's not that far."

"Joe, do you remember when we first found that spot? The woods are so thick there. We would have a heck of a time getting in on foot. Charlie's way in is about the only decent path to the tunnel. How he found that clearing in the woods I don't know."

"Well, he's been working in these woods for many years and he knows the area, so I can see how he could find the spot. I guess you're right though. We'll need to go straight to where Charlie enters. It'll be a risk going through part of Colewin to get there, but we need to do that if we're going to get to the tunnel anytime soon."

They turned onto the road heading to Colewin and tried to be as covert as they could in their approach.

CHAPTER 35

Colewin, Side Roads, a Little After 5:00 p.m.

They were just sitting on the side of the road hiding and doing nothing but looking for any sign of the people they had to take out. They knew that they had not seen anything for some time, and they were getting bored.

Vince was feeling the heat from the boss, and he knew he had to do something. He had heard that the kid they thought they had hit was in a coma in a hospital somewhere. It didn't look good for him, but that didn't matter to the boss. He wanted people out of the way. Vince was tired of this job. He wasn't an assassin. He was forced into this position, and he did not like it. He was still upset that he had to try to walk through a thick forest for no apparent reason. He felt like the guy in the bunker, Bates, just liked to give him and his two associates any dirty work that was out there. A car flew by and Vince immediately yelled, "Follow that car!"

Borya cranked the wheel and turned the vehicle around, but when he finally got on the road, he did not see the car.

"That was our marks! Both of them in the same car. Keep heading down this road. They can't be far away."

Borya pressed the pedal to the floor and flew down the street. They were just outside of Colewin, but on a side road heading to nowhere as Vince saw it. "No one's there."

"Where could they have gone? They were heading down this road and not going very fast. They must have cut into the woods somewhere along this road. Let's look." They drove down the street, turned around and began looking, but they did not see any roads. Vince made Borya drive up and down the road, but by 6:00 p.m. he decided to call it quits. "We're coming back here later, and we're going to keep looking until we find them. They had to turn into the woods somewhere."

Ron had spotted the car and the three men as they drove by, and as Ron approached a curve in the road, he saw, in his rearview mirror, the car make a U-turn, so he quickly took a left turn before they could catch his car. He sped down the road and hid in an old overgrown logging road in the woods.

Ron reacted so quickly that he surprised Joe. "That was close, Joe."

"What did I miss, Ron? What's up? Did you see something?"

As they sat hidden in the trees, Ron said, "We were lucky. That car, you see it coming down the road?"

When the car moved slowly by, Joe saw them. He could tell they were looking for something. They were dressed in camo, and all three had weapons clearly visible to both Ron and Joe. "Could that be them? The guys after us?"

They watched as the car stopped and turned back. It moved slowly along the road. They were checking each side, and then they passed out of sight.

"We were lucky we were close to this spot and could get back far enough to stay hidden."

"Lucky I've been here enough to know about it," Ron said.

"True. I guess we were fortunate today. Nice move getting us to safety! They won't quit looking though. Let's get to the tunnel as soon as we can." They kept driving until they came to the road that led to the tunnel. It was very difficult to find. No one would ever see it from the road unless they knew it was there, but if any individuals knew where the road was, they could just turn into it between two very large pine trees. The branches would push aside and a vehicle could easily drive through them.

Once a vehicle was on the other side, someone had to get out and brush the tracks made by the car turning into the woods. If done correctly, a person could totally eliminate the tracks, and once again the hidden road became invisible. Joe jumped out of the car and did his best to erase the tracks, but as he began, he saw the vehicle with Vince and his buddies round a curve and head down the road again. He jumped back into the trees and hid as the car slowly drove by. Joe knew they would not give up.

Joe went back to the car and told Ron. They drove until the hidden road ended, parked next to Matt's and Charlie's trucks, and then they walked the last two hundred yards to the tunnel. They walked past the sentry, but did not even see him.

"Hello, Mr. Joe."

Joe and Ron almost hit the ground thinking someone was after them, but they realized it was one of Joe's old students guarding the entry. "Hey, didn't see you there. You scared the crap out of me."

"Me too!" Ron said.

"Sorry. Guess I should've let you know I was here first."

"No. Stay hidden. We saw some guys back there who are looking for us. If they come this way, give us a heads up."

"Okay. Hope they don't come this way though."

"Me too."

Joe and Ron reached the tunnel and saw that the digging was still in progress. As they neared the tunnel, they saw Frank and Matt carrying someone out. It did not look good.

Frank saw Joe and said, "You made it back. Give us a hand with this kid. He's not doing well. Charlie and one of the diggers have the other kid. Hope they make it. They're breathing, but weak pulse and they look very pale. We need to take them to a hospital quickly. Matt said he would drive them, so we need to take them to the vehicles pronto."

Joe and Ron helped with the two young diggers who had been trapped. They put tarps on the ground, lowered the two on top of each, and then four of them grabbed corners and carried them to the trucks. It was a tough job carrying them around trees and over stumps and trying to squeeze between tight spots.

Joe turned to Matt as they carried them through the woods. "Matt, three guys were on the road looking for the trail. I think they were after me and Ron, or they are on to what we're doing, but I'm not sure what they know. Could we get more sentries out here? They're professionals, so we'll need to be very careful."

"We're short on people right now. We just can't trust anyone that I thought might help. Some have joined up with the bunker people. Mostly for the money, but still, they're trainin' to do somethin' and so we can't trust 'em."

"All right. We'll just have to be vigilant. You need to get these two to the hospital as soon as you can."

"I think I'd better go to the Manistique hospital. There are too many prying eyes and ears in Newberry. It's just too close."

Once they had the injured diggers in the truck, Matt jumped in and Joe took the passenger's seat. "I'll ride along until the road. I'll get out and check to see if we have company before you move through the trees." They bounced along and quickly reached the road. Joe jumped out and snuck through the branches so he could look left and right. There they were, moving slowly along the road. One of the three was walking in and out of the woods from the road.

"Not good!" Joe whispered as he rushed back to the truck and told Matt to back up until the truck was hidden. Joe went back to watch the vehicle as it moved slowly toward them. It was then that Joe realized he did not have any weapon with him. He sprinted to the truck, fell down twice on the way, and got scratched and bruised as he stumbled on the uneven ground. He reached the truck and asked Matt for a weapon. Matt had a pistol and a .30-30 Winchester. Joe took the pistol and told Matt to use the rifle to back him up if need be.

Joe moved to the tree line again and looked out. They were almost there. The guy on the road was being cautious not to go too far into the woods. This, Joe hoped, would keep him from finding their road.

The car moved close to the man who was walking. He turned and motioned to the driver and pointed to the trees. The car turned and moved between the trees into the branches and moved slowly as the driver carefully watched left and right. The man followed the vehicle. Joe could see that all three had weapons ready. The driver had an assault rifle sticking out of his window as he drove through the branches and onto the hidden road.

Joe froze. Matt had moved from where he had hidden his truck to a spot behind a large tree. Matt was ready to get the one who was walking, but he waited, knowing that if they turn around, then they would not have to do anything. The car moved slowly and was almost on him. Matt saw Joe peek out from his hiding place and motion to let them go. Matt was not sure if this was a good move, but he trusted Joe's intuition. The car passed Matt and kept heading down the hidden road.

Joe walked from tree to tree keeping hidden until he was next to Matt. They watched the car move slowly ahead. The man who was walking was right behind the car now, and he was looking left and right. Joe and Matt knew they would soon be near the spot where they would have to park the car and get out and walk. They were hoping they would not do that, but Charlie's and Matt's trucks and their car were there and they knew that would be reason for them to continue. They followed quietly until the car was at Charlie's truck. They parked.

Joe watched as the two in the car exited and the three huddled for a short time. Joe had a plan. He turned to Matt and said, "We need to do something before they get to the tunnel. We have three sentries, and they will walk right up to one of them. Hopefully, he is still hidden well. He knows not to let anyone past him, so I'm guessing he shoots as soon as he sees them. That's when we should ambush them from behind. I wish we had more than this pistol and your rifle, but they will have to do. I'm going to text Ron right now and warn him."

Joe texted Ron, but he did not respond. He decided to make a call instead. Ron picked up right away. When Joe told him about the visitors, Ron was quick to respond. He got everyone armed, and in a safe spot.

The men began walking into the woods following the small trail that had been beaten into the undergrowth. They soon split up. Adrik went to the right and Borya went to the left. Vince stayed on the path, but he kept well back of the other two. As they neared the tunnel, a shot rang out and Adrik fell. Another shot from the left took out the sentry. Borya was a crack shot, and nailed the sentry, even though he had only the sound of the shot to go by.

That's when Matt took aim and leveled Borya. Two were down, but they did not know if they were really down for good or still able to shoot. Vince panicked and looked for his buddies. He called out. No one answered. Vince turned and ran toward the car. Joe was hiding behind a tree in the path and tripped him as he tried to get by. Vince fell and his rifle discharged. Joe was on top of him in a second. Matt was right behind. Vince fired another round into the air, and Matt grabbed his rifle as Joe gave him a punch to the face with his pistol. Vince was out.

Then another shot rang out. Neither Joe nor Matt knew who took the shot, so they each jumped behind a tree. Another shot and then another. They could see that someone from the tunnel was shooting toward them. They also saw Borya kneeling down on their right, shooting toward the tunnel. More shots rang out as everyone opened fire on Borya's position, but he just slid behind a tree. He looked around and called for his buddies. No response. He decided to move out and live to fight another day, but he walked right in the direction of Matt and Joe—and they let him have it. He was down.

Joe yelled to Ron and Frank. "You all right over there?"

"We got two down. One's gone for sure. The other is hurt but will be all right!"

They all crept slowly toward Borya. Joe saw that he too was gone. Then they all crept slowly toward Adrik. They could not find him. Was he on the run? Was he still alive? Joe yelled to everyone to take cover until he was found. Matt and Ron moved toward the parked vehicles, thinking he might have tried to get away. When they got near them, they saw Adrik face down on the ground. He was alive, but he was bleeding badly, and it looked like he had passed out.

Ron decided to tie him up with rope from Matt's truck. When they turned him over, they knew he would not last. He had a hole in his chest, and he had lost too much blood.

Joe caught up with Ron and Matt and saw the situation. "He's gone," Ron said.

"Good thing that we were able to get behind them or this might have turned out differently. What are we going to do with this one?"

Frank was there now and he said, "Let's just get rid of him."

Joe said, "No, I think he might be valuable. Maybe he could give us information about the bunker. Who knows what he might be able to tell us?"

Ron agreed, "Okay, let's tie him up and take him to a secure spot. Don't let him see the tunnel."

Joe yelled to Frank who was heading back to the tunnel, "Get our injured guy and the dead one and put them in the truck with the two diggers."

Frank said, "We've got them." When Frank went to the truck, one of the diggers was sitting up in the back of the truck, coughing and wheezing. "Are you okay?"

"Yeah, I'm glad you got us out."

"How's your partner?"

"She's been moaning and rolling around, but I think she is going to be all right."

"Matt can drive you two to the hospital with these others. One of our sentries didn't make it. If you want to go along, stay in the truck. Otherwise, come with me and we'll give you something to eat and drink."

"That sounds great. I think she should go to the hospital though."

Joe was concerned. "Sounds about right. Matt, get these three out of here as quickly as you can. The hospital can take care of the one who didn't make it, and they can get him to his next of kin. We'll take care of these two bodies. No one needs to know exactly what happened."

"What about the sheriff when the dead sentry and the wounded kid report to the hospital?"

"The sheriff's no idiot. He'll once again rule it a hunting accident, and that way he can protect the base."

CHAPTER 36

About an Hour Later

Vince was sitting on the ground. Joe and Ron were not sure what to do with him, but they thought they could get some good information from him. Ron asked, "Say there, what's your name?"

"What do you care?"

"I really don't. Thought it would be a good place to start though."

Joe asked, "You're not from around here, are you?"

"And I'm glad. This place is a dump. I'd like to get back to civilization."

Ron continued with questions. "You've been hunting us here. Why?"

Vince would not answer. He decided to be tight lipped, and he knew that no matter what, he was going to be in trouble—either with these guys or with the boss. They had failed to take out their targets, and the boss did not like failure. He was brutal, and he would kill him for sure. He said aloud, "Yeah, Borya and Adrik are lucky not to face his wrath. We weren't smart enough to take you out, so much for that."

"Whose wrath? Ron asked.

"Really, don't care to get into it with you. Just shoot me now and get it over with."

"We're not going to shoot you. But, yes, you are lucky to be in our custody. However, we really would like to take you out."

Joe and Ron worked on Vince for over an hour, but they had little luck. They did decide they would have the two bodies returned to the bunker. They had not gotten the guy they shot last time to his next of kin, and Joe didn't want to just bury them. They would have someone drive a vehicle close enough to avoid the troops who were on guard, and just dump them in the road. Someone from the base would find them and, hopefully, return them to their loved ones. If not, well, there wasn't much they could do.

April 4

Charlie was elected to take his truck and drop off the two bodies. He took Sam with him, and they decided to take them during the evening just before dark. They could drop the bodies at the bottom of the hill and then get out quickly. They knew that there were sentries around the perimeter of the base, and they wanted to avoid any contact.

They arrived at the bottom of the hill near the bunker and put the bodies in the middle of the road. Sam thought it would be good if they propped the bodies up, so they would not get run over. Charlie thought he was crazy, but he went along with him. He had brought along some logs they had cut, put them behind them, propped them up as well as they could, and they left.

CHAPTER 37

At the Tunnel

Tommy, Wendy, and David returned from their trip downstate, and after checking in with Sherry and then Tommy's parents, Tommy and Wendy drove to the tunnel. David had some things to take care of and did not go. When they arrived, Tommy informed Joe about their unsuccessful trip, and what he had seen. Wendy saw her parents and gave them both a hug. Joe was sure that the place they stopped near Cheboygan was the warehouse where he and Ron were held.

Tommy asked Joe if he had heard anything from Wayne and Cathy since they were gone.

"I haven't heard anything yet. Our wives are near Marquette with Cathy and are keeping tabs on Wayne, and they'll let us know if anything changes."

"I think we're going to head up there and see how Wayne is doing. Wendy wants to give some support to Cathy too."

"That sounds good. We have some other news for you, too. You know the three who were hunting us?"

"Yeah. The ones who came to the cabin?"

"Yes. We got two of them, and we're holding the third. He's over there hidden in the woods tied up in that shed. We dropped off the two bodies near the bunker, so I'm expecting to hear from there in some way, so if you head to Marquette, be careful. Also, we had two sentries hurt. One was killed."

Tommy and Wendy were shocked. They knew all the people who were helping. "Who was it?"

"Donny was hurt and Toby, unfortunately, was killed."

Tommy was stunned. Wendy screamed. "We know both of those boys. What's next?"

"We're so sorry," Joe said. "This is bad and we need to get going on this tunnel to turn things around."

"I hope we can," Wendy cried. "We should first pay a visit to Toby's parents."

"You be careful on your trip now."

Tommy answered, "We will."

"And say hello to everyone. We're keeping in contact only if something important happens, so we haven't spoken to our wives for the past few days."

"We'll be careful, and we'll let everyone know how things are here."

"Sounds good. Take care."

Before they left, Tommy and Wendy checked out the progress of the tunnel, met Frank, and then turned to leave. Wendy's parents walked them out, and told them to stop at their house so they could freshen up a bit and get some supplies before leaving.

Joe, Ron, and Frank were waiting for Matt to return and to get word on the wounded sentry and the girl. They decided to get back to work on the tunnel, but they needed two sentries in place. Charlie was there and said he had two recruits. "One is a barber from town who is fed up with them raising cane in Colewin. He's had it. He said he would be happy to be a sentry when he could. The other one is his son, Peter. He's an ex-Marine and said he would help out when he could. They will both be here soon."

The sand from the collapse had been taken care of, and Frank had everyone working on shoring up the walls and ceiling. Things were looking a lot more secure and professional from a miner's standpoint.

"Keep adding the lagging to the right side of the tunnel near where the cave-in happened. Once we have that completed, we'll start the digging again. No digging until everything is reinforced. Got it?"

Everyone agreed. While they worked, Joe and Ron kept watch until the new guys arrived. Just about an hour later a truck pulled up and the barber and his son got out. Both were dressed in camo and had flack jackets. They also carried assault rifles. They were ready.

CHAPTER 38

The Bunker, April 4

It was around noon when a truck with six troops headed out of the bunker to get supplies. They weren't allowed to go to Colewin for supplies, so supplies were shipped to U.S. 2, and they would pick them up. The truck roared down the hill and was moving along briskly when the driver saw something in the road.

"What the hell is that?" he yelled. "Hey, everyone, get your weapons ready, we have trouble up ahead."

One of them responded. "We're always ready!"

The truck came to a stop about one hundred yards from the men in the road. The troops jumped out and walked forward slowly, backing each other up as they went. One said, "Hey, that looks like those two guys that showed up a bit ago. The ones who were always angry and didn't talk much."

"You're right," another man answered.

As they neared the two men in the road, they could see that they were not a threat, but they were cautious just the same, in case this was an ambush. "Careful everyone. Keep your eyes on the brush on each side of the road."

One walked up to the two and kicked one. "Hey, this one's dead, so's the other one. They've been dead a bit, I think. They're stiff."

The driver inched his way up to the others. He was nervous now. "Put them in the back of the truck. We need to take them to the man in the bunker. He'll know what to do. I don't want to get in the middle of this shit. Hustle, and we'll head out for the supplies later."

When they returned to the bunker, the driver walked up to the door and pounded on it. Bates saw them on his monitors. "Now what!" he blurted as he rose to head to the door. Before he took his eyes off the screen, he saw a body being lifted out of the truck. "What the f…! When are they going to send some guys with some brains? How in the world did they get hurt going for supplies? They're going to drive me over the edge. What the hell!"

Bates turned and walked to the door. He threw it open and said, "What the hell happened to you? Man, are those two dead?" Then he realized who they were, and he threw his head back and just yelled. "Noooo. What have you done? We're in a pile of shit now."

April 10

It was almost a week since the tunnel was under siege by Vince and his boys. Joe and Ron had Vince hidden with them, and they had been interrogating him, but they had gained little more knowledge than when they had captured him. He did talk about Bates a lot. Apparently, they did not get along, and Vince was happy to be done with him, or so he said. Vince was not a soldier in the sense that his two partners had been. He was more of a messenger and go-between. They found out that he was forced into the role he was playing. He did not like escorting two bullies around, but they were paying him, so he did what he was told.

"I don't think we're going to get much more out of this guy. We'd have to torture him and I'm not in for that," Joe told Ron as they took a break and went outside to take a breather.

"I'm with you on that, Joe. I don't see that he has anything that can help us, unless he knows something about where they're going and where the other bases are located. That might help the FBI."

"We might be able to make a deal for his freedom. If he tells us where the bases are and who is in charge, we'll let him go."

"Let's try it. We haven't mentioned freedom at all."

They had a few beers and ate while they contemplated their next move and how they would approach it.

"Joe, maybe we should just take him down to Ann and let her people take care of him."

"Not a bad idea." Just as Joe finished his beer, the phone rang. It was Matt.

"Joe."

"Yep."

"Say, the sentries tell me that another semi pulled up in the same place as the last two. He thinks another group is headin' out. I know you were gonna have Tommy, Wendy, and David follow again, but Tommy and Wendy left for Marquette and they won't be back for a while. David's here though. Wendy wants Tommy to take some time to enjoy life. She wants him to forget about this place for a couple of days and even stop at Pictured Rocks in Munising or maybe climb Sugarloaf in Marquette. Sounds like they'll be gone for a bit."

"Yes. I heard her the other day. That's their plan. I won't send David alone. I guess Ron and I will go again, although I'm not sure what to do with this guy we caught."

"Just leave 'im there. Tie 'im up and put 'im in that shed you have there. We'll have David stop by and check up on 'im several times a day and bring food and drink."

"That might work. We'll talk it over and plan to go when they think they're on the move. Just let us know."

"Okay."

1500 miles away

"I'm back."

"I see. You look well," the new leader said.

"I am better, but I know there are things I can't do anymore, but I can lead and that I will do."

The old boss had been disabled by Joe and Ron in February of 2021, and they had hoped to put him away, but it did not work. He survived the attack on his body, and now he was back for revenge. The only problem was that the new boss was entrenched—and had given the order for the event to occur much earlier than expected. The old boss was sure that was not a good idea. He liked to move slowly and strike at the right time, and this was not the right time.

The old boss took a deep breath and spoke, "You will move aside and become my number two man."

"Move aside? First, we must meet with the committee and see what they think. They put me in charge when you were in the hospital. I am the leader. No one has told me to move aside."

"We'll see. The committee meets soon and they will agree to put me in charge again. If you do not like their decision, you may leave. I said you could be my number two man, but maybe you do not want that, and now I'm not sure I do either."

"You're an arrogant and sloppy old man now. You're finished. You'll see."

"You are calling me old and sloppy. You will be done when I'm in charge. Just remember that."

"Oh, I'll remember. Now you can leave the headquarters. Go someplace like the old folks' home down the street. You'll fit in there."

"More insults. I'll leave, but I will see you next week at the committee meeting, and I'll make sure to take care of you!"

The new boss just smiled and sat in the chair behind his desk. He nodded to the two guards at the door to escort the man out."

They grabbed the old boss by both arms, turned him around, walked him to the door, and threw him out. This was a huge insult for a man who was once the most powerful man in the organization. He would return and set this man straight. The old boss had a lot of supporters from many years of planning the event and running the show. He would be back.

On the road to Marquette

Tommy and Wendy were headed to Marquette. Wendy was relieved. She had tried to get Tommy to leave the area a long time ago because she feared for his life. Now, she finally had him on the road, and she was going to try to keep him away for as long as she could. "This is nice, isn't it? To finally get away from all that trouble where we can trust no one, and we have to look over our shoulders wherever we go."

"It is nice, but I already miss everyone, and I fear that they need our help. I really hope nothing happens to anyone, and we can get back as soon as possible. I mean we already lost some people. Some were our age. What is that? And nothing was ever investigated like it should have been. Sheriff Daryl has that whole area under his control—and he says and does what he wants. What the heck anyway?"

"I know, but let's enjoy the time we have away and do some fun things after we see Wayne and Cathy."

"I'm not sure I'll be in the mood if Wayne is no better. That could have been me as easily as him. Like I said, I've got to get back to help so no one else gets hurt."

"We'll see, Tommy."

CHAPTER 39

The Tunnel, April 11, Early Afternoon

Frank had the tunnel going twenty-four hours per day. He had Charlie and Sam busy running all over the place for beams and lagging. They were kept busy most of the day. Charlie was ornery because he had little time to do much logging for himself, and Sam thought that he, too, was also too busy.

"A man's got to make a living, you know," said Sam.

Charlie agreed. "I know, but I think we're makin' great progress. We'll be fine if we kin get to the bunker and get all our things. We can log the rest of the year."

"Doesn't seem right to me."

"Nothin' ever does with you."

The work on the tunnel had been a lot slower since Frank made everyone do everything his way. He was able to use the excavator full time. It was a big assist. Now things were going well, and Frank thought they could make progress in the next few weeks. It was a big job, but he had faithful workers who believed in what they were doing, and that made all the difference. He enjoyed being around his brother Joe and his friend Ron, and he had gotten to be good friends with Matt. Joe had asked about how long it might take, and Frank gave his opinion.

"I think this tunnel is going to take a very long time. We don't make much progress because we run into big rocks and shaky ground, and then we have to shore it up and that takes time. The whole project might take us a year, I'm guessing, if we can work right through the winter months."

Charlie was there and he was not happy with the answer. "How's this gonna take us a year?"

"Well," Frank answered. "At best we make four or five feet a day. You have a quarter mile to go. That's over one thousand three hundred feet. Divide that by four—if we can continue to make that kind of progress. Then, as the tunnel gets longer and longer, we need to consider dust control and ventilation. Otherwise, we need to quit."

"We ain't quittin'!" Charlie boomed. "We'll find what we need, and we'll keep workin' twenty-four hours a day, seven days a week if'n we have to."

Frank responded, "If you can find the equipment we need, and you're willing to work twenty-four hours a day, it might work."

Joe was listening to the conversation and realized that what he and Ron envisioned was a much earlier attempt to get Bates, so they could interrogate him and get information to Ann at the FBI headquarters in downstate Michigan. Before Joe could say anything, Matt said he had news from the sentry by the bunker gate. "They're on the move again with more troops headin' out. Already one truck is about to leave for the semi."

"Ron, get your things. We need to head out right now."

"Everything is ready. We just need to pack some water and food and we're gone."

"All right. We'll see you all when we get back. We should go as quickly as we can. Make sure you keep an eye on our prisoner!"

"For sure," Frank answered.

The woods off U.S.-2 near the outlet for the semi, thirty minutes later

News from the sentry near U.S. 2 indicated that several trucks had arrived and everything looked ready. The driver was closing the back door and getting ready to leave. Joe and Ron were alert in their car. "I'm surprised they're leaving in daylight. The last two left in the early morning." Joe spoke quietly to Ron, not to disturb their attention on the road.

"Right. But I guess it doesn't matter since they look just like any of the other hundreds of tractor-trailers on the road."

"Yeah, you're right. There are so many going east and west on U.S. 2. I'll bet this one goes east toward lower Michigan since they'll probably be heading to D. C., like Ann said. Although that last one took us on a trip west. We'll see."

Joe's phone rang. He was surprised since he had told everyone not to call unless it was an emergency. It was David. "Joe, when was the last time you saw this guy that you tied up?"

"Yesterday. We fed him prior to getting ready."

"And where is he tied up again?"

"In the shed."

"Nope. No one is there. It looks like he escaped."

"Damn. Just get the heck out of there in case he's still there. He could hurt you."

"I think he's gone. Your four-wheeler isn't here, and I see tracks that look like he or someone tore out of here."

"All right. Get the word out to everyone. We need to find him, but if we can't, we need to be prepared."

"I'll get the word out. Are you coming back now?"

"Can't! We need to follow this semi. Let everyone know we'll return as soon as possible."

Then they saw the semi slowly poking its head out of the brush, like a spooked animal. It edged forward slowly until it was ready to turn onto U.S. 2. The driver was cautious because there was a curve in the road where a vehicle could appear at any second. His blinker was not on. When nothing happened, the driver pulled out as quickly as he could, and he was on the road.

Ron yelled, "He's pulling out to the west. I guess we'll be going through Wisconsin again. They sure are putting on a lot of extra miles doing this. It'd be a lot closer going east."

"They're probably doing this on purpose to mess with anyone trying to figure out where they're headed."

"Yes. That's a good move if that's what they're doing."

They let the semi get ahead a bit before they pulled out and began another journey to somewhere.

"This time we have to stay close. We can't lose them. If we can follow them to where they're going, that'll be a big help."

"I agree. I hope they don't catch on to us though. That could be a problem," Ron said.

"I know. Last time we lost them because of the accident. Hopefully, that doesn't happen again."

They followed closely for a time, and the route seemed the same as last time. This time they were prepared with food, drink, and other necessary camping equipment and weapons. They now knew that the semi made stops for the men to stretch and grab a snack, so they weren't as confused as to what might happen along the way.

The beginning of the trip was uneventful until they reached a road heading to Blaney Park because the semi turned north on Highway 77. Now they were on a completely different route than the one they had been on previously.

Joe said it first. "What the hell? Are they headed north?"

"I know," Ron agreed. "Where are they going? Maybe they have another base in the U.P., and they're just sending troops there."

"Maybe. At any rate we need to follow and find out for sure this time. I wonder which direction they'll take when they reach Highway 28 at Seney. They could go either way east or west. I guess we'll find out soon enough. Let's stay really close until they turn."

"That's for sure. We need to stay on their tail."

It took less than twenty minutes before they were at the junction in Seney. The truck turned west. Joe turned to Ron and said, "They aren't going to D.C. They would be crazy to go north, then west, and then south and then east again, unless they're trying intentionally to mess up anyone who might follow them. They are definitely headed someplace else. We have to make sure we know where this leads us—and what's there when they arrive."

"Agree. This changes what we know and have learned about these trips and possibly the event."

CHAPTER 40

A Meeting on a Remote Island in the Pacific, April 11

Those who could attend, did so on an island in the Pacific. The committee decided to meet, but they did not want to force their members to travel, so they had a video conference. The membership wasn't so large that they could not have a face-to-face meeting, and they for sure, had the means to travel anywhere, but travel was a way to advertise their group, and they did not want the attention. It was just a matter of convenience for members in high state-level positions, some rogue leaders around the world, billionaires who wanted to be in charge, and politicians who sought power.

The group had a serious concern. They needed a powerful leader to run the now very large group of people who were like a small army spread all across the U.S. They knew the current temporary boss was ruthless, but cunning. The old leader who had been put out of commission for some time through some type of poisoning was more cautious, but just as ruthless—and that is what they wanted.

This operation needed someone at the top who could think through all the variables that come with an event such as the one they had planned. Thus, a decision had to be made as to whether the old leader should be returned to his position, or if the current leader was the man for the job.

The new leader opened the meeting from his headquarters.

"We are here to vote on whether you want to continue with me in charge. I'm telling you I have everything in place to have the event occur in a few months, and I can assure you that all of the bases are quite in order and ready to go. I have been able to direct the key representatives at all seven sites to be ready at that time, and they have said they are close. Also, we need to take over as quickly as we can to ensure our success."

The new boss's demeanor was terrifying. His wide, unblinking eyes bulged, and he moved his clenched fists up and down as he ranted. "We will also need to eliminate many in the government right now. An expedited event is to our advantage. We'll have some people who will oppose the move, so we might need our troops to secure key cities. We know that we will have many individuals who will immediately join the cause. We have politicians at all levels that we can turn right away, and some who are already with us. We also have infiltrated the military at all levels, even some at the top."

At this point the old boss began to clarify his concerns, and he said, "This is crazy. We are nowhere near ready to do this. It's going to take a year or two before the event can be pulled off the way we want it to happen. There is a lot of training that should be completed for the troops we have enlisted. We also need to prove to the people that this is necessary, and we do that through the media and by convincing the public that this has got to happen to save the country. You all know that this is a fact. The more people we can convince, especially those in the government, the more power we'll have. We also need to elect more of our people in local, state, and federal positions. If we do this right, we can move in quickly and not have as much bloodshed as the current leader indicates is needed."

"You are just weak, and you can't handle a little bloodshed," said the current leader.

"That's not true, but I would like to keep the bloodshed to a minimum. You say you have people in the military at all levels, but

I know for a fact that you don't. We never have. We knew last year that there was one general who was on the fence, but when he heard what the plan was, he has not been on board. Yes, we have some lower-level people, but really, we need to rethink the timeline right now. Moving too quickly will doom this event. Most of the troops need more training anyway. I've spoken to the trainers and the leaders on site, and they feel that we have people who do not know what they are doing."

Both leaders had decided to attend the meeting electronically, but several of the committee had joined the group at the site. One man in particular who had loads of influence, spoke up. "Enough of the arguing. It is not for you two to decide who is in charge or when the event takes place. It's up to the committee."

Another member, a strong leader and demagogue in his own country agreed. "This is correct. We will decide who leads, and when the event takes place. We need a thorough report from both of you on what you know to be the condition at each base, and what you each might think is lacking at this point."

One of the billionaires spoke next. "Listen, we've spent a lot of money so far on this, and we need it to go exactly right. We cannot afford any missteps. If we don't plan better than those idiots on January 6, we will be doomed, and so planning and readiness are essential."

There was an agreed-upon murmur that came through loud and clear on the screens that the two leaders were watching. Everyone in the room at the site felt it too.

An old man with perfectly combed white hair and an immaculate presence spoke up. Everyone listened. "I agree with what has been said by our committee members. This is the first time we did not have a real mediator. The leader usually takes that role, but today we are not sure who will be in charge, so I suggest that you two give us your take on the situation and readiness as it stands today. You can also tell us why you should be the leader going forward. Does everyone agree?"

Several hands shot up on the screen. "Then it is agreed. Let's hear it."

CHAPTER 41

On M-28 Heading West, 5:00 p.m.

An hour later, Joe turned to Ron and said, "As I said before, I think that Ann's theory that they were all going to D.C. may be wrong, but where are they going and why through the U.P.? Unless they are going to another base in the Keweenaw Bay area. We know that there is another militia there, but they are not as big as the one near Colewin."

"I remember talking about that last year. Ann did not think that it was very active, but she knew they had a number of members."

"We'll see where they end up, and we'll have to let Ann know."

They passed Munising around 5:30 p.m., and the semi stayed north on M-28 through the little town of Christmas and then on to Harvey. They stayed north, and they were now headed for Marquette. Joe guessed that the only route out of Marquette was U.S. 41, and he realized that they were near where their wives were staying. They might be in Marquette right now with Cathy.

Wayne was in an induced coma, and Joe had not heard from any of them in a while. He knew Tommy was there with Wendy, and Joe thought he might give his wife a call. They had decided not to use their phones unless it was an emergency, but he was right here, and he wanted to get an update, but he was guarded with his words.

"Hello?" Joette answered and was happy to hear Joe's voice, but nervous at the same time. "Joe, is everything all right?"

"Yes. We're following a semi. We're traveling close to where you are right now. We can't stop because we need to stay on their tail."

"Joe, we're not where you think we are. I won't say on the phone where, but you know. The place that you sent us. All is well, but Shanice and I are going to head back and help out. We have the kids settled, and we can't do anything here. Cathy told us to go back and help. She'll keep us informed."

"Are you sure you girls want to do that?"

"Yes. We could help with whatever is needed."

"Okay. We'll keep you informed about where we are. We're not sure where they're headed, so I'm not sure where we'll end up, but we'll keep you up to date."

"Sounds good. Take care."

"Will do."

"Say. If we come back this way, we could travel together. Not sure how long we'll be on the road though."

"We'll hang back for a day or two, but if you're not here by then, we'll head out. By the way, do you have any other help besides Ron?"

"Not really. Why?"

"It just seems like you should have somebody backing you up."

In the background Joette heard Shanice exclaim, "You mean those two are alone again? They don't have anyone helping them? For Pete's sake, tell them to get help!"

"Shanice agrees. You need some help."

"No worries. We'll see you soon. Take care."

Joe hung up and let Ron know about the plans. Ron was not happy that the women had decided to go back when he and Joe were not there. "I know together that they can take care of themselves, and they won't do anything crazy. Hopefully, we can find out where this truck is going and get back soon."

"We'll see." Joe decided to make one more phone call before they passed Negaunee and Ishpeming.

"Who you calling, Joe?"

"Just making a little insurance call. Hope it works."

It was slow-going because the road was not heavily traveled at this time of the year. Joe and Ron had to keep back and hope they would not lose the semi. They had been on the road for some time, and they were getting hungry, so they grabbed the sandwiches that they had packed and washed them down with bottled water.

"Yummy," Ron said, "Good old peanut butter and jelly sandwiches. My favorite."

"Best I could do with the time we had. I made several and packed a cooler of water. We should be good. Also, I packed some of those fizzy waters and power bars if you want something different."

"I'm good." Just as Ron answered, the semi reached the intersection of 41 and 141, and turned left to follow Highway 28 and 141. This surprised Joe and Ron. They thought that they would be heading to L'Anse and Baraga and then into the Keweenaw.

"Now where are they going? Maybe they will go north at Bruce Crossing or will they head south on 141?"

Ron wasn't really aware of the roads heading north or south, so he just said, "Not sure where they're going, but wherever it is, I'm confused."

April 11, 7:30 p.m.

His mirrors did not lie. That same view kept popping up, and it was the car they expected to see. He murmured before he picked up his phone and called. "Now just to let the plan unfold. It'll be some time before we need to stop. Then we'll finally get them."

The driver thought the guy was losing it, talking to himself until his passenger made a call.

"Yeah. Who's this?" Bates answered.

"It's your man on the road."

"This better be good."

"Oh, it's good all right. Got 'em spotted. We're somewhere on M-28, and we're headed to a little town called Bruce Crossing. We'll let them follow until we get to the resting spot. We have a place fixed up for us to stop just past another small town called Ewen. Not sure yet how far it is, but it can't be too far. We'll pass it, and then there's a stop we've planned for the troops in the trailer to take a break. I'll be looking for the locals you contacted up ahead, and who set this up. I'll get back to you then."

"This time don't mess it up. We have them out of this area away from any help, so it's up to you to do this, Vince."

"Don't worry. They've pissed me off for the last time. If needed, I have almost one-hundred troops to help. We got this."

"Like I said, don't fuck up, and keep our troops out of this. Work with the guys that I had set this up over there. They know the area and have enough fire power if needed."

The truck lumbered on through a desolate area of the U.P. until they came to Ewen. They drove through and then passed a small roadside park. The area was all trees and dense forests, but it wasn't long before Vince saw his signal. It wouldn't be long before it was dark, and Vince thought that they should wait until darkness to pull off their plan. Out here, at night, a person could not see a foot in front of his face because it gets so dark. No lights anywhere. His next signal was just a small flag on the side of the road. "There it is. Next road we turn right and set the plan in action."

CHAPTER 42

Earlier in the Day Near the Tunnel, April 11, 4:30 p.m.
David was nervous, but at the same time he was sure that the guy was no longer nearby, yet he feared for the people at the tunnel. Could he have gone there? No. He probably went straight to the bunker, and if he did that, he would probably have people heading to the tunnel right now. David turned off the road and drove through the trees. He reached the parking spot, concealed his vehicle, and walked briskly to the tunnel.

"Matt, Matt, are you here?"

"Right over here. What's up?"

"The guy that Joe and Ron had at the shed is gone. I called Joe and Ron, and they're still after the semi. He told us to prepare for anything. My guess is that they'll have people out here soon. What's your take?"

"I agree. Let's shut the place down for a few days and hide out and keep the surveillance team up here. The rest of us will have to head out. We'll need to hide the tunnel. Let's move a small tree in front of the entrance. We can uproot one with the excavator and plant it right in front. I'll get everyone to cover our tracks and the equipment we have here. We should hide it all in the tunnel."

When everyone got the message, they all pitched in to get the area ready for visitors. Matt and Charlie gave everyone places to hide. They all had weapons. Most were hidden around the tunnel ready for any intruders. They figured if they were going to be attacked, it would be soon. It didn't take long to get everything in place. All the vehicles were taken out of the area, and the trail in was hidden as best they could. Now they just had to wait.

Earlier in the day at the bunker, April 11

Bates met with Vince, and they discussed all that had happened to him and his cohorts. Bates was not sure if he should inform the boss. Vince had arrived on a four-wheeler that belonged to someone in Colewin. How would this affect the bunker? Was Vince seen heading here? Would it involve the cops? Whatever the possibilities, Bates knew this presented some problems and some possibilities for him and Vince. Vince told Bates about Joe and Ron, and how they had kept him hostage. He was upset and wanted revenge.

"I think I know just how to get some of that revenge for you," Bates said.

"You mean go and blast them out of that hiding place in the woods? I'm not sure exactly what they're doing there, but it isn't that far from the bunker. Should we storm the place?"

"No. That's not a good idea. Look how it turned out for you and your buddies. Storming the place wouldn't do as much good as the idea I have."

"And what's that?"

"We have it on good info that the two older guys who held you captive followed our trucks through Wisconsin, and one of the others followed in Michigan. We've had to make numerous adjustments in order to lose them. The last trip through lower Michigan was a mess until we employed several other truckers to help us lose them."

"What does this have to do with me?"

"I'm going to send you on the next mission. If these two are the same ones following again, then we'll get them. We'll drive through the U.P. in some very remote areas where there is little law enforcement. We have some militia cells who would do just about anything in some sections of the U.P.—and we'll employ them to help us get them once and for all."

"How?"

"You'll ride along with the driver of the next group that goes out of here today. You can identify these two, and if they are the ones who are following, you can take them down."

"Sound good. I'm not sure I'm getting the whole picture here, but let's talk and see what we can do to make this work."

"Oh, it'll work once you're out of the area. They'll have no one to help, and the guys I can get to help you will know the area and won't be on anyone's radar if we eliminate these two. It'll be good for all of us—and the new boss will be very happy. We won't let him know anything until the deed is done."

The road between Ewen and Bergland, April 11, 8:00 p.m.
The truck drove to Matchwood, Michigan, a ghost town. Joe and Ron saw the truck take a right turn on Norwich Road. Joe said, "We'll have to check the place out and make sure it isn't a destination, but just a scheduled pitstop."

"For sure, Joe. Pull up ahead, and let's find a spot to hide the car. Not many roads around here. We might have to drive ahead a little to get off the road, and then walk back to the spot where they turned."

Joe and Ron drove past until they reached a road with a few houses on it. They ditched the car in the trees and both got out. They knew they needed a plan, one in which they would have to separate to back each other up. Joe decided to walk along the highway until he came to the road where the truck turned. Ron was to keep back a bit and stay hidden in the trees.

Joe did not expect that this was going to be easy following a semi for so many miles, but he did not anticipate anything bad happening. As he moved slowly along the road, daylight was receding and he looked over to see if Ron was in place. He saw him moving slowly near the tree line.

CHAPTER 43

Nearby, a Truck and Six Men, past Ewen, after 8:00 p.m.

"The guy said that dis is the place. You see dat car coming along?"

The driver, Brad, responded, "Yah! They're turning on dat dead-end road up ahead. That's gotta be dem. I know most everyone 'round here and they ain't from here."

"Let's just move slow like in that direction, eh? No. Maybe just pull over right here. We can keep dem two boys with the truck, ya know, and the rest of us can sneak up on 'em."

"Hey, dis ain't good. What if they're armed?"

"So, what! There are six of us and we're armed. Even if we keep two wit' the truck. We still got four, ya know."

"If they got only two, we'll be fine. What if dey got more?"

"We'll take it slow and easy."

They exited the truck and told the other four what they were going to do. They kept two young guys with the truck, and the other four walked slowly near the tree line. In just a few minutes, they saw someone walk to the road and head in the direction of the semi. Then they noticed someone else walking along the tree line just like they were doing.

"Yah, that's dem for sure, eh? Let dem get a little down the road and we'll come up behind 'em. It's almost dark, so we have to do dis quick like."

"You two walk on da road and get close to dat guy. We'll move ahead and catch up to the one near the woods. Get ready. Make sure your safety's off. We may need to do some shootin' right away, ya know."

Everyone nodded. They moved quietly like well-trained military. They were on them in no time.

As Joe turned back to the road in front of him, he and Ron were grabbed from behind and quickly tossed to the ground. They had no chance to react. Before they realized what was happening, they were staring down the barrels of four assault rifles and looking at four men in camo gear. No chance to escape.

One of them was in Ron's face. "You move up to da road. On the ground, now. Face down."

Joe and Ron capitulated. They were tied up on the spot and rolled on to their faces and zipped tied. Joe tried to yell to Ron again, but they told Joe to settle down or they'd shut him up. All Joe could think about was what had he gotten Ron into this time, and what would their wives do if they disappeared? He knew these guys were not from Colewin, nor were they some of the troops. They sounded like they were from this area—the western U.P. Joe tried to say something to Ron once again, but he suddenly felt a severe pain and he was out. Then a rag was stuffed in Ron's mouth, and he lost his sight when a cloth bag was shoved over his head. They did the same to Joe who was lying on the ground. Ron didn't know what to think!

"You," the head man spoke to Ron. "Don't try nothin'. Your buddy is lucky he ain't dead."

One of them spoke up right away. "Brad, we ain't here to hurt no one, jest to take dese two prisoners for dat dude."

"Yah, well, too bad, eh?"

"Brad, we agreed to do dis, but we ain't gonna be any part of any hurtin' or killin' for sure."

"You just shut up and do what I say. Get the zip ties out and get their legs tied up so we can deliver 'em."

Ron could hear the men continue to argue, and it did not sound very good. He heard them discuss getting rid of the evidence at a spot well-hidden in the woods. His mind raced with thoughts of the past. *This did not sound like fun. Was this the end? After their escape a year ago, Ron never thought they would be in this type of situation again. What a mess! How had they been so careless?*

The men responded quickly and had Joe and Ron bound on the road. It was almost dark, and the leader sent a signal to the truck, and it began moving toward them. As they were loading Joe and Ron in the back, another car drove quickly by and then another. The men looked at each other and stopped when the first car slowed, but it kept going, and the second sped by.

"Let's get dem delivered and den get the hell outta here."

The truck stayed hidden up the road from where Vince was with the semi. The head man, Brad, had told him where the best spot was to get rid of any evidence. He knew a place where he had two of his men dig a hole big enough to get rid of whatever. It was a desolate spot off the road past where the semi had stopped, down the road a bit to keep whatever was going to happen away from the people in the trailer. All Brad and his men had to do was wait.

The men were loaded on the trailers and the doors shut. Vince waved to the semi driver and told him to stay put until he returned.

"You got half an hour. That's it. If you aren't back then, I'm leaving. I have orders to have these troops in place on time. I'm going to let them out for another fifteen minutes because we have a long trip ahead. I'll have them load in fifteen, and you had better be here five minutes later."

"Yeah, yeah. I'll be there. If I'm not, I'll figure something out." Then he walked down the road until he found the truck. It was dark now and he could not see much, but thanks to Brad, he could see the truck about fifty yards away, a light beaming in the cab.

Vince reached the truck and hopped in the cab with the other two. "Where is it?"

"It's down the road a bit, eh? Hang on. It's a great spot. No one will ever find it. My boys dug the hole you wanted. We won't stay with you like you said. Once we drop you off, I'll send two of my men to head back in twenty minutes. You should be gone by then. They'll cover the hole and get the hell outta there. We don't want no connection to what you're doing."

Vince had a big smile and just breathed a loud, relieved breath. "That's the plan. We'll be out of your way in no time, and you can all get out of here."

They drove to the spot and then stopped by a very dense wooded area. They got out and pulled Ron and Joe off the bed of the truck. They had rags in their mouths and blindfolds over their heads, and they made them walk ahead of them. They waddled like a couple of drunk penguins. Three of the guys flicked on flashlights. There was no trail. It was all brush, rocks, and twigs. Joe and Ron both stumbled several times. They just laughed at them. Vince was ecstatic. He mumbled something that the others did not understand, "Finally, I get revenge and can let the boss know that we did what he wanted." Then he asked, "How much farther?"

"Just down the hill a bit and den to your right. You'll see the spot. It was the only place we could dig a good enough hole, but you can see it's not someplace anyone is going to find. Do you have a flashlight to get out of there?"

"Yes. I have a good one."

"Can you find your way out?"

"It's not that difficult. If I can't, I'll wait for your boys to get here and they can help. Hey, have one of your guys get their car. You got the keys, right? Just to be sure, can you leave a trail of flashlights out of this spot?"

"I have the keys, and I can place four or five flashlights leadin'
out. What do ya want with the car?"

"Just in case I need a ride. Otherwise, I'll leave it nearby and
you can ditch it. Have them leave the keys in the ignition."

"You got twenty minutes to take care of dis, ya know. The
two boys I'll send will throw the dirt in, and I'll have dem check
on the car. Where will you want it?"

"The car should be either here or where the semi is parked
right now."

"Okay. Sounds good. Here's your hole."

CHAPTER 44

The Tunnel, Same Day, Evening

They had waited most of the day, but nothing happened. The sentries around the bunker said they did not see any movement or anything out of the ordinary. Matt told Charlie that maybe there wasn't much to worry about, and they could continue work the next day if all remained quiet at the bunker. They had been at it almost every hour of every day—and still they were only about fifty feet in. The tunnel was good, but to get over 1400 feet total, it was going to take a while, but Charlie was not deterred. He figured they would make better progress as they gained experience, and he had all the time in the world.

Matt did not. He thought they would be farther along than fifty feet, but he too was willing to see if they might get better at this, yet he was concerned. "I don't know, Charlie. This here tunnel will take us a year at this pace. We might have to find another way into the bunker."

"No. No. We just need more people is all," Charlie said.

"That could help, but we don't have any other people we can trust, and we lost Wayne, Cathy, Joe, and Ron, plus Wendy and Tommy for the next week or so."

"We'll manage. Let's just keep at it."

"I guess we have to, but let's see if we can think up some other way to get what we need. Maybe we should shut 'er down for a few days."

"What? Go ahead. Think. I'm going to keep workin'."

The virtual meeting somewhere in the Pacific

Through video conferencing, both men gave their best version of what they thought should happen—and when it should happen. It took quite some time because both had a lot to say. The new leader kept getting more and more belligerent and threatening, and he kept insisting that the event had to happen before the next election cycle. The members had already listened for more than an hour when he finished and slammed his fist on his desk. Luckily, the meeting was via electronic conferencing—and he wasn't in the same room as many of the members because he was very intimidating. Some of the members squirmed in their seats.

When he was finished, the members waited for the old leader who also spoke for over an hour. He went on and on about how they needed to wait. He spoke of people who needed to be in place in specific positions. He mentioned over and over again how they would fail if they had the event too soon. It would be another attempt to overthrow the government without any real planning. He was not any more convincing than his competition, but he was a lot smoother and less frightening. The members knew what they had with him since he had led the group for many years without any problems—except for his failure earlier this year when he let those two guys get the best of him.

When both were finished, the electronic meeting ended, and another meeting for committee members only was held.

"We need to handle this correctly or it is going to be a bad situation," one of the members said.

"Agreed," sounded from several.

The discussion lasted quite a while, but when they were finished, they decided to go with the old leader who was less prone to overreacting and more toward a cool, calm demeanor. When they finally voted, they called the old leader and gave him the good news. They also gave him permission to handle the new boss whatever way he wanted.

He knew what that meant.

A spot in the woods

Vince had a good laugh. Joe and Ron were now kneeling in front of a hole in the ground. They knew what would come next, and they were both trying to come up with something, but hands and feet were tied and a bag was over their heads. This was it.

Vince decided he had a few minutes to play around with their minds, so he said, "Do you want to live? Just bow your head if you do." Joe and Ron did not. They knew what was in store, and they would not bow down to this animal.

"Isn't this great? I'm going to leave here in your vehicle, and then we're going to get rid of any trace of it and you two. No one will ever find you. Isn't that too bad. You gave me headache after headache and wasted my friends. Well, "friends" might be stretching it, but we worked together. You almost had me. I would have been killed, I guess, if I hadn't escaped, but tonight, this is good-bye."

Vince moved close to Joe and put the barrel of his rifle right at the back of his head. "This shouldn't hurt much." Joe flinched. "Oh, maybe you want your friend to go first." He moved the rifle to the back of Ron's head. Vince kept laughing and playing with their sanity as he moved back and forth, finally settling on Ron.

Vince ranted on, "So, you think you're tough and can take out anyone. Right? A big mistake. What are you looking for anyway? You think you can stop this train that's moving full steam ahead? You can't. It won't be long, and we'll wipe out all of you bleepin' idiots, who think you can tell everyone else all your bullshit about life in a free country. This country is not free! It ties the hands of anyone who thinks differently. Too much government, too many politicians, too many laws. Good-bye you asses. See you in hell!"

Joe tried to talk, but the cloth in his mouth made it impossible, and he was weak with fear. His head was spinning and he wanted to do something, anything, but how? He could not breathe well, and he wanted to say something, anything to Ron before…

"Ahhh, I'm going to call Bates and let him know I finally have you." He rested his rifle on the crook of his arm, pulled out his phone, and called Bates. "Hey, Bates, guess what? I got those two you been moaning about. I told you we'd get 'em."

"We? How is *you* a *we*? Your buddies are dead."

"I got 'em anyway. They're kneeling in front of me. Blindfolded and ready to drop in a grave. That Joe and his buddy!" And Vince laughed.

"You mean they're still alive? That's the trouble with you. You brag before anything is done. Even if you get them, you got another one to take care of—that Tommy guy. One of our troops, Bill something, said that Tommy's headed for Marquette and is staying in some place called Ishpeming. Bill knew him from Colewin and they talk. Unfortunately, Tommy didn't know that Bill was fed up with his shit, so you can head to Ishpeming next."

"Yeah, yeah, we'll see you soon. Gotta finish this off." Vince saw that he had only about five more minutes before the semi left, so he hung up to finish the job.

Ron was thinking of all that he had left unfinished in his life, but what bothered him most was that he would not get to say good-bye to his wife, children, and grandchildren. His stomach was queasy and he felt like he would throw up. Then he felt the barrel of the rifle on the back of his head.

Joe heard a shot and a body fall and tumble into the hole in front of him, and tears filled Joe's eyes.

CHAPTER 45

On the Highway

Tommy found the car and knew he did not have much time. He had been following them for some time, ever since Joe called and asked for backup. Wendy wanted to go along, but Tommy was firm in his belief that it might be too dangerous. She didn't listen and had borrowed Cathy's car and she was following him, but she had lost him somewhere around Covington.

Tommy knew when he passed the truck on the side of the road that this had to be where Mr. Joe and Ron must be. He saw something that looked suspicious. It was nearly dark when he saw several men with assault rifles on the side of the road. That was not normal, even for the U.P. He passed a truck and kept going in hopes that they would not suspect him. He traveled until he was well beyond the truck where they could no longer see him, and then he turned around. When he did, he saw a car approach his as he maneuvered to head east again. The car slowed and pulled to the other side of the road.

It was Wendy.

He rolled his window down and she did the same. "What in the ever-loving hell are you doing? This is dangerous stuff!"

"I can tell. When I passed that truck back there, I saw them lift a man into the back of a pickup truck. Who was that? What is going on?"

"I'm not sure, but Mr. Joe and Ron have to be around here someplace. I lost the truck, but I know it can't be far away. They had to stop for a break. They'd been on the road for over four hours."

"Let's look to see if we can find their car. If that was them that they were loading into the back of that truck, their car can't be far from here. Then we'll know for sure that it's them. Otherwise, we'll have to keep going until we find them."

"Let's go back and search any roads near there. They would have to have hidden the car nearby if they were trying to stay near that semi."

Wendy was shaking and her voice was wavering. "First we have to make sure that truck is gone."

As they drove back to the scene where the truck was, they saw it turn left at a road about one-hundred yards away. Both Tommy and Wendy pulled into the first road that they saw to get out of view of the people in the truck. As they drove down the road, they spotted Mr. Joe's car.

Tommy stopped and Wendy pulled in behind him. They checked the car and saw there were no keys in the ignition. Tommy thought they should hide one of their vehicles farther down the road and then jump in together and search for Mr. Joe and Ron. They decided to search the road where the truck had pulled in to see if they could find any evidence of the semi or of Mr. Joe and Ron.

1,500 miles away

Now that the old boss was back in business, he called his old team together and decided to make quick work of the new boss. This was serious business. The new boss was ruthless and had a good following. Many of the people he had on the payroll wanted the event to take place quickly and violently. That's not the way it should go. The old boss wanted to get people in place and do this quickly with as little killing as possible, so he knew that this guy had to go.

After getting his people together, the old boss gave them their instructions. They knew where the new boss was, but they felt it was impossible to get to him. One of his aides asked, "Does he even know he's been ousted?"

"I don't think so. They wanted this to be a surprise so he did not prepare a way out and try to take over again. From what I understand, even the committee members are afraid of him, so we have to move quickly and with precision."

On the road

As they drove down the road, they passed a side road where Tommy could see lights. "That has to be the semi they were following. Are they here?"

Wendy was worried. "I don't see the pickup truck anywhere. Let's drive down this road a bit first to see if we can spot it. I'm sure they were in the back of the truck."

"We can, but I hope they're not here. We could be too late to help if they are."

They drove down the road for a short distance and then they spotted the pickup. Tommy drove past and then turned around. He cut the lights and moved slowly toward the pickup and hid the car in the trees. As soon as he parked, someone came wandering out of the woods, jumped in the truck, pulled a U-turn and drove away.

"I see some lights in the woods," Wendy said.

"Where?"

"Look to your right. See?"

"Yes, Let's pull up and check it out."

Wendy was nervous. "I don't think we should take any chances, but what if Mr. Joe and Ron are hurt or worse?"

"You stay with the car and keep it running. Don't leave the car! I'm going to see what the lights are in the woods. I'll take my .30-30. It's really dark out here. Hopefully those lights will guide me."

There was enough light from the flashlights for Tommy to walk to the spot where Vince had Joe and Ron. When he reached an opening, there were flashlights giving off enough light for him to see, and he could see two men kneeling on the ground and one man in camo holding a gun at the back of one of the kneeling men. He heard someone talking and noticed that the guy with the gun had a phone out and was talking with someone. Tommy listened and crept as close as he could. What he heard shocked him, but at the same time, confirmed to him that this was Mr. Joe and Ron. He heard the following:

"I got 'em anyway. They're kneeling in front of me. Blindfolded and ready to die and drop in a grave. That Joe and his buddy!" And then the guy with the phone laughed.

Tommy realized he had little time to think and no time to hesitate. He aimed his rifle and pulled off a shot. The man twisted and turned and fell into a hole in front of him.

Wendy had heard the shot and stiffened, but she knew better than to leave the car.

Tommy was sweating profusely as he crawled closer and yelled, "Mr. Joe, Ron is that you?"

Both Ron and Joe tried to turn and fell to the ground. Joe recognized Tommy's voice, but he could not respond. Tommy moved carefully right to the hole and checked on the body to make sure he was not going to be a problem. He turned to Joe and Ron and pulled off the bags covering their heads. Tommy was relieved that it was Mr. Joe and Ron. He pulled the cloth out of their mouths so they could speak, took out his hunting knife, and cut them loose. They were both free now, but as they rose to give Tommy a hug, a car horn blew near the road.

"That's got to be Wendy. I told her to do that if she saw anyone. Follow the lights and we'll get out of here."

There wasn't time for any thank-yous as they dashed to the car. When they reached the road, they could see lights heading toward them. They all jumped in and Wendy was elated to see all three. Tommy yelled, "Drive!" They passed a car heading right to them.

The two men in the car wondered who it might be. "Hey, was anyone else supposed to be here?"

His buddy answered. "Hell if I know. Let's just get dis done and get out of here."

"Yah!"

They drove to the lights, took out their shovels, and walked into the woods. It was very dark now, so they didn't even look in the hole as they started throwing dirt in as fast as they could. When the hole was filled, they packed it down as best they could, put leaves and shrubbery over the top, and began to collect the flashlights.

Wendy drove toward where the semi had been and mentioned that she had seen it pull out a few minutes before the car came down the road. Joe thought the car they passed looked a lot like his car, but he could not be sure in the dark. Wendy kept driving, and when she reached the road where the semi had been, Joe said to pull in.

They waited until the other car stopped and then Joe told Wendy to return slowly. When they arrived, the people inside were gone, and Joe saw that it was his car. He had spare keys attached to a magnetic container under the front wheel well, but he didn't need them. The keys were in the ignition. He slid into the car, grabbed the keys and got going as quickly as he could. They agreed to meet at the spot where Wendy had left her car. Ron jumped in with Joe and they turned around and left, and Wendy followed Joe to the road where she had parked her car.

When the two guys picked up the last flashlight near the road, they saw two cars pull away. Their first thought was to hide, but then they guessed that their buddies were playing another trick on them. When they reached the road, the car they had used was gone. "Dose damn fools. They're playing games again. I guess we walk out. Wonder if they're going to be hiding down dis here road, eh?"

"Yah, Dey give us all da crap jobs 'cause we're the youngest. I'm tired of all dis. Let's get out of here." They took the flashlights and shovels and walked to the highway, mumbling all the way.

CHAPTER 46

Earlier, the Semi in the Woods

It was very dark and the driver had waited twenty-five minutes. He had let the troops out again for a short time, but he had them climb back in fifteen minutes later, and now he was getting impatient. "I'm outta here," he said as he drove straight ahead and turned right. He was on the highway in no time heading west.

The driver kept wondering what Vince was doing, but he could not wait any longer. They had been here a lot longer than they should have, and he did not want to explain why he was late. He was on the road past Bergland when he checked his GPS to make sure he was on the right road. He would head west to a place they had prepared for the troops. They would stay there until the signal was given to move. Where they would move, he did not know, but he knew it was going to be significant.

It would be a lonely drive through a lot of desolate areas in the U.P. and through much of northern Wisconsin. He had plenty of fuel, and he had packed some munchies to keep him awake. He wondered what the next trip would be for him. He'd been all over the Midwest, but this was the farthest west he had gone. He had heard that he might have to go as far as North Dakota next. Well, so be it. Wherever they want—as long as they keep paying me.

The road was very dark in spots, but he did drive through a few small towns. He did not see much traffic, and he kept wondering if Vince was going to catch up and jump in with him, but he was a little crazy anyway. Better if he didn't. He decided to call Bates at the bunker where he had started. "Hey, this Bates?"

"Who's this?"

"Hey, man, your truck driver. Just wanted to let you know we won't be having any people follow us anymore. Vince took care of your problem."

"I know. He called me just a bit ago. Guess he eliminated any problems we've been having. Just one more to take care of and our main problems are over."

"Well, hope you get 'em. Okay, just thought I should let you know."

"Okay. Get those troops where they're headed. Did you pick up Vince?"

"No. He didn't show. Had a car of his own he stole, I guess."

"That idiot! Keep moving and let me know when you arrive."

"Gotcha!"

Occasionally he would see a deer on the side of the road, and he hoped he did not hit one and splatter it all over his cab. He had never been through the U.P. on M-28; he had always traveled on U.S. 2. He wondered why they had gone so far north, but now he understood. Fewer people and quieter roads. It might take him a bit longer, but he would be safer up here. He knew he would intersect with U.S. 2 soon. Nothing like a trip in the dark. He passed several resorts and rental shops, and realized this must be a real vacation area, and he was liking it.

Just off of the highway on a dirt road

Once they arrived at the car that Wendy had driven, there were thank-yous and hugs. Joe and Ron were still sick to their stomachs, and a bit dizzy from what they had just experienced. "That's the closest we've come to checking out since Cheboygan in 2019.

Thank you! Thank you!" Ron said. "We were really too sloppy this time, and we didn't even have a weapon on us."

It would take Ron and Joe a while to calm down from the terror they had just faced, but they knew they had a job to do. They knew that this may be the only chance they would get to find out what's going on with these people, so Joe and Ron decided to hunt for the truck. They had to stamp out their fear for the time being and move on. Coming that close to death was terrifying.

Joe said, "You head back to Ishpeming and take it easy for a while. I don't know how we can thank you for saving our lives. We'll never be able to really thank you enough."

Tommy looked at Joe with disbelief. "There's no way we're letting you follow them without backing you up. We'll both jump in one car and follow. We can pick up this other car when we return."

"Are you sure?" Joe asked.

Wendy looked him in the eyes and very forcefully said, "Yes. You won't be able to talk us out of this."

"Well, in that case, why don't you park this other car in Bergland near the school. Get it out of this area where these guys are. It's right by the road. It'll be safe in a parking lot there. We're not far from there, about ten minutes.

"Okay. We'll follow," Tommy said.

They knew there would not be much traffic in the area, or hoped there would not be. Joe said, "I think we can catch them. They won't be able to go that fast on these roads and we should be able to make good time in the car."

They drove for about ten minutes and found Bergland, and Wendy parked in an abandoned school parking lot. It said temporarily closed, so they thought it would be a good place to keep the car until they returned. Joe led the way and drove as fast as he could. He knew he could not go too fast since there was a state police post in Wakefield where they were headed, so he kept it just above the speed limit.

It took them about thirty minutes, but they reached Wakefield after 10:30 p.m. The last time Joe had remembered was 8:00 p.m. What had happened in that short time? They drove around a big curve and saw the state police post on their left. They took a right and hit U.S. 2. There would be more traffic now that they were leaving Wakefield and heading toward Bessemer and Ironwood. They had not seen the truck yet. Really, they had not seen any trucks on the road, but Joe knew they would find it if they stayed on this route.

Joe and Ron kept in the lead, while Tommy and Wendy stayed back an acceptable distance. Most times Tommy could not see the car ahead, but sometime on straightaways, he'd get a glimpse of Joe's tail lights.

As they drove through Ironwood, Joe spotted the truck up ahead. They were driving slowly through the town. It was after 11:00 p.m. when Ron yelled, "There it is! At least that looks like the truck. Let's get closer and see for sure."

Joe pulled up as close as he could. "Sure enough. That's the semi that we've been following. Check the plate!"

Tommy was close enough to see that they had gotten behind a semi. "I bet that's the truck they were looking for. We need to back off now and keep our distance." Wendy agreed.

When the truck did not pull south on any of the southbound highways, Joe and Ron were not sure where they were going. "Maybe they'll go south on U.S. 53 or 35 out of Superior, Wisconsin. They had no idea where they might be headed, but as they approached Superior, the truck took a right onto the Blatnik Bridge heading to Duluth, Minnesota. "Wow, Joe, we're headed toward Duluth. Think that's the destination?"

"I would really like to know. Maybe they're headed up the North Shore."

"I guess we'll find out," Ron said.

As they crossed the bridge, the semi took a left and moved onto Interstate 35. Now they were headed south.

Once the semi crossed the bridge, they were in Minnesota. Ron looked at Joe and shook his head. "Never too sure where we're going to end up. There is no way they're going to D.C.," Ron added.

"We really need to get ahold of Ann tomorrow and tell her about this. We'll have to be sure though, so we'll need to follow them to the spot where they're stopping, and that may take some time."

Ron was thinking the same thing. "For sure. We need to know the final destination for these boys."

The trip took them down I-35. Joe and Ron recognized many of the towns and the trip went quickly from Duluth until the semi took a right turn in Pine City. Joe looked at Ron and they both had surprised looks on their faces. "Why here?" Ron asked.

"Not sure what's going on. They're about an hour from the Twin Cities, so there's that. We'll have to follow until we can figure this out. Why in the world did they take the route they did? It would have been closer and quicker to drive through Wisconsin."

Ron looked at Joe. "I guess the plan they had for us went through parts of the U.P. that they wanted. No one would have found us in that place."

They took a right and then another right. They were now in a forested area. They kept driving until they were off the beaten path. It was after 2:00 a.m. and there wasn't much either Joe or Ron could see. It was very dark, and there was nothing but trees and brush on each side of the road. They came to a stop and let Tommy and Wendy catch up. They were not sure what to do next, but they did not want to follow too closely and get spotted by the driver. They thought there was no way out of the road, so they were confidant that this was the end of the line for now. Maybe it was just a rest break for the troops who had been in the trailer for almost four hours. Joe was quite confident that was the plan.

When Tommy pulled up, Joe and Ron got out to stretch their legs and take a needed break. Joe thought that they should drive one car to see what was up and keep the other back unless Tommy and Wendy were needed. They figured if the semi stopped that Joe could get out and quietly sneak up to see what was going on.

"Okay, Ron, you drive until we see something. If we need to turn around, it could be tough, so let's proceed slowly."

"Got it."

They drove for a short time until they could see the lights of the truck. Ron stopped the car and Joe exited. He walked slowly toward the light. When he was close, he could see that the driver had opened the back and the troops were getting out. It was quite dark, but he got closer and could see that the troops were headed to what looked like a barracks. As a matter of fact, he could see very little, but the building stood out on his far right.

Each man jumped down and walked straight to the building. Joe watched for some time before the driver shut the back doors and walked to the cab. Around 2:30 a.m. the truck driver looked like he was going to drive somewhere, maybe park it, but he turned the truck and began heading out.

Joe sprinted as fast as he could. He had to get the cars out of the way or this guy would know they had followed him.

He reached the car and jumped in. "Ron, drive out of here as fast as you can. That semi is coming down the road. Don't turn on your lights."

But it was too late. The driver saw the taillights when Ron turned around and stopped to back up to go forward again.

"What the hell is that?" The driver stopped his truck and radioed to the camp. Several troop members were out in no time, jumping into a small truck and heading toward the semi. Fortunately for Ron and Joe, the troops could not get around the tractor-trailer. They jumped out and began pursuing, but Ron had reached Tommy and Wendy, and both cars roared out of the place.

CHAPTER 47

The Bunker Near Colewin, April 12, 9:00 a.m.
Bates was glad Vince had told him what he was about to do. Then he thought he should contact Bill and have him get to the bunker. He knew Bill was local and could help. When Bill arrived, Bates said, "Now we have few problems left in this area."

"That's not so true."

"Why do you say that?"

"You know Charlie? Well, he has something going on in the woods not far from here. I'm not sure where, but I think we need to eliminate him, too."

"That's partly why I called you out here. Vince did mention something going on near that road that leads out of Colewin to the north. It's difficult to find, but he gave me fairly good directions."

"I bet I could find it. Give me the directions and about ten troop members and we'll check it out. If anything is going on, we'll take care of it."

"Just make sure if you find anything that *you don't leave any loose ends*, if you know what I mean."

The road leading to Colewin near the tunnel, April 12, noon
Bill was leading a team of ten men. They were all armed and ready to engage anyone they could find. The troops were happy to get out of the bunker area for a while. They were bored with the training and wanted some action, and they knew this would be a nice break.

Bill was confident he could find the spot that Bates described. "I think we're close to the area. See those trees over there? That could be the entry."

The troops spread out along the road and kept searching inside the tree line near the road. One of the troops called out. "Bill, I found something. Look. Tire tracks inside the tree line, and what looks like a road."

Bill ran over and checked it out. It wasn't much, but he could see that there must have been some vehicles here. "Okay, call the troops—and get everyone here to spread out and be careful."

They walked slowly forward. When they reached a spot that looked like an opening in the dense area, they kept moving.

The sentry nearest the parking area saw them first and sent a message to the other two guards.

We have company. Stay put and don't engage unless they spot you or they shoot first.

The first sentry could hear his heart beating. He crouched as low as he could and stayed hidden, hoping no one would look his way. Bill and his group moved slowly and carefully. They passed the first sentry without seeing him. When they came to the opening, Bill said, "This has to be the spot that Bates talked about. Spread out and search until you find anything that might show that people were here."

They spent the better part of an hour when one of the troops yelled, "Over here. Behind this tree. Looks like someone spent a lot of time trying to hide something."

The men came together and began pulling branches and shrubbery from around the tunnel. "Here's something."

Bill took a look. "It looks like a cave. Let's clean out this area."

Once they had the area clear, they found pails, wheelbarrows, a small excavator, and a lot of beams. They could tell someone was building a tunnel of sorts. "We have to report this to Bates. We'll keep you guys near here. You can stay out by the road if you want while I call Bates."

Bates wasn't surprised. He told them to search the area for anyone who might be around. They went back and searched for another hour or so, and then they gave up. "There's no one here, Bill. We might as well head back. You want to keep any guys here?"

"Not now. Nothing's going to happen."

Earlier that day, the tunnel, April 12, early morning

Matt was still concerned about the safety of the crew. He thought it's important that they should be safe—and not just move forward at any cost. Matt finally got to Charlie. He kept it up until Charlie agreed to shut the work down for a day or two. They would keep three sentries there to keep an eye on things, but they would send everyone else home for a while.

"All right everyone, we're going to shut the work down for a few days just to be on the safe side. We'll clean up everything, put all the tools and supports in the tunnel. We're going to move a tree to the front of the tunnel to disguise the opening. You three go and find a tree about eight feet high that's easy to dig out. Get it and then plant it in front of the tunnel."

Charlie thought that was overkill. "If we just clean up the area, we'll be good."

"Not if they send the troops here. We need to do the best job we can of hiding what we're doing. Get a couple of people to the parking area and clean that up too. Cover our tracks as best we can."

Before they left, Matt called everyone together and told them to keep their eyes and ears open. "Keep me and Charlie informed. Those troops are all over Colewin some days, and we can find out if they know what's going on here, so stay alert to any news."

They worked for the better part of three hours, but they had the place looking like nothing had ever happened there. They moved out, went to the few vehicles they had hidden, and left two people to cover the tracks. Then they all loaded up and left.

1,500 miles away

When they arrived at the new boss's headquarters, they realized that they would not be able to do anything. It was well-guarded, and the new boss had several well-armed men. The old boss looked at his men and realized that they would not be able to overtake the compound. Instead, he told them that he would go in alone and work out a deal. This was no time for a rift in the organization. He knew they would need everyone on board with the same goals, and this guy had a good following, and he might be valuable.

He drove his car to the gate. After much discussion and phone calls, he was let in. In a few minutes, he was standing in front of the new boss. "You know the committee has made a decision."

"Not really. No one has said anything to me. I can guess what is going on though because those guys are afraid of me, and they want me gone. Right?"

"Something like that, but it doesn't have to be the way they want it. After all, we're the ones that the leaders at each base listen to."

"And…?"

"Why can't we do this together? We can be a powerful force. The committee will have to listen to us. We can be completely in charge after the event. We just need to slow it down a bit, and make sure everything is in place."

The new boss was skeptical, "And you will become the president, I take it?"

"We can work that out, but we could both be in powerful positions, plus we'll be controlling the money and will have power to raise more. The men will follow us."

"That's true. We need to be sure that we can take full power—and get rid of those guys who want this done quietly."

The old boss did not answer right away. He looked at the new boss and just stared past him. "I'm guessing we can cross that bridge when we get to it, but right now we have to let the committee know that we are in charge. They know we have the power, and they'll do what we want when they know we have joined forces. As far as doing anything quietly without any more violence, I think we both know that won't work. Let's sit down and plan what we can do to make the event take place as soon as possible, but let's make sure everything is in order."

"I'm not really sure I want to share what I have."

"You won't have to. There's plenty for everyone. I mean money, power, and control."

"All right. Let's talk."

CHAPTER 48

Colewin, April 13

Sometimes things happen when a person least expects them. They had been unable to work on the tunnel for a couple of days, and the barber was back at work sitting in his chair waiting for the next customer. He kept his business going while working on the tunnel after work and on weekends.

His shop was not very spacious. He had just the one barber's chair and a few chairs for his customers. As he sat looking out from his perch, he could see the three chairs on his right side, and to his left he could look out a window, and just beyond the window, he saw one chair and a shoeshine stand where his sons had shined shoes when they were younger. Next to that was a very large radiator that stood almost three feet high. Above the radiator was a shelf holding hair supplies. His shop was not fancy, like the ones you see in the city, but it was clean and tidy. He had made most of his barber's cabinets for his equipment and towels when he first started, and he still used them today.

He left the shoeshine stand in place for old times' sake, and when people would come in, it was a conversation piece. He was a very gregarious person, but he was also a good listener, learning after many years to let his patrons speak. He never criticized what they said, he just let them talk. He would answer when he had to, but he tried not to ever upset his patrons. He had a knack for steering conversations when he felt that they might go awry and cause him stress, and so he learned to avoid such topics as politics and religion.

That day, Bill came in for a haircut. He had been a customer for many years, and he always tried to get the barber into an argument about anything. He was one of those guys who liked aggravating a person and then leaving, knowing he had stirred the pot in whatever direction he wanted that day, but the barber was smarter than that.

When Bill walked in, the barber realized that he had not seen him in a while. "Hey, Bill, long time no see. What's up?"

"Not much. Just been busy."

"Well, come on and have a seat and relax."

Now the barber knew that Bill had joined with the people at the bunker, but that was all he knew. "So, how's the family?"

"Good, everyone is good."

"You been doing any fishing this spring?"

"No time."

Bill was being somewhat terse in his answers, and this was not like Bill, so the barber just stopped talking. He knew Bill wouldn't be able to stand the silence.

It didn't take too long before Bill started. "I'm sick and tired of the way this country's goin', you know?"

The barber said nothing.

"It's like we don't got no say in what we want to do. You know what I mean."

The barber grunted.

"You know. I mean look at these elections and stuff. These liberals are going nuts. Next thing you know, they'll be making us give up our guns."

The barber only said, "Oh."

"Yeah. I like my AR-15. That's why I joined up with them."

The barber said, "Hmmm…"

"Yep. I get to practice any time I'm at the base, and they provide the ammunition. Not bad. I also get to work with people who think like I do. We need to change this country."

Again. "Oh…"

"Yep."

The barber took his time trimming Bill's hair. This would be a long haircut.

"Yeah, I'm doing stuff I never thought I'd be able to do, and people listen to me."

"They do?" the barber responded.

Now some people just like to hear the sound of their own voices, and they go on and on, not even thinking about what they're saying. Bill was one of these guys. He loved the sound of his voice, and he thought he had all the answers for what was wrong with the world. You only had to listen. And the barber listened.

"Hey, I got these new duds. Did you see when I came in? Real camo stuff, for free. You should join up with us."

"Join up?"

"Yeah. We need more troops. Got a lot coming and going out there, but we can always use more. You interested?"

"Keep talking."

"Sure."

The door opened and another customer came in. This made the barber nervous, and Bill stopped talking.

The new customer asked, "How long?"

The barber answered, "Won't be too long. Ten minutes."

The man sat. The barber had watched him walk across the street from the local garage. Then the customer stood and said, "I'll be right back. I need to make sure that the mechanic checks my brakes. Forgot to mention that when I dropped off the car for the oil change. I'll be right back."

"Sure. No problem."

The barber got back to work and said nothing. He wondered if Bill would continue.

"That guy is an ass. I don't like him. He pissed me off a while back, and I can't get over it."

"Uh," is all the barber said.

CHAPTER 49

Bergland, Michigan, April 13

Joe and Ron had stayed near Pine City trying to find out what might be going on in the woods where they had followed the truck. They had Tommy and Wendy follow the now-empty semi. When it left, it headed back north toward Duluth, and they wanted to know where it might end up.

Tommy and Wendy had an uneventful trip back to Colewin. The semi went right back to where it had been a few days earlier. The driver spent a night at a motel in Ironwood, Michigan. He slept late and did not get going until after 2:00 p.m. They called Joe to let him know. "Joe, this is Tommy. We followed the semi back to Ironwood, and the guy took a break, so we are stopped too. We're on the road again and will keep you informed."

They followed the semi, and this time the driver didn't get very far before he stopped in Wakefield and ate. Tommy and Wendy drove through a Dairy Queen and waited. At 4:00 p.m. they were on the road again.

That was the last stop, and they followed the semi into Colewin where the truck parked around 9:30 p.m. in the same place it had been days ago.

Tommy called Joe again. "Joe, Tommy here. Hey, the semi is back in Colewin at the loading spot."

Joe was not surprised, "All right, sorry I had you cut your vacation short. Have the sentries keep us updated on what happens there. I'm sure another group will go out soon."

"Got it. We'll stay in touch."

"Good. Be careful and get some rest."

"We're fine. Are you heading this way?"

"In a few days."

"Have a safe trip back."

"Thanks!"

Joe and Ron decided to stick around, but they learned nothing. They kept watch and the troops trained during the day and seemed to party during the evening. They watched that evening until they felt they needed to head back and somehow give Ann all the details.

Ron was driving when they stopped in Bergland. They had planned to pick up the car Wendy had driven since it belonged to Cathy who was staying in Ishpeming. They went right to the parking lot, Joe jumped in, and they both drove to Ishpeming, planning to stop and rest a day there.

The trip was uneventful. They were disappointed that they had little more to discuss about what was going on, but they did have a lot of information for Ann, which they would share once they arrived in Ishpeming. Joe knew that the trip they had just made had changed everything, or, at least, he thought it did. He was going to try to convince Ann to head to the U.P. and have the FBI take over the bunker. He knew it was a big wish, but he thought they might learn a lot if they could get the key man, Bates, out of the bunker. What they had been trying to do was not working and would take forever. They needed help.

They drove to the house where Cathy was staying with some of Joe's relatives. Their wives were there also, and they were happy to spend some time with them, and to thank them for the suggestion that saved their lives. When they arrived, Cathy asked, "Are Wendy and Tommy with you?"

"No, we had to have them follow the semi. We weren't sure where it was going next, and Ron and I needed time to investigate the area where they sent the troops. We didn't find out much, but Tommy and Wendy are back in Colewin now."

"Oh, so they're back. I was hoping they could spend more time here. Well, thanks for returning my car."

"How's Wayne doing? Any change?"

"No, they still have him in a coma. He's fighting though. I hope some day to take him home. Has there been any news from the police? Do they know who did this yet?"

"The investigation has stalled because of Sheriff Daryl. It's still active, but you know what he's going to do. He says it was a hunting accident, so who knows where this will go?"

Cathy was anxious, "We couldn't go back to Colewin now, at least until all this scary stuff is over. Our house is damaged, our truck is gone, and who knows what else is lurking there. Wayne is better here and so am I."

"We agree, Cathy."

At that point Joette and Shanice entered the conversation. Joette spoke first, "We feel the same way, but we also want to help get those people out of there."

Shanice agreed, "This has to end. We think you two have done enough. It's time to turn this over to the authorities. Go to someone you can trust and have them take care of this. You guys are getting too old to be running around like this and taking chances."

Joe and Ron looked at each other, thinking about the previous evening and their close call. They had agreed not to say anything to anyone about what had happened. Tommy had agreed it would be best. They decided to stay the night and rest and then leave in the morning to see if they could do just what Shanice had suggested—get the authorities involved. This had been going on too long, and they needed it to end, or they needed to find out what these people were planning to do.

CHAPTER 50

Somewhere Near Lansing, Michigan, April 14

Ann was deeply involved with the investigation around a proposed event. She had heard last year from some friends in the U.P. that something was going on. She was spread so thin these days with all of the investigations since the January 6 insurgence, the Governor's problems, and other investigations around the election that she was not sure what to address next. That's when her phone rang. "Hello, this is Ann."

"Ann, Joe DeLuca here."

"Joe, I was just thinking about you and Ron in the U.P. Any news?"

"We have followed three semis now full of troops heading somewhere. Ron and I are almost certain now that this whole thing is not only about D.C."

"I told you not to get involved, but you don't listen, but I guess what you are doing is going to help. I have some information that I would like to share with you, but we cannot talk on the phone. We'll have to meet somewhere. I need to know exactly what you have found out, and I need to give you some information that is very interesting."

"Do you want to meet like we did the last few times, and if so, where?"

"I don't want to say right now. I can't let you know why, but do you remember several years ago when you met me and my family?"

"I remember, if you're talking about a letter drop at a certain location."

"Yes. Do you want to meet there again?"

"That would work. There shouldn't be many people around in April."

"Ron and I can be there in a day or two. How does that work?"

"I can work that into my schedule. It can't be right away, but let's say April 23. That's a Friday. Try not to let anyone else in on this."

"We won't, but we'll have our wives along."

"Not sure I want anyone else involved, but if you have to, we can make that work."

"See you then."

Ann hung up. She did not say anything else, but Joe was surprised at her tone and her quick exit. "Something is up, Ron. That was not like the Ann I know."

"Must be something serious I would guess."

"Yep. It must be."

1,500 miles away

The two bosses met several times trying to agree on things and to coordinate their small armies of security personnel. Spending time with each other made them realize that together they could run this whole organization if everything went as they planned. The committee was afraid of both of them, and they knew it. They spent many hours on the event and came to some conclusions. They had to agree on the training of the troops, and when they could pull everything off. The new boss was very pushy, but the old boss knew how to manipulate him and get him to agree. He just had to make it sound like it was the new boss's idea. Easy for a schemer like the old boss. It took several meetings, but they had it down.

The last meeting had them deciding on a date. The election in November 2022 was kicked around, but they did not want to go right before or during, so they settled on a January date. The old boss pondered, "How about January 6, 2024?"

"That would be sweet. Everyone will think it was the same people who tried to overthrow the politicians back in 2021."

"Exactly. They'll never figure out it is us."

"All right. We need to coordinate the date with each site then. Can we do that?"

The old boss smiled. "Of course. We'll use our network—and it'll be important to keep it to just our network. No other groups. Just our troops. Both the small and large teams will have to be in place a month or two ahead of time. The largest group will have to be ready on a moment's notice. We also have to make sure we have infiltrated all of the organizations. Let's check to ensure we have some sympathizers in each one."

"I have been working on that. I have some in the senate, several in the house, a few in the CIA and FBI, and several in each capitol, not only the capitols, I mean we have people in each legislature. We can solidify that in the coming months."

"What about the other branches of the military?"

"Working on them. We still have one high-ranking Navy admiral who is with us."

"Then we really don't need to do anything during the '22 elections, except make the elections look bad. If that date we set doesn't work, we'll go for the next January 6, 2025, but we should be able to pull it off sooner."

The new boss was ecstatic. He knew several pieces were in place, and he knew he had a few details to work out so he could claim himself supreme ruler. Getting the old boss to accept him in that position might be a problem, but he had ideas.

CHAPTER 51

Colewin, the Barber Shop, April 22

The barber had let Bill talk for a while and told him to meet him later to discuss joining the group. Bill was elated. He would get a promotion for helping to enlist another guy. The barber really wasn't eager to join up, but he said he knew of others who would do that. They were tired of the country, and they wanted a change. Just what Bill wanted to hear.

They met several days later. The barber had gotten enough information from Bill on how he could join the group at the bunker, but he knew he was too old for that kind of stuff, so he involved his son, Peter. Peter was excited, but he did not want to do it alone so he convinced his friends Michael and Tony to join with him. They were quite curious and didn't know much about troops and a bunker, but they were in. The barber contacted Bill and they decided where they would meet him.

Peter knew that the three could outsmart Bill, but they did not have any idea just what was involved. "Hey, Dad, are you sure we'll be all right?"

"I don't really know. It'll be serious. You'll have to really fit in to get accepted."

"What do you mean, *fit in?*"

"Well, you have to say the right things. You're tired of the country and the fact that you can't do anything without government interference. You want a change of government. You don't really care for democracy as it is. You might say that we need to change the constitution too. Anything like that they like to hear. At least that's what I got from Bill."

"That's easy enough. I'll get Michael and Tony up to par on what they need to know."

Colewin, later that day

The four of them were all at the barber shop when Bill showed up. "Good to see you. You all in for this? Man, I'm excited to have four people."

The barber spoke up. "Three people. I'm too old for this kind of traipsing around."

"You sure? You don't know what you're missing."

"I'm sure, but I've got you three people who are ready to go."

Bill was cautious but excited. "All righty. Can you boys be ready tomorrow morning around 6:00 a.m.?"

Peter answered yes for all three. Then he asked Bill about the base. "What's it like there? Do we have to stay there all the time? Will we get paid?"

"I'll answer all of your questions tomorrow. Be on time. We can meet right here in front of the barber shop."

They agreed and Bill left.

CHAPTER 52

St. Ignace, April 23, 10:00 a.m.

Ann was on a mission and arrived in St. Ignace early on April 23. She had plans to meet with friends for a short vacation, but she turned it into an important meeting with Joe. She needed to find the rock where she had deposited messages for Joe years ago. Hopefully, he would remember. She had left Lansing by herself, and she did not want anyone with her on this trip, and she hoped that she was not followed or tracked in any way. She had purchased a new phone just for this undertaking. Hopefully, it would not cause Joe any trouble or doubt.

Joe and Ron were back, planning their trip to St. Ignace. Joe remembered that the place Ann had chosen would be the St. Ignace boat launch to Mackinac Island. Joe knew that if Ann followed the pattern from years ago that he would have to get a text message from her. After that, there would be no calls or texts. He did not want to leave until he had received it. If he did not, he would know something was wrong.

Ann drove out to the parking lot and parked as near as she could to the rock where she would hide the letter. There weren't many places to hide anything here, but she had always left messages for Joe in the same spot. *Where was the rock where she had placed messages many years ago? Would it still be there?* She looked where she thought it would be, but she could not find it. She walked around the lot and spotted it. "I'm going to have to move the darn thing if this is going to work," she breathed quietly. It was a large stone, but she managed to roll it some distance that was closer to the original spot.

After she moved the rock, she went back to her car and grabbed the letter sealed in plastic. Before exiting, she sent a message to Joe.

Joe. Not my usual phone. Will explain later. Hope you have help with you. Note will be in same place.

Joe and Ron were at their new hiding place. They knew Vince had escaped from their old cabin, and even though he was no longer with the living, he probably had told everyone where they were hiding. He and Ron were debating what their next move would be.

Their wives had returned with them, and they were not in agreement on the trip to St. Ignace. Joette was insistent that they send someone else, but Joe knew that was impossible.

"Can't you send some of those guys who have been helping you?"

"I wish we could, but they would not know our procedures with Ann, and I don't want to give away any of our strategies with Ann and the FBI. Too many situations could evolve from it, and they would not be good."

"Well, you are not going alone again. Shanice and I will back you up. You don't have to worry about us giving away your strategies. We'll use a backup vehicle, and we'll be armed."

Ron spoke up, "I really don't think that is necessary. We can take care of ourselves, and this shouldn't lead to any scary situations."

"Ron, listen to yourself," Shanice broke in. "You two get in trouble wherever you go. You're both older and aren't as spry as you used to be. We aren't either, but we are two stealthy broads who can back you up."

Joe had been listening, but now decided to call Ann since he had not heard anything yet. Then he saw the text. "Hey, I have something here. It's from Ann, but it's not her phone." Joe read the message and read it again before he said anything. "This is a weird message. This is not typical Ann. She sounds kind of guarded again. Listen."

"Joe, not my usual phone. Will explain later. Hope you have help with you. Note will be in same place. Heading out right after I drop this."

"So, it's a go!?" Ron said.

"Yes, but it's just not like her. She's always so clear and confident, and she would never text me from a different phone prior to a meeting like this. Something's up."

"Let me see," Joette said. "I don't know Ann well anymore, but I understand what you're saying, Joe. I think we should do what she says and leave quickly."

Ron and Shanice agreed. They were ready for whatever. Ron said, "I'm not sure what's happening to this country, but I know it's a challenge to our democracy, and we need to do whatever we can to help, even if it means doing things that could get us in trouble. We were almost killed the last time, and we have had nothing but trouble from these people, so let's go. This time though, we will be extra careful. No one gets the drop on us again."

"All right. Agreed. Let's get ready and move out. We need to let Tommy, Matt, and Charlie know that we'll be gone, but that's all we say. Everyone get ready."

St. Ignace, 11:00 a.m.

Ann was fortunate that the boats were running. It was very cool, but the sky was clear and there was just a light breeze on shore. She could see the Island stately in the distance, and she could also see Mighty Mac, the Mackinac Bridge, five miles of concrete, steel, and wire spanning the spot where Lake Huron and Lake Michigan met.

She purchased her ticket and waited until she could board. There were a few other people, and she was glad that she was not alone, but, at the same time, glad there were not a lot of tourists. She took a seat that allowed her a view of both her destination and the dock where her car was parked. She was nervous but confident, but she was concerned that everything she had fought for these past twenty some years was all going down.

"Where are you, Joe?" she whispered. She kept her eyes on the dock as the boat pulled away and she saw a few cars enter, but she was not sure who they were. At any rate, they would have to wait until the next boat. She was going to meet with friends and stay at the Grand Hotel, but until then, she had already gotten a room at a bed and breakfast with a nice view of the Mackinac Bridge—and hoped Joe and Ron would find her.

After meeting with Joe and Ron, she would begin her stay with her friends. She and Joe were to meet the next day at Arch Rock, a place they had met several times for passing clandestine information through the years. They chose Mackinac Island, and this time of year because of the scarcity of tourists, as well as the ability to avoid having to use phones or computers that can be tracked so easily. Everything was completed orally and on paper in this remote spot.

She arrived at the Island's dock about twenty minutes later and took a carriage to her room.

Joe realized they would have to look like tourists, so they decided to travel in three cars with Joe and Joette in one, Ron and Shanice in the second, and Tommy and Wendy, who wanted to help, in his truck. Joe and Joette pulled into the parking lot around noon. They were followed by Ron and Shanice, and a bit later, Tommy and Wendy. They were taking no chances this time.

Joe knew the letter would be under a rock, and it would give him directions for the next twenty-four hours. After they pulled into a parking spot, Joe jumped out of the car and began looking. He was not exactly sure where the rock would be since it had been a long time since they used it. He went to the exact spot he thought, but there was nothing under the rock. He kept looking around and turning over every stone he found, but he had no luck. He walked to Ron and Shanice. "Ron, did you see any other people out here?"

"Just those two over there. They've been walking around the parking lot. They look like a couple of tourists."

"Maybe. They don't look like tourists to me. Wondering why they're here in April? We'll see when we board. By the way, I can't find the letter. I know where it was supposed to be. We need to locate it."

"I can help."

"Ann always puts it under the rock in the same place. I found the rock, but there was no letter."

"Maybe she didn't get a chance to place it, or maybe she's not here yet."

"No. She's here. I don't see her car, but she may have driven something we haven't seen."

"Can we text her?"

"I could, but we usually stay away from any electronics. That's why the letter and Mackinac Island."

"Yes. I recall."

"We'll have to go to the Island. She's probably there."

"Why Mackinac Island anyway?"

"You remember that we started doing that a long time ago. It took us to very remote spots with few people around at this time of year. My family and I had many vacations there, and Joette and I thought it would be a good place to vacation when the kids got older, and then I could meet with Ann who also vacationed here. It was all part of the journey and the business. Kept us out of the main stream."

"Yes. The good old days."

Joe recalled many days with his family on the Island and secret meetings with Ann. He would be the go-to guy. Ron was not there. He would always meet with Joe later once the information was available. "I forget that I did many of those trips by myself or with my family. It was a long trip in those days, but it was worth it."

They saw a few people head to the dock, and they knew it must be time to board. They grabbed their suitcases to make it look good and headed to the boat. Their backups, Ron and Shanice, would also go on the boat, and Tommy and Wendy would stay at the dock just in case.

"Joe," Ron breathed, "look at those men. No luggage. You think they live there?"

"Not those two."

"Let's keep an eye on them, and stay as far away as we can."

Before they left, they informed Tommy and Wendy about the letter and the two guys, just in case.

Everyone was on board and the boat began its trek to Mackinac Island. Joe and Ron decided to talk over their next move and so were seated together on the lower deck where it was much warmer. The two tourists were on the top deck as were Joette and Shanice. It didn't take long before they arrived. The only problem was that without the letter they had no knowledge of where Ann might be.

Joe watched as the two men left the boat, and he noticed one had a paper in his hand that he was studying. He turned to Ron. "Could that be the letter?"

"Let's follow them. We'll have to keep our distance."

They walked near their wives who were getting the luggage. Joe said, "Follow us, but not too close."

"Got ya!" Shanice answered.

CHAPTER 53

Earlier, the Barber Shop, April 23

It was early and the three young men were a bit sleepy. They had decided to hang together that night and discuss their future with Bill. Unfortunately, some beer and pizza kept them up quite late. They had gotten up at 5:00 a.m., dressed, and headed for the meeting place near the barber shop.

A car pulled up at five after six. Bill rolled down the window and said, "Jump in. We gotta move. I don't want to be late. Bates has this thing for being on time. He said six-thirty, so we can't delay.

Tony, Peter, and Michael all jumped in. Michael asked, "Hey, are we going to get any neat weapons out there?"

"You sure will. We all get either M-16s or another assault weapon. Some guys even got AK-47s, not sure where they came from. Ammunition is a problem though. They have an abundance of NATO ammunition. You'll have all the gear you want. They have a lot of equipment. Some of it, Charlie had collected back in the day. He's still sore about losing his trucks, weapons, and clothes. Our gain." He laughed a big hearty laugh that even brought a smile to the three men, although they knew that was not really funny.

Bill drove right to a spot in the woods where a military truck was waiting for him. He parked his car and had everyone get out. "You guys go in the back and relax. I'll sit in the front with the driver. We'll be there in no time."

They bounced around for about fifteen minutes, and, after climbing a steep hill, they arrived at a gate in the middle of the woods. The driver hit the horn and the gate opened.

"What in the hell is this?" Tony asked.

Peter motioned to him to be quiet. Tony took the hint.

"Here we are, gents. Get out and follow me. We'll talk to Bates."

Bill pounded on the door. Bates was watching from inside. He could see who Bill had brought in. Bates was cautious. He did not want any more people from the area. The boss was firm on that point. Unfortunately, the boss wanted some new blood though and a lot of it, and so far, they were not coming fast enough. Bates wondered if he should just send them home. He looked at the four of them standing at the door and decided to let them in. Bill entered first and tried to shake Bates' hand. Bates looked at him and turned around, walked to his computer desk, and sat.

"Pull up some chairs."

The four of them got chairs that were up against the wall behind Bates. They sat near him and waited.

Bates looked around at each one and then turned to Bill. "What makes you think these guys will make good troops for us? Are you sure we can trust them?"

Bill looked a bit nervous. He hadn't thought about trusting anyone. His only thought had been to get the barber in. It all kind of moved on to the barber's son and these guys. He really didn't know them. "Ah, yeah, we can trust them."

"You'd better be right. We weren't going to take any more local people, remember?"

"Oh, I wasn't sure about that." Bill was sure. He just wanted to get some points for bringing in people because he knew they needed more help.

"I'm telling you. The new boss is not high on any more local people, but now you've got them here, so I suggest you dig into their lives a bit." He turned to the three. "You better be good, and you had better not try anything. We'll keep you here training for the next four weeks, and then you'll be sent somewhere."

Peter spoke up. "What do you mean, we'll be here four weeks? Does that mean we can't go home at night?"

"That's right. Why, you need to see your mommy?" Bates said.

"No. Just wondering."

"Well wonder no more. You're here for the duration. If you can't do that, then we have a problem. No one leaves here unless I give them permission."

Peter spoke up. "We see your guys in town all the time."

"Sure. We let some go. Those we can trust. We can't trust you. You just got here. We'll see how it goes." Bates turned to Bill. "Did you take their electronics? Phones and any others they might have."

"No, should I?"

"You idiot. Do it now. Then get these three to the barracks out by the woods on the far left when facing the bunker. Get them all the things they'll need and have them meet the trainers on the field with the other new troops."

"Gotcha."

CHAPTER 54

Colewin, April 23

Matt and Charlie realized that the tunnel was not feasible for the time being. They called their tunnel people, including the sentries, and told them they would not be going back for a while. They decided to spread people out with the other sentries around the bunker to give the regular sentries some relief. Trying to work as a sentry during the nights and having a job during the days or vice-versa was difficult. They knew everyone needed a break, and having more people for the bunker reconnaissance would help relieve some of the time constraints for people.

Charlie and Matt were planning their next move when the barber pulled up to Charlie's place. Neither knew who it was at first until they recognized the barber in his vehicle.

"It's the barber," Matt said.

Charlie knew that he was on the way. "He said he had somethin' to discuss at our meetin', but he wanted to speak in private. Wonder what it is."

"I'm not sure, but he's got a sharp mind. Always comin' up with great ideas for the tunnel."

"Hey, Matt, Charlie."

"How you doin'?" Charlie asked.

"Great. Got a good plan for you guys while we're out of the tunnel business."

Matt was curious. "Let's have it."

"I think we can infiltrate that bunker. I've got a great idea."

"Oh, yeah, what's that?" Charlie was dubious because of all the ideas that they tried—they had little luck with any.

Matt, on the other hand, was excited. "What's the plan? How do we get into that place?"

The barber was quiet at first and just stood there thinking. Then he asked, "What if you could get someone in the bunker?"

"Can't. Tried. They ain't takin' no one from here anymore." Charlie was certain they could not get anyone inside.

"What if I said I got someone inside right now? Would you believe me?"

Matt was excited now. "Sure. If you say you do, I believe you, but how?"

Charlie said, "We tried that so many times, and it backfired on us every time. Most of them ended up joinin' with 'em when they heard that they would have a good income—and only have to play war games. Others were caught, and we haven't heard from 'em since. Your guys are doomed. Either they'll get sucked in or they're dead."

"I hope not. I got three guys in. My son's one of them."

Matt was shocked. "What? You sent your son in? Are you crazy?"

"Nope. I'm just tired of these interlopers. Sick and tired. Bill for sure. He keeps trying to get me to join."

"Yeah, he does that. We lost a lot of people because of him. They offer good money. Most people can't turn it down," Matt said.

"You won't hear from 'im again. They'll take his cell phone and anything he has on 'im. They even give 'im new clothes. If he has anything on 'im that shows he's a spy of some kind, he won't las' the night."

"He's got like three cell phones. They might get two, but they won't get the last one."

"How's that?"

"It's hidden in a hole in the bottom of his boot. He has those heavy work boots with thick soles, and we got the smallest cell phone, and we cut out most of the heel and sealed it in there and replaced the liner over the hole. They won't look there after they get the other two. We planned that they would take them. The other two don't know much about what we're doing. They can flip if they want. We just need my son to find out what's up, and maybe get info on how we can get in there."

CHAPTER 55

Mackinac Island, Afternoon

Joe watched the two men. They looked around once they were off the pier and took a good look at everyone. Ron and Shanice were standing together. Joe was off to the side while Joette stood nearest the boat getting her suitcase. After they made a good scan of the pier and the people on it, they turned and began a trek up the main road.

Joe observed. They seemed to be on a mission. "Where are they headed?" he whispered to Ron who was close by.

"Let's watch, but let's also get this luggage somewhere so we have a room if we need it."

Joe agreed. "You find someplace for us to stay. I'll follow as best I can."

"You sure you want to do that alone?"

"I'll keep you in the loop. Have your phone ready and then follow my directions when you have the women set up somewhere. Tell them to be ready to assist at a minute's notice if we run into something."

"They're on it. They don't like what we're doing. I think they thought this would actually be a vacation."

"I thought it would be too, but I knew I had to meet Ann, but I didn't expect any trouble."

The two men kept walking down the main street. Joe was behind, but he did not want to get too close. He followed for some time. They did not seem to be in a hurry. They must have known that in April, since there were no cars on Mackinac Island, that the carriage taxi was by appointment only because they did not stop to rent a bike or try another form of transportation. They just kept walking. Joe was in good shape, but they were walking at a very fast pace, and Joe was not young anymore. His knee started to hurt a bit. He had hurt it a few years back, and it still gave him trouble.

The two men stopped. They were conversing in a casual way. Joe ducked to the side of the road and hid behind the stairs of a Catholic Church. He could see them motioning. Were they lost? Were they really just tourists? But then, where was the letter? Had he missed it? Joe took a deep breath and walked out of his hiding place, and as he returned his gaze up the road, he did not see the two men. Where had they gone? Joe called Ron and the girls. He needed all three to help him find these guys again. If they had his letter, they knew where Ann was—and that could be a problem. Hopefully, they were just tourists, but Joe had a premonition that they were after Ann.

Ann settled in her room and took out her phone. She knew Joe would probably not use his phone, but she had to check. Nothing. Had Joe not arrived yet? Did he find the letter? It gave him the information he needed to find her. She had given explicit directions to the B&B where she was staying, and she had told him to be careful because she had found incriminating evidence that someone in her FBI office was working for the same group that Joe was investigating in the U.P.—the same place that Joe had been warning her about. She figured that this person had been diverting assets from the U.P. for some reason—she did not know why, but now she realized that she had been influenced by someone who was directing efforts and the workforce elsewhere.

Joe had been following them for about five minutes when he lost them. Could they have gone straight to where Ann was staying? Was it close to here or did he just miss where they went? Then he saw the two men dash out of a bed-and-breakfast, and he saw them continue up the main street, but they now moved at a faster pace, and he lost them again. As he attempted to get behind them, Ron, Shanice, and Joette showed up. He told them what had happened, and Joette said, "Maybe Ann is planning to stay at a bed and breakfast."

"That's a good point," Ron agreed.

"If that's the case, we should split up and find all the bed and breakfasts on the main street," Shanice said.

"Good. Let's bring up Mackinac Island on our phones and look for every B&B we can find."

Joe said, "You do that, and I'll hustle and try to catch up to these two."

Joette was quick to have a picture on her phone, and she had a great map of the main street. She looked it over and the only other B&B she could find was about five minutes away. Joe was just up the road, and they all quickly headed his way. This had to be it.

Ann was being cautious. Unfortunately, she did not know who to trust in her office until she identified the enemy collaborator. This made her nervous for herself and for Joe and Ron and their families. That's why she had gone to extreme lengths to get to Joe, someone she knew she could trust, to see what he might know and how they might be able to assist each other.

There was a knock at the door. Someone said, "Hello, we're here to welcome you. If you need anything, let us know."

It was a man's voice. Ann considered the situation. She wondered *why would anyone welcome her again? The person who showed her the room welcomed her and told her what she needed to know.* "Something's up," she said. Ann had her guard up, and she wasn't going to fall for anything like this. She pulled out her Glock.

CHAPTER 56

Colewin, April 23

Charlie and Matt were sitting together in the local bar, the Sportsman's. They had just left the barber and wanted to discuss his plan to infiltrate the bunker. They were both thirsty and each ordered a beer and some peanuts. Charlie was dubious. "This ain't gonna work, you know. We tried all that stuff over and over. The bunker wasn't even takin' any more people from Colewin or Poplar or any local towns. Why did they change now?"

"I'm not sure, Charlie, but I know that Bill is a talker, and he can convince people to do stuff. He's a blowhard, but he's sneaky and gets what he wants. I just can't believe that he convinced that guy in the bunker. What's his name again?"

"Bates."

"Yeah, Bates." Matt was mystified too, in ways he could not figure out.

"I know they need more troops. They been hurtin' for some time accordin' to those guys who come to town las' week. I overhead 'em here in the bar. That could be the reason."

Matt took a sip of his beer and threw a few peanuts back and then he said, "Sure could. Why do they need all them anyway? Has anyone figured that out?"

"Not that I know. Joe has ideas, but he ain't talkin'." Charlie drained his beer.

"I'm gonna check with him when he comes back." Matt looked around the bar, waved to Todd, the owner, and held up two fingers.

"Where did he go again?" Charlie asked.

"Not sure this time. They didn't really say."

The bunker

Peter, Tony, and Michael were put up in the far barracks. There were a lot of guys there, and they wanted to keep together, so they had beds next to each other. Tony and Michael shared a bunk, Peter had the top of another. There was someone assigned to the lower bunk, but he wasn't there.

"You believe what they're going to pay us to play these games?" Michael said.

Tony was amazed. "Crazy. Who would have thought you could make this kind of money around here?"

"Well, just be sure that you don't let this go to your heads. We're here for a reason."

"And what's that?" Michael asked.

Peter thought he might have said too much, so he backed off. "I just mean, let's keep our noses clean and not get into any trouble."

Michael was excited, "We will. Your dad will be proud when we're finished."

"Good."

None of them were happy that they could not go to town for quite a while, but they decided to just do what they had to do, and they would let Peter do what he had to do. Peter didn't tell them much, and they kept it that way. Neither Michael nor Tony wanted to get too involved. They were out just to have some fun. They hoped this would not last too long, but the money was good, and they would have fun training.

Peter was on the top bunk and took out his cell phone. He had the smallest phone made. It wasn't easy, but when they gave him his new military boots, he was able to salvage the phone before they took his old ones. He quickly sent a text to his father.

All good. We're in. Will keep you posted.
Going to pay us by the way.

The barber looked at his phone and smiled. He said to no one in particular, "Step one is taken care of—on to the next one."

CHAPTER 57

The Island, That Evening

Tommy and Wendy had been parked for several hours. They were going to stay as long as they had to and head to the Island if they were called. The boats did not run as often in April, but they knew they could get one in the morning. Hopefully, they would not be needed tonight.

Joe texted them as they planned—short and to the point:

Everything good. Eyes on the targets.

Tommy responded with one letter.

K

Joe and Ron were headed to the B&B that Joette had identified. They had their wives about fifty yards behind, just in case. Each one was armed and ready.

When they reached the B&B, they entered and were greeted by a young man. "Hello, welcome, what can I do for you?"

Joe looked him over as if to wonder if this guy was in on something. "Say, have two men come in here recently looking for a room?"

"Why do you ask?"

"They're friends of ours, and we're supposed to meet up," Ron said.

"Oh, sure, they're in the room at the top of the stairs, first door to your left."

"Would you like a room next to them?"

Joe looked at Ron, "Sure. Ron, can you take care of this? I need to go and speak to our friends."

"Got it, Joe."

Joe turned and asked the person behind the desk. "Oh, and our friend Ann is also here. Could we get her room number?"

"Listen, I gave you the one room. I'm not doing that again. Find your own friends."

"All right, thanks." Joe moved slowly up the stairs and right to the room where the two men were supposed to be. He moved to his left at the top of the stairs and wondered if he should just knock, and he did. "Room service."

"We don't need anything," someone answered.

Ron took the stairs and found Joe. "Anything?"

"No. They didn't bite. Maybe they're just tourists. Could Ann not have made it here?"

"Why don't we just keep an eye on these guys and see what they do? You could text Ann."

"No. We always have stayed away from anything electronic. Too many eyes out there with the ability to effortlessly spy on us. No texts or calls. I kept it very short for Tommy, too."

"I sent Shanice and Joette outside to keep an eye on the place just in case."

"Which room is ours?"

"To the right of the stairs."

"Let's go there and keep an eye on this door."

They entered the room and had a good view of the hallway if they kept the door open. Joe put a chair near the door and sat and watched. It didn't take long before the two guys left their room. They moved to the stairs and walked down. Joe immediately motioned to Ron that they were moving. Joe walked to the stairs and saw that they stayed in the building. He walked down the stairs and the two men were knocking on the bedroom downstairs. Now Joe was sure something was up. At that same moment, the door opened and the two men forced their way in.

Ron was right behind Joe and saw the same thing. "We've got to get in there!"

"I'm going to knock and see what happens. Stay back."

Joe knocked, but no one answered. He knocked again. "Anyone in here? This is room service. We have towels and the information you requested."

No one answered. Joe looked at Ron and they decided to come up with another plan. Joe knocked again. "I'll leave the towels and information on the floor. You can get them at your leisure."

Inside the room, Ann was sitting in a chair and the two men were deciding what to do. They did not anticipate anyone knocking or interrupting. Ann was not surprised when they pushed the door open. She knew she was being investigated, but she did not think that the investigation would follow her to the Island. She remained calm and confident. When she saw who it was, she put her Glock down, and she figured she could reason with these guys. She had worked with them before in her office, and she knew they were newer agents. She would try convincing them that she was not the one to be followed—that she had done nothing wrong.

After they pushed through the door, they read Ann her rights and cuffed her. They had Ann tied in a chair and decided to gag her because she kept talking about how the two guys had no idea what was going on, and that she had to notify her friends who were going to meet her on the Island.

The two men decided that they needed to think how to stop her constant interruptions. The first guy, the taller of the two, spoke, "We need to take her back to Lansing. The boss was specific that she is in on some type of insurgent activities."

"Yes, but he never said what. What is she up to?"

They knew that someone was there to make trouble when they arrested Ann. They saw a guy following them and then the knock on the door. "We need to be careful and get her back to the pier so we can get off the Island first."

"Agreed."

The first man said, "I'm going out to see if anyone is there. You take Ann and get her ready to go if I motion the coast is clear. Our only problem right now is to figure out who the letter was for. Obviously, she was meeting someone here, but who?"

"Hey, it had to be one of those couples who was on the boat. There weren't that many people. It's got to be them. We just need to avoid those people. I'm sure that guy who followed us was one of them."

"Yes, but how do we get her out of here?"

Joe and Ron walked away from the room. They thought they could come up with something to get Ann out.

Then the door opened and a man looked out. Joe saw that he had a gun in his hand. This was no time for heroics. They'd have to see what happens before jeopardizing everyone, including Ann.

The man walked out of the room, motioned to his partner who had Ann in front of him. She was still handcuffed and gagged.

"Hey, what's going on?" the man who was in charge asked.

"FBI. We're arresting a possible traitor. We're taking her in for questioning."

"Oh, wow. Good luck with that."

Joe and Ron heard the talk about Ann. That shook them both. Was this true?

Joe turned to Ron. Both had wide eyes and panicked faces. "What if that's true?" Ron asked.

"I know. That would explain a lot of things, but I still can't get myself to believe Ann is in on this."

"Let's follow these two and ask what's up."

Joe agreed. As the men led Ann out of the B&B, Joe motioned to their wives to follow. Then he yelled, "Hey, wait up!"

The two men turned, both with their weapons out. "Don't try anything or you'll be in big trouble."

"We're not trying anything. We just want to know what's up."

"FBI business. None of yours."

"Come on. Ann is our friend. We deserve to know something."

As they talked, a carriage pulled up. The men had called for one to take them quickly to the pier. They jumped in and drove off.

Joe looked at Ron and at their wives. They were all a bit shocked. What in the world was going on? They needed to speak with Ann. They all walked as briskly as they could to the pier. They knew it would be a while before the next boat would leave the Island. They had time to make some kind of plan, but they had to be on that same boat with the FBI agents.

When they arrived at the pier, they did not see Ann at first. They split up and wandered around. Then Shanice found them sitting in a restaurant, waiting. She notified the others and they met to think through their plan while they all waited.

Ron spoke first. "We could plan something around Tommy and Wendy when we get back."

"We could," Joe said, "but we have to realize that we'd have to hold two FBI agents. If caught, we'd have a real mess on our hands."

"Do you have to capture them? They might understand if you explain what's going on and give Ann a chance to talk," Joette said.

"I agree with Joette," Shanice said, "we might get more help from them if we don't try to do something that could get us all in trouble."

Joe was very perplexed. "How do we do that?"

1,500 miles away

The two bosses had met several times, and they felt that all the preparations for the event were going rather well. They had agreed on the date and knew what had to be done in each area.

The old boss was confident. "We have infiltrated most of the organizations we need. We have also been able to enlist some of the groups who wanted to change the government. We have them on our side now, and they will be a force. They bring an attitude that we need."

"I agree," the new boss said. "I like that we have now gotten several FBI agents involved. That was one area where we were behind. It will help us when the day comes. They can arrest some of the people we need to get out of the way."

"Yes! I agree," the old boss said.

"I know it will work."

The old boss began to philosophize about how important their work was. "I have studied many leaders around the world. Most lose power because they get soft or lose their way. They forget to think of the goal. Ours is domination and power. We will change this country and turn it into a country that allows freedom in all areas. Today's laws are too restrictive and downright stifling."

Then he looked at the new boss and thought… *how will I get rid of this guy? I want to be a supreme ruler for life. No voting. This guy wants to be in charge. What can I do with him? How do I get rid of him and his followers?*

The new boss saw the look in his eyes. He too was thinking *how can I eliminate the guy?* He turned and said, "We need to get someone of high rank in the military. That is one area that we are deficient. Without the military, we'll have a rough time keeping all of the areas secure."

"I think we can work on that. That is the last piece of the puzzle. We were able to get the FBI after many tries. We'll get the military." The old boss thought about the military bases they had established around the country. That lead him to the base in the U.P. where the two men had come from who put him in the hospital for some time. He was glad that Bates finally got the word that they were eliminated. He also knew that the base was now secure, and that the local police had been neutralized. He even had word that the FBI agent who was sneaking around and getting close to finding their conspirator was now being picked up. He must make sure that the agent was also eliminated.

CHAPTER 58

Colewin, April 23

The barber decided to finally let Matt in on what he had planned. He did not want Charlie to know because Charlie had his own ideas of how to get at the bunker, but it wasn't practical. When he saw Matt in Colewin one day, he walked over to him and asked if he could meet him later at his barber shop. He did not say anything else.

Matt was surprised and, at the same time, very curious. He knew the barber many years ago, but he hadn't been personally involved with him until the bunker. Matt had some errands to run, which he completed, and then headed to the barber shop.

"What's this all about?" he asked the barber.

"You know you have been working hard to get to the bunker, right?"

Matt agreed, "Yep, as you know, we've been on it a long time."

"And you want to get into the place to get Charlie's military gear and to find out what's happening, right?"

"That's as close as I can tell."

"Well, here's the thing. You know the three I told you about earlier, including my son? Well, I got my son casing out the place."

"Sure you do. We've tried that over and over. As we said earlier, it doesn't work. They don't want any more men from Colewin, and everyone we've sent there has either joined up for the cash, or they were outed."

"Let me guess, by Bill, right?"

"Yep, as far as I know that's who turns on 'em."

"I thought so. See I been cutting Bill's hair for years. He's a big talker, and he likes to think he's the big man around Colewin."

"Some say he is."

"Right, but like I said, he's come to my shop for years. He tried to get me to join that outfit. I never bit, but I kept listening. He's got the ear of that man out there, ah, Bates, right?"

"Right."

"They like Bill because he fills them in on anything that's going on in Colewin. Like you said, he also outed some troops, so he's got their trust. I figured I could take advantage of that, and I did. Got the three in there. Bill trusts me too because he wants to think I'm his buddy and would do anything for him, but I just listen and don't say anything, so he's become a fount of information for me."

"Well, I'll be damned. You really got inside Bill, haven't you?"

"For sure. We're going to find out if we can take that place over when the time is right. They could get into that bunker and force Bates to let us in or anyone we want in."

"Maybe. Maybe not. That seems like a big order."

"We could even find out what they're up to. Joe said he's been following these troops they've been sending out, but he can't tell why or where they're going. Maybe we can get that information if nothing else. It'd help us to take them down."

"Could."

"Anyway, I wanted you to know, so if I get any information, I'll pass it along to you and you can let Joe know. I'd keep Charlie out of it. You understand? He'd want to keep digging the tunnel, and this plan would kind of eliminate that."

"Yeah, he wants his stuff back. Can't blame him."

"No, for sure, but he'll get it if we can get in there this way."

Matt said, "Yeah, if it'll work, but it makes more sense than the tunnel."

CHAPTER 59

Later, on the Island, April 23, 5:00 p.m.

Ann sat in the restaurant between the two agents. They were going to order something to eat, and they told her she could order too, but she would have to keep the handcuffs on. They did take the gag off, so she could eat, and they decided they did not need it anymore anyway.

"Order what you want."

"Am I supposed to eat with these things on my hands?"

"You'll have to. We're not taking them off. You should be glad you don't have shackles on your legs."

"Oh, I'm so happy. You boys have no idea what you're doing. You have the wrong person."

"Just shut up or we'll gag you again and let you go hungry."

The waitress walked over and asked if they were ready to order. The tall agent answered, "Yes, we are."

Ann ordered a turkey sandwich and onion rings, and the two agents ordered pulled-pork sandwiches. Ann also ordered a drink, but they would not let her get it. They ate quickly and quietly. The two men each went to the restroom, one at a time, and then they let Ann go. They escorted her to the door, but they had the waitress keep an eye on her after explaining what was going on. She was very happy to oblige the two young men.

It was the last boat for the day, and Joe and Ron had to hurry to make sure they made it. They had retrieved their luggage from the room they had rented. Joe, Ron, Joette, and Shanice were eating protein bars, disappointed that they could not get a hot meal as they watched the restaurant. They saw the two men and Ann leave the place and head to the pier. They decided to follow, but they kept their distance. They wanted them to get on the boat first. Joe had purchased four tickets earlier, so they just had to wait.

Both agents were being cautious, and the tall agent said, "We need to keep our eyes out for that guy and his partner who were following us. They look like trouble."

Ann was not going to let them turn Joe and Ron into criminals. "You know those are two ex-Army veterans. The one has served over twenty years, and they both fought in Vietnam. They also worked with us for many years in some serious operations. They are good people and they know more about what's going on with the insurgence than anyone we have."

Neither agent said anything. They just kept walking.

The three hustled down the pier and arrived just as the boat was available to board. The wind had picked up, so they went below and took the seats near the middle of the boat. Once again, Ann was in the middle of the two agents. This time she talked. "You know that you're making a big mistake. The person you need to arrest is the traitor in our organization. The one who has been keeping us from heading to the U.P. to check out what's going on there."

"Sure, sure. I bet. A traitor."

Ann knew she had her work cut out for her, but she kept trying. They listened.

Joe and Joette entered the boat together and sat in the lower level in the back. Ron and Shanice entered and sat on the other side of the boat about three seats behind Ann and the agents.

Joe had decided to play this situation in a way so they did not cause any more trouble for Ann. He thought they should just level with the two men and tell them all they knew. His plan was to sit behind the two once the boat started moving and just talk to them.

He wouldn't do anything that might cause them to pull their weapons. He would just be super careful.

The boat roared and began its trip to St. Ignace. The noise was loud, but not so loud that they would not be able to hear Joe. The boat bumped along as the waves grew higher and made the ride feel like being on a dune buggy. It wasn't the most pleasant ride, but no one was complaining.

Joe stood up and walked leisurely to where the three were sitting. He reached the seat and slid between the seats right behind them. All three turned around and saw Joe take a seat right behind Ann. "How are you doing, Ann?"

"All right. Nothing I can't handle to this point."

One of the agents pulled out his Glock and held it just above the seats. "Don't be stupid, man. You'll pay. We have a job to do, and we're going to do it."

Joe looked at the weapon and laughed. "So, you think we're the bad ones? You think Ann is the enemy? You need to examine what you're doing."

"We're doing what we were told to do. You're getting in the way of a federal agency, and you could get yourself in trouble if you interfere."

Ann said, "Will you lay off the official stuff? This is a friend of mine. I told you he's a good person. He will not interfere."

"No, I won't, but I would like to know why Ann is being arrested, while so many others, who should be, are running free."

The tall agent said, "I'm not sure what you're saying, but Ann has committed a serious crime."

"Oh, yeah, what's that?"

"None of your business. This is an official FBI investigation, and you need to stop now. We're taking her to Lansing, and if you want to get hurt, just try to stop us."

"I could have both of you in trouble in five minutes if I wanted to. We have several people here and on shore who could take you out."

At the mention of others, the agent on Ann's right pulled out his phone and made a quick call. He spoke loud enough for everyone to hear. "This is Agent Maxwell. We have a problem and need back-up." He remained silent for a while; then realized the two were on their own. He hung up, but as he did, he said, "Now we have backup, too. They'll be here in no time."

Joe smiled, "No, they won't."

The man was silent. He looked at his partner and shook his head. They already knew they were on their own, but it was worth a try.

"Don't worry. We have no plans to hurt you or try anything that could cause a problem."

Ann spoke up. "Really, I'll be all right. I've done nothing wrong, and I know who the traitor is now, and who ordered this, and I know some of what they're planning, but I can't say now. I just need to be able to convince some people. Joe, you take care of yourselves and keep doing what you're doing. I'll try to keep in touch."

"Not what I thought you'd say, but I understand and will keep in touch." At that Joe walked back to his seat with Joette and texted Tommy.

Looks like we won't interfere. Ann okay. Stay close in case and be armed.

Joe sat back and closed his eyes. Joette looked at him and said, "Bad news?"

"We can't help Ann here. There's a real problem. She said there's someone in the hierarchy where she works who has flipped—a traitor. That explains a lot. Probably why she wanted to meet, but now it's out there. These two know, but I'm sure they don't believe her, but they'll tell their boss and she could be in real trouble."

CHAPTER 60

Colewin, May 20

Joe had been in Colewin for some time and not much had happened, but when he had returned from Mackinac Island about a month ago, Matt informed him about the barber and his plan. Joe thought if it worked, it could really help. It might be a way to get the place shut down. Also, not long after he had returned, he received word from Matt and the barber that a semi was heading out, but this time they had information on where it was going. That meant they did not have to follow.

A semi full of troops was headed for North Dakota, and it was going to leave in late May. They got word that the number of troops was thinning, and that there would be only one more transport, and this one would be to South Dakota.

Among the first group of men would be two of the barber's son's friends. His son was not going this time, so they figured he would be among the last to leave. The word was that after the South Dakota group, less than two hundred men would remain at the bunker—and they had no idea where they would go.

Joe had been trying to find out about Ann. He did not have any word yet of where she might be or what happened to her. He and Ron decided to put their sons on it to see if they could find out anything on the dark web. There had to be something somewhere, but so far, they had nothing.

Charlie wanted to get back to digging the tunnel, but everyone thought that since the bunker was scaling down, it would not make sense to put their energy into the tunnel. They did increase the number of sentries around the base in hopes that, if they moved equipment, they would be able to do something, maybe intercept them.

Yet, Joe thought getting equipment back was not the top priority. He felt that finding out when the event might occur and what it would entail was most important, and knowing what happened to Ann would be extremely helpful too. Hopefully, she was still alive.

Also, Cathy had sent word from Marquette that Wayne was out of a coma and recovering, but he would need a lot of physical therapy before he would be able to make it back to a somewhat normal life. This helped everyone a bit, knowing that Wayne was improving. Joette and Shanice decided to head back to Marquette to see Cathy and Wayne, and Tommy and Wendy wanted to go too, but they left on different days.

Shortly after their wives left Colewin, Ron and Joe met again with Matt to learn of any further updates. The barber's son had just sent some information about his possible move. He said he and his group of troops had been training to take over a building. He said this was the typical training for all the men who had gone through the bunker. He had word that this was also going on in other parts of the country. His trainer had come from the west coast late last year, and he told them that they were doing the same thing. He had been trained to take his knowledge to the U.P. to add to their readiness. Joe wondered what he meant by "take over a building." Did they know which building it would be?

Matt did not know, but he said he would ask the barber if he had any information that would help. He would check back with Joe and Ron when he found out, and he would get the barber to meet with them in a day or two.

"That's great." Joe said. "I know he's been keeping a low profile, so he would not jeopardize the safety of his son and his son's friends. What does he say about Bill? Is he still at the bunker?"

Matt was not sure where Bill was. "That's another question for the barber. He'll know. I'm sure. Bill is creepy in how he gets information from people—super smart. Before this is over, the barber may be able to answer all of our questions."

"I hope you're right," Ron added. "He's the only one to get a person inside that place. All the other attempts ended in death— or they joined up."

Matt agreed. "As I've said before. They pay well, and that sways people."

CHAPTER 61

Lansing, Michigan, May 21

Ann had been brought back to Lansing in April, and was immediately turned over to the boss. He had her stripped of her duties, took away her badge and weapon, and had her locked up for the duration. Her boss had been in the Bureau for many years and had a good reputation, but she had no idea what turned him. After several weeks, he visited Ann at an abandoned building.

"How has your time been here?" he asked.

"Everyone has treated me well, but what's up with you? You know I'm not an insurgent."

"Who knows? My boss thinks you are."

"Your boss. And who would that be? The boss I know would not say that."

"Sorry, Ann, you need to get with the times. We need change and we need the type of change that gets rid of all these damn bleeding liberals. They're a bunch of socialists, and they will take this country down. We need people running this country who aren't afraid of stopping a lot of the crap that is going on. A man can't even own a gun or he's looked at as bad, and immigration, I'm not even going to get into that."

"So, you work for them then? Not the FBI."

"You can say what you will. I work for the country to make it better."

"So, you work for them!" Ann repeated.

"I work for myself. I work for fair elections and everything that goes with that."

"No, you work for yourself and the money you can make by putting people like me in jail."

"No sense talking to you. You don't understand."

"When do I get out of here, or even speak to a lawyer?"

"Lawyer? You're not getting a lawyer, nor will you ever get out of here until we've taken over."

"WE?"

"That's all I'm saying. Enjoy your time while you still have time."

"What the hell does that mean? Are you going to eliminate me? What about my family? My husband must be crazy worried by now. It's been almost a month. Can I call my husband?"

"Can't call from here. This is a dead zone. No Wi-Fi, nothing."

"My family must know something is wrong!"

"We've taken care of that. You're on a special assignment for the duration. We even gave him your extra duty pay to appease his doubts. He's fine."

"You're a bully and a rat. You'll never get away with this."

"I will, and I am. See ya!" He left and slammed the door as hard as he could. He knew Ann was a good agent, but she was in the way, and he could not have that. She had almost figured out that Michigan was a hotspot for the Midwest training. He knew that the last two groups would be leaving soon for South and North Dakota, and then most everything was in place for the event.

1500 miles away, Florida Keys, electronic meeting

The committee had agreed on the dates that the two bosses had devised. The members gave them their full support and reassured them that they had the final say. Both bosses were delighted. They also guaranteed that money would roll until the event was over—

and their people were running the country. At that time, the money would freeze up and all troops and those they had bribed would no longer receive payments. The members did want a report on the current progress at all seven sites.

The new boss's eyes glistened while he spoke, and he had a devious look on his face. The old boss saw the look and had a smirk of his own. The new boss began, "Well, we have thirty states with everyone in place. The troops are being trained to secure buildings, and the elite groups are being informed about the people they will be arresting. The other states do not have their people in place, but it shouldn't be too many more weeks until they are."

The old boss added, "We have enlisted members in every state house, and we have police in every state on the payroll. We don't have large numbers, but we have people who are in high places, so we should be good. We've talked about the military, and you know that we have some soldiers and officers on the payroll. We hope to have more soon. Getting those who direct troops is our goal, so they do not send soldiers out once the event takes place."

When one of the members spoke, his remarks were translated for the bosses. His main concern was that they would not have a strong military presence in opposition to their troops. The old boss spoke, "Once we take over the buildings, we'll be in charge, so I doubt any response will be quick enough or strong enough to oppose us."

The same member spoke once again, and his concern was translated. "I hope you're right. We cannot afford for this not to work. It is a one-time chance. Get it right!"

The new boss answered, "We will. It'll work and we'll be in charge in a few hours once the event begins."

"Good," was the only response and the meeting ended.

CHAPTER 62

Lansing, Michigan, Sunday, May 23

It was a Sunday, and Loretta, who was also an FBI agent, was dismayed. She had not heard from her best friend and agent in the FBI for almost a month, no, it was a month. The last she had heard from Ann, she had said that she was going up north for a quick vacation with some old friends. She assumed it was Mackinac Island since Ann had been vacationing there for years with some friends from up north. The funny thing was she was keeping it quiet—and did not want Loretta to say anything to anyone.

Loretta had checked with the boss, and he said Ann was on a special assignment, but Loretta knew that when she returned from Mackinac Island, she would have been contacted by Ann before going on any clandestine operation. Not that she would have said anything about it, but she would have let Loretta know that she was back. She had heard nothing.

Loretta was a wily character who was afraid of nothing. She had been through many tight situations and had come out on top each time. She could hold her own in any situation and even had hand-to-hand combat training when she was in the military. Her most accomplished credits were that she had a knack for strategizing. She thought this would be a time to be at her best.

Loretta started checking around, talking to a few agents who might know something. She had checked with everyone in the office, but she had gotten nothing. However, a couple of agents had been a little off when she talked to them, so she was returning to one of their homes to ask some more questions. She had worked with Jerry Maxwell on several cases during the past year. She knew he was okay and very honest and candid. She knocked, "Hey, Jerry, me again."

"Yeah, what's up? It's Sunday you know."

"Yes, it is, but I still have a few questions. Mind if I come in? I'm trying to get some word on Ann. She always checks in with me, but it's been a month and nothing. That's not like her."

"Sure, come in. She's on special assignment, I guess."

"Really? How would you know that?"

"I don't. I'm just guessing. With all the crap that's been going on with this militia stuff, I just assumed she was."

"Well, she was on vacation, you know," Loretta said.

"Yes, I guess she was up north—Mackinac Island from what I heard."

"Oh, the Island. And how do you know that?" Loretta was now sure that Jerry knew something because Ann was keeping her trip quiet for some reason. Now she had to force the issue.

"Come on, Jerry. How do you know that? Did someone say something?"

"Not really. Why?"

"Why? Because she's missing."

"No. She's not. I'm sure of that."

"And how are you so sure?"

Jerry was excited. For a newer agent, he felt like he was in on something, especially if Loretta didn't know. His chest swelled. "If I tell you something, it'll be just between us, right?"

"Sure. No problem. I just want to know that Ann is all right."

"Great. Here's the thing." Jerry went on telling Loretta all about Ann, and how she was being kept in a nice place for some time until the boss could figure things out.

Loretta was shocked and, yet, at the same time, not surprised at all. "Where is she being kept?"

"I can't say, but she's fine and in a nice place. They say she's even in good spirits, so it can't be all that bad."

"Right, right. I'm sure she's fine. Must be in that old building then. Nice place and all. Still kept up." Loretta was fishing and hoped for a response.

"Ah, yeah, can't say." But his voice gave it away.

Loretta was silent, and then looked at him and turned toward the door. "If she is all right, that's all I care. Thanks."

Jerry was happy to help. "Okay then. See ya."

"Bye, take care." And Loretta was on her way to get some information.

CHAPTER 63

Colewin, Monday, May 24, 12:30 p.m.
Joe called a meeting with the key players that he felt needed to find out what they could do now that they had someone inside the bunker—which they had been trying to do for a long time. He decided to meet with Matt and the barber, and he felt he probably should also include Charlie. They needed to find out just what the situation was at the bunker, and what information the barber's son could give them.

They set the meeting for May 24 at the hideaway where Joe and Ron were staying. Matt and the barber were there early. Charlie came about twenty minutes later. Joe set everyone up with beer and pizza that Joette had made from scratch when she returned from Marquette. It looked great. "Everyone, take a seat and help yourself. This could take some time."

"Looks good," Matt said.

The barber agreed. "I love pizza, but I can't drink beer. You have any water?"

"Sure," Ron said. He gave the barber a big glass of cold water.

Joe turned to the barber and said, "We are here to try to piece together as much information as we can. I know you have an informer inside the bunker. Is there anything you can tell me about the place that we don't already know?"

"I'm not sure what you know, but I can tell you what I found out so far."

"That's a good start."

"Okay, my son is inside. He told me that they are going to start sending all of their equipment out to several places. He doesn't know exactly what they have, but he knows that trucks and armaments of all kinds will be sent out. He also said they are preparing for two helicopters to be delivered there, and then they will be sent to two different states. He doesn't know which ones. The important thing is that after they send out the last group, there will be fewer than two hundred men at the camp. He will be among them."

"Wow, that sounds like they're ready to do something. I wonder if the event is planned to happen soon," Joe said.

"I don't know. We communicate daily, and he sends me information every evening, so I can ask anything you want."

"Good. I have an idea. Can you ask him about how many guards they post at the bunker and where they are? Will that number change after the next group goes out? We know they have two guard towers on each side of the gate, and one person who guards the gate. They used to have several more, but lately they have thinned out. Can he tell us where the other guards are, and where they're posted?

"I can see what he knows, or if he can find out."

"Get that information tonight if you can, and then let's meet tomorrow at the same place and time."

Matt said, "Sounds good."

Ron agreed, "That will be valuable information. Eat up everyone. We have a lot of work to do in the next couple of days."

CHAPTER 64

Lansing, Michigan, Monday, May 24, Early Morning
Loretta had gone back to the office after talking to Jerry. She was certain she knew where Ann was, but she needed to check on how to get into the place without being seen. She had found the blueprints and realized that getting in was going to be a problem if they had agents watching the place. Her best bet might be to just act like she belonged and barge into the place, and that was her plan.

Ann was bored. She had been in this prison of sorts for about a month, and she was beginning to wonder if she would ever get out alive. "If only I had some way to contact anyone," she said out loud. She knew it was impossible. Her boss had planned the whole thing, and he wouldn't have left any loose ends.

Loretta planned to find Ann, but she knew she had to let someone know what she was doing, so she made sure her friend, Mary, also an agent, knew where she was going and what she was doing, and she gave her a minimum of details.

Then early the next day, she got into her car and decided to drive across town to check out the building she suspected. She kept wondering what she could actually do once she got there. It took her longer than she expected even in the early morning hours. After forty-five minutes, she arrived at the building.

It was quiet and still dark out. She knew exactly which door to enter, but it was locked. She walked around the building and found another entrance that looked like it was being used. She walked to the door and pulled it open. She thought that it was too easy. There's probably video out here. It was just getting light out, and when Loretta surveyed the area, she noticed a small camera above the corner of the door.

She slipped ahead anyway. She was met a few minutes later by an agent from her office. Tall and gangly, she recognized him right away. "Hello, Aaron, how's everything?"

"I'm not too sure. What are you doing here? I was told we would not get any more visitors this week."

"Oh, you've had other people here?" Loretta was wondering what that might mean. *Who else knows about Ann, or is Ann even here?*

"No. I mean I haven't. The boss meets here with these others almost three times a week. He's had me here for almost a month. I switch off with another agent, but this has been our duty. Very boring, but it's what I'm ordered to do. Hey, why are you here? The boss never said anything about you."

Loretta was careful and guarded, but she was going to take a chance. "I'm here to see Ann. Didn't anyone say anything?"

"How do you know about Ann? I thought no one else knew about this."

"What do you mean? We all know." Loretta thought she could confuse him a bit by saying this.

"All I know is the boss said that the two of us who watch the place were the only ones who know that Ann is here."

"What exactly do you mean? That's crazy. We know she's kept here, and I'm supposed to check on her to see that she's all right."

"That's not what I've been told, but this whole thing is really weird. The boss meets here with some men who are not FBI. They look a little out of place here."

"Who are they?"

"I don't know, but they are very confidential about their meetings. I see them walk in, but they meet in a room over there. I can't figure out what's going on, and I'm really confused. Ann doesn't seem like the type he has made her out to be, but these meetings, they scare me. I think the boss might be up to something."

"I think you're right, but could I see Ann first and we can talk later?"

"I can't do that. I have orders that no one sees her."

"And why is that?"

"Not sure. Those are the orders I have. Man, I've been bored here. Not much to do."

"How about just letting me talk to her for a minute? Let me make sure she's good."

"I can't do that."

"Sure, you can. I know we haven't worked all that much together, but we have worked together a little. You know you can trust me, and that I'm not going to do anything stupid."

"You know I'm nervous about what is going on here. The three who meet with the boss look like militia. They always have camo on every time they come here. They also carry guns—and I know they're not FBI."

"That should tell you something. I bet Ann knows about it. Let's ask her."

"I don't know."

"Just for a minute. That's it. You can tell the boss if you want that I was here when he comes in. He won't care."

"All right. One minute, no more. You have to hurry because the boss meets with them almost every morning at this time, so he could be here soon."

"If he shows up, just don't say anything right away!"

"Sure. I'll give you some time." The agent led Loretta down a long hall, then took several steps up to a landing, turned right and stopped in front of a door.

CHAPTER 65

Colewin, Later in the Day, Monday, May 24

The barber did not expect to see Bill again for some time, but when he was going to his shop, he met him on the street. The barber was not sure what to say. He did not want to give away anything that was going on, but he knew he could possibly get something out of Bill. "Hey, Bill, how's it going? You got anything going on out there?"

"Good. Got your son set up at the base. His friends have orders to move out soon. They're headed west as far as I know."

The barber knew. His son had told him that his two friends were not very happy about it, but they would play along because the money was good. "So, what's up? Anything new?"

Bill looked at the barber funny because he usually never said anything like that. He usually didn't even talk. He walked with the barber down the street until he reached the shop. Then he said, "Not much. Heading to the bunker. See ya."

The barber saw the look in Bill's eyes, and he knew he had screwed up. He should have just let Bill talk. In a subdued voice he said, "Hopefully, he doesn't think anything about this."

Bill walked down the street, stopped at the grocery store for a minute, and then took what he had purchased and walked to his car and jumped in. He headed for the bunker. When he arrived, he went straight to Bates. He pounded on the door. Bates saw him on the screen, but he ignored him for a while. Bates mumbled, "That guy pisses me off. He always has some lame-brained idea. He's helped weed out a few traitors though, so I suppose I better let him in."

Bates opened the door and immediately asked, "What now?"

Bill tried to enter, but Bates kept his foot on the door, so he could not squeeze through. "I just got a bad feeling in town. It was the barber."

"The barber? What about the barber? Did he give you a bad haircut?"

"No. I don't know. I just thought he was fishing for something, or he knew something."

"What do you mean?"

"I really don't know, but I got a feeling."

"If you can't give me anything other than you have a feeling, then this conversation is over." Bates rolled his eyes and pushed the door tighter on Bill. "If you find out anything, then let me know. Otherwise, keep it to yourself."

"I'll see if I can get anything out of his son."

"Who?"

"His son. One of the three that we let in last month. You remember?"

"Yes, I do. If he is a problem, we have to get rid of him."

"I'm not sure, but I'll let you know."

Bill walked to the barracks where the barber's son was staying and walked over to the barber's son who was sitting on his bunk.

CHAPTER 66

Lansing, Monday, May 24, Morning

The agent unlocked the door and let Loretta in, and then he walked back to his post and waited for the boss. He wasn't sure what he was going to say, but he knew he wasn't going to give Loretta away. She had always been nice to him and treated him as an equal. He had faith in her that she was a good person and agent, but he did not have that same feeling for his boss.

Loretta entered the room. Ann was asleep on a sofa in the center of the room near a barred window. She looked relaxed. Loretta examined the room and saw a small kitchen area with a fridge and microwave, a stacked clothes washer and dryer stuffed into a corner, a pile of books off to the side of the sofa, a table and two chairs, but not much else. Comfortable enough. Loretta walked close and said, "Ann."

At the sound of her name Ann threw off her covers and sat up on the sofa. She blinked twice and shook her head. Then she said, "Is that you, Loretta?"

"It's me."

"Oh, my gosh, don't tell me you're in on this too? I would never have guessed!"

"In on what?"

"This conspiracy to take down the government."

"No, I'm here to see how you are. I was able to get by the agent on guard. He seems all right. I think he doesn't trust the boss."

"How did you figure out where I am being held?"

Loretta explained the process she used, and how she figured it out. They talked for a few minutes and Ann finally realized that Loretta was on her side and wanted to get her out of there. Loretta mentioned that the boss might be there soon, and they would have to hurry if they were going to get Ann out.

Ann told Loretta to slow down. "I need to give you some information in case I don't get out of here and you can. "First, contact Joe DeLuca in the U.P. You remember the guy I used to work with many years ago?"

"I remember."

"He's hiding out in Colewin, a small community near Lake Michigan. He's been involved in this mess for a few years. He was the first to bring it to my attention. He can help us with where the base is and what is going on now. Next, you need to get word to the Governor about a base in the U.P. where a bunch of revolutionaries are plotting to take down the government. I think our boss has joined up. He's kept us from investigating that U.P. base, and I think it has cost us. There are at least six other bases across the continental U.S., so we need to involve the Governor and the President too, but we have to be careful because we don't know who's involved in the plan. Keep it to yourself and only one other you fully trust."

"Is that what you've been working on this past year?"

"Sort of. I haven't had the full blessing from our office, so I've been on my own really, but I don't know who to trust."

"Well, you can trust me."

The door opened quickly and in walked the agent. "You've got to get out of here. The boss is here and he wants to check on Ann. He's meeting with those militia guys right now, and they're armed like I was telling you. You only have about one minute. Get moving, and I can't let you take Ann out of here. It'd be my neck."

"I understand," Ann said. "Please, don't say anything to my husband right now. I'm all right. If things change, then give him the full story."

"Right. Will do. Since we can't get you out right now, I'll work on something to free you. Be safe."

As Loretta left, she narrowly got by the men coming out of the room where they had met. The agent stood between Loretta and the meeting door—and the boss's gaze was left, not right where Loretta was leaving.

CHAPTER 67

Colewin, Monday, May 25

The barber had talked to his son, and Peter had given him information on sentries, number of troops left, and equipment that had left the day before. He was concerned because Peter had said that Bill had talked to him the previous evening and was acting quite strange. It had made him a bit nervous because Bill was asking questions about his friends and his father. He wasn't too concerned, but he knew it wasn't like Bill. The barber knew what had happened and explained it to Peter. "Won't happen again. I'm smarter than that. I should have just let him talk."

The barber knew he had to get to Joe's later that morning, but he thought he should go sooner and let him know what had happened. He arrived around 8:00 a.m., about an hour early for the meeting. He knocked on the door and Ron answered. "Hey, come on in."

"How are you today?" the barber asked as he stepped into the room. Then he saw Joe who was making coffee and had eggs frying in a pan. He was making one-eyed sandwiches, as the barber called them. Then he looked up at Joe and said, "I love those sandwiches. I used to make them all the time for my kids. I still make them for my wife."

"We love them," Ron said. "Have them a couple times a week. Old army habit, I guess."

Joe said, "Say, we aren't supposed to meet for another hour, but you're welcome to sit and have some breakfast with us."

"Sounds great, but I've eaten already. I just came early because I spoke with my son last night, and he gave me some valuable information. He repeated everything Peter had passed along. He also mentioned his awkward meeting with Bill. "I think if we are going to act, we should do it soon. When Bill gets nosey, he doesn't stop looking around. He's one meddler that I don't trust."

Joe agreed. "I think you're right about moving quickly. Once they send out that last group, we need to act. I would like some help from the government, but who the heck can we trust these days?"

Ron said, "And we'll have to get as many people to help as we can. People we can trust."

"Let's start by making a list of things and people we'll need to pull this off. Let's keep to as few as we can and as little equipment as possible. We'll have to travel light."

The barber immediately volunteered. "I'm in. No matter what. My wife could help too."

All three were getting excited about their chances. "Let's see, we need Matt, Charlie, Tommy and Wendy, Paul and Sarah, the five diggers who are now also helping with the sentry duties, all six of the other sentries, Frank, our wives, Shanice and Joette, and our sons, you and your wife, Ron, and me. That's about twenty-six of us. Let's keep Sam out of this. He's been a problem in the past. We'll have to plan what, how, and when we're going to do this. We need to include Charlie, and let's wait for Tommy and Wendy and get this right.

CHAPTER 68

Colewin, a Hideout in the Woods, Wednesday, May 26
Joe started the planning right away. His initial idea was to somehow breach the bunker. He and Ron decided to contact each person they would like to have help. They had just under thirty people, and they knew this might not be enough, especially since several were older. However, they did have a good group of young people that they had been training throughout the year, and they were ready.

Joe made sure that everyone would be in Colewin by the end of the month. He and Ron made several calls and had Matt and Charlie very quietly spread the word in Colewin. No one was to be given any knowledge of what they were to do except for the individuals they mentioned.

Ron's and Joe's sons were enlisted to help with the tech part of the plan. They also knew they had some individuals who were going to have to take out some of the troops who were on guard at the bunker. They would have to find more silencers to accomplish that task.

Right now, Joe thought there were about five guards, but he knew that the hill on the back side, not far from the tunnel, would probably have more than two. He told the barber to keep checking with his son to see if he knew of any others who might be armed guards at night anywhere near the bunker.

Ron was in charge of getting as many military-style rifles as he could. Charlie was going to help him since he already had access to several. They also needed trucks, probably two to carry them to the bunker, and to be ready to take them back if there was a mishap or something did not work. Some of the young people were working on getting a very sophisticated drone to search the base and to be ready to get a clear picture of the layout.

Next, since they were outnumbered, they knew they had to have a fool-proof plan, and they needed people who were willing to put their lives on the line. The barber had come back with information that the semi was leaving on Monday, May 31. Joe thought that they had to make their move right away after that. The plan would take some time before it was finalized, and the group came up with Monday, June 7, or if that didn't work, Wednesday, June 9. Any time later than that, they thought would be to the advantage of Bates and the people in the bunker. Joe's group had to hit while they were still adjusting to much smaller numbers.

The young people came up with their first drone, but Joe thought it was too large. He wanted something small that they could fly around during the day, and something that would not be very noticeable, especially while the troops were busy training. He wanted clear aerial pictures of the bunker area and of any buildings or other structures, besides the barracks, to give his team a picture of the area so they could be properly prepared.

CHAPTER 69

The Bunker, Wednesday, May 26, Morning

Bates was busy scheduling the last semi. He was hoping the new boss's timeline would be a go. Then it would soon be time to stand-down as much of the base as he could prior to abandoning it in a few months if things went as planned. By September all of the bases that had been established were to be closed. Troops were to be in place, and training would continue in the places where they had all been sent. These other training areas would have just over one hundred to two hundred troops each, and there were almost fifty of them. Plus, they had about two hundred troops in other spots in each state who would back them up.

They would also have backup from the individuals that they had enlisted, but who had not joined the training. They were members of local, state, and federal agencies of all kinds. How many others they had, Bates was not sure, but he knew they had a significant force to pull this off. They also had many helicopters, drones, tanks, and other armored equipment all over the country.

Bates was happy that his time at the bunker was coming to an end. He had amassed a pile of cash and could do just about anything he wanted now. He knew there was a lot more cash to be had, and so he volunteered to help after the takeover. He was a bit nervous about his next post, but he was so focused on the money he would make that he didn't much care what he had to do. He knew some of the work involved eliminating some key figures, but, what the hell, money was money.

As Bates stood and turned to grab another beer from the fridge, he saw Bill on the screen. "Not again. He's going to drive me crazy."

Bill pounded on the door, but, of course, Bates could not hear it in the bunker. He walked to the door and opened it and in a rather irritated voice said, "What now?"

"Hey, how you doin', man? Just stopped by to give you some ideas again."

"What this time?"

"I was guessing that since the next group is moving out at the end of the month that we should probably increase the lookouts around the base. We'll be under two hundred, you know."

"I know, but we have sentries."

"You have only three troops guarding the gate and two in the woods. Why not double them, just in case? I just sense that we need more protection."

"I don't really care. Take it up with the trainers. They take care of that stuff."

"I did. They didn't think it was necessary, but I do. I know this area and the people, and if they are going to try something, this would be the time. Remember what I mentioned earlier when I got a funny feeling when I spoke to the barber in town on Monday? His son is one of us now. I spoke with him before going in to town to see his father, and he was jittery. Not sure why. I think something is up."

"Okay, okay. Tell them to double the sentries. We'll need four in the woods above the barracks, and six at the gate. The rest of the grounds are impassable, so no one is going to get in any other way. How's that?"

"What about the old road?"

"Put two guards there. That should do it!"

"Great. Thanks. I'll get on it right away. What about the barber's son?"

CHAPTER 70

Colewin, the Hideout, Thursday, May 27

Joe wanted to call everyone together, but he did not want them all to head for the same place—and then have someone suspect something. He knew he was being paranoid, but he did not know if anyone was being followed or if there was any electronic surveillance going on, so his best bet was to work in small groups in different places.

Joe and Ron called the young people together because they wanted them to do surveillance with the drone. Joe also had his son and Ron's son included, so they could help with the electronics part of it. The discussion centered around how and where they would send up the drone. The new one was much smaller, and everyone thought it would be very effective. The time of day was the issue right now.

Joe had received information from the barber's son that the best time would be around lunch time since most of the troops—because the numbers were so low—would be either training or in the mess hall. Joe asked, "Do you think you could get this in the air by Sunday, and where would you like to launch it?"

The leader of the young people said they could actually launch it anywhere Joe would want. The tunnel would be a nice place, but they were afraid that the place was still compromised and troops might be there at any time. They decided to take the road to the hill, stop about a mile from the turn, and hide in the woods. Their drone had a range of a little over two miles, so they wanted to get as close as they could. They could fly the drone about four hundred feet off the ground, but Joe wanted it to be just above the tree level to get the best view. They would have to be in the air only a few minutes to get a good look at the layout. The barber's son had given them a lot of information, so they just needed everyone to see exactly where they would be when they entered the gate.

Joe was satisfied. "If for some reason the drone is spotted, stop immediately and get back."

"For sure, we'll be able to see if anyone spots us. We'll be in and out quickly, and we'll have good pictures for you to use."

Ron said, "Great. Thank you for all the work you've done. Be safe and don't take any chances."

"So, you're ready for tomorrow?" Joe asked.

"Ready," the leader answered.

CHAPTER 71

Lansing, Before First Light, Thursday, May 27

Loretta was still upset about what she had seen on Monday. It had been a whirlwind since she saw Ann—and she could not find out anything. She wanted to get Ann out of that place, but she had to have evidence that something strange was going on. She knew and trusted Ann, and she wanted to do what Ann asked, but she had to be sure. She kept pacing around her apartment and looking over information she had gathered, but there were no answers.

She talked to the papers on her table like they were actually listening. "Maybe I just have to do something without proof. I have to help Ann. Who could I get to help? Who can I trust?" Only a few names came to Loretta, but she was certain there was one person she could trust, but then she knew she might have to do this herself. "I'm going to get Ann out of there."

Loretta checked her Glock and grabbed a backup weapon and a knife. She went to her garage and pulled out another Glock she had in her car. She said, "This will be for Ann. We're going to get her out."

Loretta took out the floor plan again and decided she knew how she was going to get Ann out. She gathered some tools from her garage, placed them in her trunk, folded the blueprint of the building, packed some food and drink, and she was ready.

Well, almost ready. "What am I forgetting?" she whispered to herself. "I better take two bulletproof vests, some zip ties, something to jimmy the lock on the door, and pepper spray."

She packed a few more items and she was off. Forty-five minutes later, she was at the building. It was still dark, but she could not see any lights on. "Is everyone asleep?" she asked herself. Then she said, "I better stop talking to myself or, if someone hears me, they are going to put me away."

She parked the car in an inconspicuous place not far from the building, then she took out the bag of things she would need and headed to the side door. It was locked. She knew this and took out her tools. It wasn't long before she was inside. She knew where to go, but she was a lot farther from the room where Ann was than where she entered on Monday.

Loretta walked slowly, Glock in her hands, quiet as a mouse. She slipped down a very long, dark hallway. She was depending on her memory to get her to the room. Soon she was near the place where she saw the sentry. No one was there. She climbed the stairs, got to the landing, turned right and tried the door. It was open, and it was dark. She moved slowly to the couch, clicked on her flashlight, but there was no one there. She walked around the room, but Ann was nowhere to be seen. She searched every corner. No Ann.

Loretta turned to leave when she mouthed, "Oh, no!" as the lights went on.

CHAPTER 72

The Bunker, May 27, Afternoon

After talking to the trainers and getting the extra troops in place, Bill started pestering the barber's son. He felt something was not quite right, and he knew he was the one who had brought Peter to the bunker, so that made him nervous.

When Bill was nervous, he talked even more than he usually did. Later when he was on the parade grounds talking to some of the troops about this and that, he asked, "Do you think anyone here is not one-hundred percent into the plan?"

One of the guys who was standing nearby said, "I don't know for sure, but I think there are quite a few here who just want the money. They're not interested in being a part of the real action."

Bill was surprised. "You think there are more than one then? Do you think they will act when it's time?"

"Not sure if they will, but what the heck, we have a lot who are in it for the right reasons."

"Is there anyone in particular you would single out? I mean anyone who might not fight when the time comes?"

"Who knows for sure? What about you? Are you in it for the right reasons?"

Bill was insulted. This man was asking him if he was one-hundred percent in. "Of course!"

"Well, you're from Colewin, right? Seems like a lot of you are just here for the wrong reasons."

Bill thought he had better end the conversation. He did not like being the one who was being questioned. "Yeah, well, I'm good. See ya!"

"We're going to keep our eyes on you." A few of the others joined in and agreed. Bill left the group, muttering as he walked away. He was upset and confused. How could they question him? He had been a big part of identifying others who were working against them. He decided to keep to himself for the rest of the day.

CHAPTER 73

Lansing, Michigan, May 27, Morning

Loretta's first instinct was to point her Glock. It was a quick move, and she ducked behind a chair in the room, but when she looked, it was the agent who had let her in previously, and he was not in an offensive position. In fact, he had his hands up and he looked stressed. Loretta said, "And where is Ann?"

"I wish I knew."

"What's going on?"

"Let me explain. Could you please put your weapon away?"

"Not yet. I want some answers. First of all, where were you when I came in here? Were you waiting to ambush me?"

"Hardly. Let me tell you what's happened since yesterday morning."

"Go ahead."

"I came in at my usual time and checked on Ann. She was fine. She had just gotten up and was having some breakfast. The boss came in as usual with those three I told you about, and he came right to me and said that I was no longer needed here because Ann would be released soon."

"Released? When?"

"Well, I'm not sure."

"The boss told me to leave, and I packed up all my stuff, but then I noticed that he went right to the room where they met all the time. I took a chance and snuck close to see what was going on. They were in a heated discussion. I couldn't tell what it was, but the door was ajar, so I walked closer and then I could hear. They were plotting some type of takeover. It involved the

Governor. I'm really not sure of that, but it sounded like that's where the conversation was going at first, so I kept listening."

"And…?"

"They were definitely planning some type of takeover of the government in Michigan. They also had someone on speaker phone, and that surprised me—they were on a land line and the boss had told me there were no phones or Wi-Fi in this place—and they were for sure discussing taking down the federal government with that person—not real soon, but down the road."

"Ann was right, then. I should have acted on her requests."

"What requests?"

"She begged me to contact the Governor and Joe Deluca in the U.P. She said I need to learn what was going on in the U.P., and then I would understand why we weren't allowed to investigate up there. She also wanted a line to the President to discuss these issues. She gave me a couple of numbers to try."

"Man, we have to do something. I had to leave when they started to break up the meeting, but I stayed outside hiding in my vehicle. They all left, but I did not see Ann. I went back in to get her, but she was gone. Somehow, they took her out of here. It looked like a struggle when I came in. Look at the kitchen."

Loretta turned and saw the mess in the kitchen. Everything was out of place and some of the kitchen utensils were on the floor. "We have to act, and we have to act now."

"How do we find Ann?"

"I'm not sure. Let's make a few phone calls and see what we can do."

CHAPTER 74

Near the Bunker, the South Side in the Woods, Friday, May 28

The troops had already finished breakfast and had gotten ready for their daily training. The last group was preparing to leave on Tuesday as planned, so their training was complete, and they were packing things in a few trucks and getting everything in order to leave. They had only two more nights left at the bunker, so they had a lot of time on their hands. Most of the troops were just loafing around doing a lot of nothing while the trucks were readied.

The drone was set to go. Only two people were with it to keep the numbers down, just in case. The drone had a great camera, and the pictures would be perfect for what they needed. They sent it aloft and directed it to the area they needed to probe. It was the woods around the bunker, and the open area between the bunker on the north and the trees on the south. They also needed to see how the barracks lined up with their sight lines from the front of the bunker in case they had opposition, and they needed to know what type of protection they would have to bring in, if any. Of course, it all depended on the layout of the trees.

The drone was up less than five minutes and their reconnaissance turned out well. As they were flying over the area near the barracks, they were spotted. Someone yelled, "Hey, is that one of our drones?"

The trainers looked up and realized they were being observed. They ordered everyone to open fire on the drone. When the two young people saw what was about to happen, they directed the drone out of the area as fast as they could. It made it.

The problem was that now the bunker people would be on high alert after spotting the drone—and that could be a problem. The drone was retrieved and the two young people packed it away, jumped on their machines, and drove as fast as they could to Colewin.

The trainers ordered ten men to take a truck and head in the direction of the drone. They were on it in no time. They flew down the hill, took a wild right turn onto the road below the hill and immediately saw two vehicles in the distance. The truck bounced around and jostled the troops inside. They began to yell. "Hey, take it easy. We're getting knocked around back here."

The driver didn't much care. He kept pursuing. The road smoothed out and the truck was able to make good time.

CHAPTER 75

The Hideout, May 28

Joe had just heard from the young people who had the drone. Everything went well they said. They got great video, and they were about to leave. Joe was happy the first part of the plan had gone well; however, he did not know about the truck.

He and Ron were discussing the video from the drone that they had received. It was exactly what they needed. Ron was ready to do some training with some of the inexperienced people, so he stepped out of the cabin. That's when Joe's phone rang.

Joe looked at the number, but he did not recognize it—so he did not pick up. A few minutes later Joe's phone buzzed. He received a text that said the following:

Joe, you don't know
me, but I work with
Ann. She gave me
your number. She's in
trouble and we need
to talk.

Joe took a look at the text and was instantly uncertain about what he should do. He thought, *who is this?* Could he be sure it was Ann's co-worker? Is it someone trying to identify our position? If so, they probably already have it. Do we need to move again? On the other hand, the last time he saw Ann, she was being escorted by those two agents. She said not to worry, but now he knew he should be worried. The phone rang again. This time he picked it up.

Someone said, "Hello."

Joe did not answer. He waited a few seconds, and then the person on the other end continued.

"Joe, this is Loretta, I'm a close friend of Ann's and an FBI agent. I also have another agent here with me. You need to trust us. Ann is in trouble."

Joe finally spoke, "What kind of trouble?"

"She's missing, and she had earlier given me your number and said I need to listen to what you have to say about what is going on in the U.P. She said there is some group trying to overthrow the government. They want to set up their own governor here. She also said I need to contact our Governor because someone is planning to kidnap her like they did in 2020."

"Sounds about right, Loretta. We've been tracking this group for some time now. That is exactly what they're doing. Do you know anything about the troops they have been sending all over the country?"

"A little. Ann did not go into many details. We have been tracking some type of paramilitary groups down here. They turn up here and there, but this is the first that I've been this close to what is going on. Our boss has intentionally kept us out of the loop."

"Figures. They have people in all sorts of places: political, military, and corporate, you name it. They have several places all over the country training men to join their ranks. They are very persuasive because they pay very well, and a lot of men have joined. By the way, they don't enlist women in the ranks, but they do in government and politics. Again, they pay well and they prey on people who are dissatisfied with the way things are going."

"I wasn't aware how widespread this was. I guess we've been kept in the dark."

"What about Ann?"

"We don't know what happened to her. We're going to begin an investigation, but we can't trust anyone. So far, it's one of the agents you met that I just mentioned and me. Not such a great start, but we'll do what we can to find Ann."

"All right. We have quite an operation going on up here. I can't speak about it, but it should be over soon, I hope. Maybe we can get some information for you if everything goes well."

"That sounds good."

"I can't stay on any longer, but keep in touch. I'll fill you in about some things if we can meet soon. I'd rather not put information over the airwaves."

"Good point. Thanks. Will keep you informed."

CHAPTER 76

The Bunker, May 28

Bill had seethed most of the previous day, and he had talked to the trainers, but they thought he was crazy. He wasn't satisfied—and he was dismayed that anyone would think he was not totally into this. He decided to visit Bates again.

Bates saw Bill walk up and pound on the door. "That guy drives me crazy. Here he is again. What could he want this time?" Bates opened the door, but again he did not let Bill in. He kept his foot jammed into the back of the door. "What in hell's name do you want now? You can't keep coming in here like you're my buddy. I don't appreciate it, and I don't like people in general, and you in particular."

Bill was not phased. "I know, I know, but I think some of these troops are not into doing what has to be done. They're not in one hundred percent!"

"What makes you think that?"

"I, I'm not sure. Just a feeling."

"Let me tell you. The people who have come through this place have all been vetted by several of us. That's how we were able to weed out so many. You should know. You helped us catch some of the bad ones. The only ones that haven't had a thorough vetting are the three you sent in, but I've been checking and they seem all right, so stop your crying and don't come in here anymore. You'll be shipping out soon anyway, so enjoy the last few weeks you have."

Bill did not say anything. He just turned and left. He talked to himself as he meandered back to the barracks. "If they don't care, then I don't either. I just hope this all works."

The hideout and other places, May 28

Joe and Ron were both concerned about Ann, but there was not much they could do from Colewin. They hoped that Loretta could find her soon and let them know. Joe and Ron had been working on a plan for some time to take over the bunker and take Bates captive. It would be an ambitious endeavor, but they thought it might be their only chance. Their current plan involved everyone that they could. Most kept training with Ron each day, but they had to work around people's lives and schedules. It all made Joe very anxious.

Right now, their only job was to wait for the two young people to return from the bunker area. Joe thought they should be back soon, but he did not know if they ran into anything, so he was concerned.

Back on the road the two young people were moving as fast as they could, one in front of the other. They knew they were in trouble if the truck got close enough because they would probably shoot at them. They rounded a curve and took it on two wheels, the first four-wheeler shuddered and trembled, but it made it through. The second machine did the same, but it hit a bump and the machine flew into the air, catapulting the driver into a large pine tree, high up in the branches. The machine continued to fly through the woods and bounced several times, turned over, and crashed into a large stump. The machine was deep in the woods and concealed from view.

The driver was unconscious, cut and scraped badly, lying high on a branch, and hidden from view. It did not look good since she was bleeding profusely, and the young man on the first four-wheeler did not even see what happened!

The troop truck made the same curve and took it on two wheels. One of the troops in the back almost fell out, and the rest had to hang on for dear life. The driver did not stop even though the guys in the back yelled and pounded on the back window. He was determined to catch the machines.

The young man on the first machine reached the road to Colewin and looked back to check on his friend, but she was not there. He panicked. He just sat and looked down the road. Then he saw the truck, and he knew he had to lose them and then go back and look for the girl. He thought that if they were still following him, they must not have caught her, so he blew out of there, heading for Joe's hideaway. He knew they would not pursue him in Colewin.

The driver in the truck followed until they came to the road to Colewin. Then they had a decision to make. Their orders did not allow them to enter the town. Should they follow the machine? They did.

The hideout, same day

Joe was sure that the plan they had prepared was a good one, but like all operations, he knew it must have flaws, and he was worried he might get some people hurt and not even succeed.

Ron came running in and yelled to Joe. "The young kid is back from the drone operation, but the girl is lost. He was followed for most of the escape from the area, but he lost them in the last few miles. He's not sure where she is, but we're going to take a few people and head that way to look. He said he probably lost her on the big curve because he had seen her just prior to that. We'll also need to keep people on guard to make sure they don't find this place."

Joe was stunned. "What do you mean he was followed?"

"There was a military truck with armed troops that was chasing after them."

"That's bad if they're coming into Colewin with weapons now! I hope you can find her, and that she's okay. Those young people have been a great help. Go ahead. Take three others and see what you can find. Keep me informed."

CHAPTER 77

Lansing, Michigan, May 28

Loretta and her agent friend had scoured the areas where they felt would be places that the boss might keep Ann, but they had no luck. They wanted to involve other people, but they did not know who they could trust. They needed to know what the boss was planning to do. Loretta had called Ann's husband, and he said that he had not heard anything, but that the boss said her operation might take some time, so he was not worried.

Loretta was.

It took some doing, but Loretta convinced the young agent, Aaron, to get his partner involved. She asked him if he thought he might be involved in the mess that the boss was in, but Aaron was sure he wasn't. "We're close, and we have worked cases together for a year, and I've known him for ten years before that. I know him. He's good."

"All right. Now, I'm not sure you want to do what I am planning, but it is the only way out of this. Unless you think that the boss will meet with the militia again."

"He might. He's been meeting with them often for the last month. We could watch the place and follow one of them."

"We could. Do you think your partner would help?"

"He might. He was upset when we had to get Ann from Mackinac Island. He worked with her and said she was top-notch FBI, but he also took orders from our boss like we all do."

"If he's willing to help, and we can get to one of them, we won't have to go after the boss."

"Go after the boss! Are you kidding?"

"We have to find out what happened to Ann, or this whole thing goes out of control."

"I'm in if we follow one of the three, but I'm not sure about going after the boss."

"We wouldn't hurt him. We'd just interrogate him. We'd try to keep it as secret as possible and hold him hostage in his office."

"Let's see if we can first follow one of those he meets with."

"That'll be the plan for now. Contact your buddy and see what he says. Then give me a call. I'll be at the building where Ann was held so I can do some surveillance."

"I'll see what I can do."

CHAPTER 78

The Road to the Bunker, Earlier on May 28

Ron and the young person and the two people they chose, drove to the spot where the girl had last been seen. Ron noted the bump in the road and looked around at the very thick woods. It was a dense forest, and the pine trees were very tall and thick with foliage. They drove right past the curve in the road and then turned around and headed back toward Colewin, searching for any sign of the girl and her four-wheeler. They were moving very slowly looking for any sign when they heard a vehicle coming from the direction of Colewin. Ron yelled, "Hide in the woods. This could be trouble."

They all moved their four-wheelers off the road, two to one side and two to the other. Ron was hiding on the left side facing Colewin. He backed in as far as he could to conceal his machine and himself when he backed into a recently broken small tree. Ron turned and looked and saw something strange near a huge stump. He walked farther and saw the four-wheeler.

Ron did not investigate right away because the noise of a vehicle from town was heading closer. He turned and saw a military truck. As it passed, he saw several men with assault rifles crammed in the back. This was not good.

Once the truck was passed, he called the others who investigated. The young guy, Jacob, knew that the four-wheeler was the one the girl had been riding.

"She must not have negotiated the curve, but what happened to her?"

Ron told the others, "Move out and look everywhere on this side of the road. If we don't see anything, we'll move to the other side."

Jacob said, "Maybe she walked away from this."

Ron looked at him with wide eyes and said, "No way. She was thrown off her machine."

They searched for thirty minutes with no luck.

Suddenly Jacob called to Ron, "Hey, if she was thrown off her machine, she could be in a tree somewhere."

Ron had two people go to the other side of the road to search, and he and Jacob searched the side with the four-wheeler. Ron spotted something in one of the trees. It was her. "Hey, she's up here. Help me get her down."

The others came, and Jacob climbed the tree. She had cuts and scratches all over, her head was bleeding, and it looked like her arm was severely broken. He could see the bone sticking out.

After much maneuvering, he was able to get her down. She looked pale, unconscious, and had lost a lot of blood. They did as much as they could. Ron said, "We need to get her to the hospital, now!" Ron knew they needed help and a vehicle to put her in, so he called Joe and he sent Paul out with a truck. Twenty-five minutes later, they were heading for the hospital.

When Ron returned, he told Joe the whole story.

Joe's first reaction was fear for the young girl. His face was red and he broke out in a sweat. "How is she? Will she make it?"

"Not sure, Joe. It did not look good."

"I feel responsible. I sent them out there to fly the drone. I should have had one of us or one of the others go with them."

"I'm not sure that would have helped, Joe. You might have gotten more people in trouble."

"I just hope she's all right."

Ron said, "We need to do something soon. They had a truck full of troops out on the road. They are getting very aggressive. We have to stop them. They have never sent military vehicles into town. We've seen their troops before, but they never openly carried guns in Colewin!"

"I know. We have to go in as planned. We'll probably have two fewer people."

Ron agreed. "Right, one of the young guys went with the girl. He contacted her parents and they are on the way. Paul will return and help. How many does that give us?"

"We'll have about two dozen. That should work. We're at a disadvantage no matter what, but we'll have the barber's son on the inside and the element of surprise, so that should help."

CHAPTER 79

Lansing, Michigan, Friday, May 28

Aaron visited his buddy and fellow FBI agent after work on Friday. They had a plan every Friday to meet at a bar in downtown Lansing. It was an old family bar, and they liked the clientele. Neither was big on loud and crazy music, and this place just played old quiet songs. You could visit and actually hear each other, plus they had old high booths so their conversation was somewhat private.

Jerry was alone in the booth when Aaron walked in. He had a smile and two beers on the table. They both liked to drink the local brews, and Jerry had ordered that.

"How's it going, Aaron? You still working on that case with Ann?"

"That's *exactly* what I want to talk to you about." Aaron said this with a lot of force and sat down hard on the padded seat.

"Whoa! Take it easy on the furniture! You look and sound upset, man. What's up?"

"We've got a problem. Not us exactly. I'd say Ann has a problem. I've been watching her as I told you, but she suddenly disappeared."

"Disappeared? People don't just disappear!"

"This one did, and I think I know who made her disappear." Aaron went into a long explanation about what had transpired the last several days. He explained about the boss meeting with the militia and about how Loretta had approached him.

Jerry was not surprised. If anything, he was nodding his head and agreeing. "I hear you. Loretta's been driving me crazy. She's been asking all kinds of questions."

Aaron was nervous about asking him to help, but he had to find out where Jerry stood. He finally came out and asked him. "So, could you see yourself helping us find Ann?"

"Us. You mean you and Loretta?"

"Yes."

"Hey, I wouldn't mess with that lady. Like I said she's been driving me crazy, but I like her, and if you believe her, and if she says something is amiss, then it is. She's one tough lady who knows her stuff. I was always a little upset about the trip we made to Mackinac Island. Ann and Loretta are the best. We need to do something."

CHAPTER 80

The Hideout, Sunday, May 30

It was just over a week until the day that Joe wanted to go after the bunker and hopefully get some answers. He had a very good picture of what the place looked like, thanks to the drone pictures, so now he could plan the attack. He told Ron they had to get everyone together, but they could not have everyone at the hideout. Too many people heading in this direction would give everything away, and they would probably be compromised.

Ron agreed. "Can we plan to meet at Paul and Sarah's place?"

"Exactly what I was thinking. Let's do that. I'll okay it with Paul and Sarah, and we'll have to get the word to everyone without using phones. Let's pass the word to Matt, Charlie, and the barber when they come here today. They can each contact a group. That should do it."

"Good idea."

Joe and Ron brought up the video they had of the base and began to plan their attack. They drew a picture on a large sheet of paper and transferred it to a transparency to project it when the group was together. They did not want to put anything about the plan on their phones for obvious reasons, so they decided to use some old tech.

When the drawing was completed, both Ron and Joe looked at it and laughed.

Ron just chuckled, "Man, that's the best we could do? I guess we aren't artists in any way."

"No, I never did do well with that kind of work, but I think they'll get the point, don't you?"

"I think it's good enough for what we need. We just have to have everyone pay attention to the plan we've come up with, and we'll need to practice a bit too. There won't be any room for error. If one thing goes wrong, it could blow everything up. Remember, after the next truck leaves, there'll still be about one hundred and seventy-five troops there."

'Yeah, that's too bad, but it'll be our best chance. Twenty-four against one hundred and seventy-five—seven to one odds. Not very good."

"But we have one other problem," Ron added.

"I know. How do we get inside the bunker? Do we blow the doors off? If we do, we have all the troops to contend with, but we can't pry that door. It's thick and solid. We could run a vehicle into it."

"That might work. It wouldn't make as much noise, and it would be quick."

Joe was concerned about this part of the plan. He paced back and forth shaking his head. He finally sat down, with elbows on the table and hands on his chin. "We've got to figure this out as quickly as possible. We need to meet with everyone soon to get the plan out there."

"I wonder," Ron added, "if Bates sleeps all night or if he still works late. I know we've heard he works late into the night. If he's up, could we do something to get him to open the door?"

"That's something to think about."

"The girls are coming back from getting supplies, let's see what they think," Ron said.

"We could check with Charlie. He has access to a lot more military equipment than anyone around here except for the bunker. Maybe he has an idea."

CHAPTER 81

Lansing, Michigan, Sunday, May 30

Loretta and the two agents had been doing their homework and had also been watching the building where Ann had been held in hopes of following someone. On Sunday, she decided to meet with Ann's husband, and then go back to the building to keep watch. She knew she finally had to tell Ann's husband that something was amiss. She thought they might need his help, and she wanted him updated on everything. He did not take it well.

"The boss said she was on a mission—something clandestine, he said. How is she now in trouble? Is it about the mission?"

"There never was a mission. She was held captive like I said, and it was the boss who was keeping her there. I have two other agents who can corroborate this whole story."

"But the boss? Why would he get Ann in trouble and keep her captive?"

"It's a long story, but it has to do with a plan to take down the government." Loretta went on to discuss all that she knew. When she was finished, Ann's husband was now on board and ready to do anything he could to get her back. Unfortunately, he had no training as her partners had, but he had been in the military, so he knew something about weapons and had some basic training, but little training for what would come next.

Jerry sat in the car parked outside of Ann's home. He was waiting for Loretta. Aaron was watching the building for any activity. Jerry, Aaron, and Loretta were going to follow one of the men if the boss met with anyone today, if he followed his regular routine. Loretta came out and jumped into the driver's seat. "He's in," she said, "but I'm not sure how we can use him. Do you think the boss will meet with the militia today? It is a Sunday."

Jerry answered, "I'm not sure, but the way things have been moving lately, Aaron thinks he might. No call from Aaron yet, so we might as well go over and park on the far side of the building."

"Good idea. I really can't believe this is happening." Loretta cranked the car, put it in gear, and sped out as quickly as she could. They weren't far from the place, but she was in a hurry to do something. On the way, Jerry's phone buzzed. It was Aaron. "Our boss is here and so are three others. All in camo and armed."

"We're on the way. Sit tight until we get there."

CHAPTER 82

The Hideout, Sunday, May 30

Charlie, Matt, and the barber showed up on time. The barber had another report from his son that the semi would leave late today. They would load and probably be off by 11:00 p.m. He also said that Bill was getting nosy and was hanging around his son and was still acting weird. He gave them all the details about the guards. It looked like they would have two guards on the old road along with the four on the hill, and six at the gate, two in each tower.

"That's a change then. However, we'll need three people on the old road to take out those two guards, if necessary," Joe said. "Any other information?"

"Not much," Matt said.

Charlie spoke up. "I wasn't able to get a whole lot of silencers. We had five. I picked up four more. Will that be enough?"

"It'll have to do." Joe was concerned, but no plan is perfect, and he knew he would have to do without some things. "One thing we might need is some vehicle to ram the door. We'd rather not use explosives. That would alert everyone."

Ron said, "We think one good ram of the door wouldn't make enough noise to wake everyone and it would be over quickly—but we're not sure if a vehicle could take out that door."

Charlie was all smiles. "Don't you worry none. I got this. How many days do I got?"

"We're still planning on Sunday, if all goes well, so we have a week." Joe was not sure if they had to move the date up, but as of now it was June 7.

"I can get just the thing you need. It's used by the military and law enforcement. I know just the guy. We might need some cash though."

"What is it that you're referring to?"

"It's a vehicle made to ram structures. It's armored and has a battering ram on the front. It'll do the job."

"How much cash?" Ron asked.

"Not sure. Let me get aholt a him and I'll let you know."

"Charlie, can't he just help us out?" Joe said.

"I don' know. Well, all right, I'll talk to him and see what he can do."

"Good. I mean we really need the vehicle." Joe had never seen the vehicle, but he had heard about it, and he knew it was exactly what they needed, but he was hoping Charlie's friend would be with them and just want to help. He knew he could come up with some cash, if need be, but…

"Is there anything else I should ask my son?" the barber inquired.

"Not right now, but we need to get the group together soon. We have a plan and a diagram, over there on the table. It's not much, but they'll be able to get the picture. Who are our best shots, Ron?"

"We have some good ones. The two sentries who watch the gate are crack shots, and I'm working with two other sentries who are good. They'll pick off a bullseye at 100 meters. Tommy is a good one and so is my wife, Shanice. They're the best. Joette can shoot that compound bow too. She hits the target every time, and is accurate at 30 meters, and it's quiet, so it's like having another silencer. Paul is very good using his own rifle. The rest use the M-16. It's a good weapon for what we need.

"All right. Let's set the meeting for tomorrow evening when everyone can get there. Let's say eight-thirty. How's that?"

Everyone agreed. They took the time to look at the map Joe had drawn and seemed confident it would do the job. They talked for another thirty minutes about the plan and then broke up until Monday.

CHAPTER 83

Lansing, Sunday, May 30, Afternoon

They had decided to use three vehicles just in case, so Loretta drove Jerry to get his car. They waited at the building where the boss was meeting. It was about two hours from the time that Aaron had told them about the meeting when three men walked out of the front door. The boss left by a side entrance. Aaron spotted the boss, and Loretta saw the three men head to separate vehicles.

She noticed that two were older and a third was much younger. The two older guys moved to their trucks and stood in front and talked for some time. The young person who was driving a smaller truck, left by himself while the two were talking. Loretta was on the phone with the other two agents and gave them a heads-up. "We're following a black Ford Ranger. Let's be smart and follow at a distance. We can't afford to lose him."

"Where is he?"

"I'm at the front door. He's heading east on Michigan Avenue. Follow my car."

Aaron was right there in no time. "I see you, and I see the truck."

"Same here," Jerry said.

They followed for a bit and then he turned. Loretta said, "He's turning left on Beal Street. Don't stay too close to me. I'll relay everything. Keep your lines open."

"Gotcha," Jerry said.

Aaron repeated the same thing.

"Say, he's turning into an apartment building. This might be his place. Do you see it on the right?"

"Got it." Jerry said.

"Make sure we all park in different places. Spread out."

Loretta entered the parking lot and parked about four spaces down from the Ford Ranger. She watched as he parked the truck and walked to the front door. Aaron and Jerry parked several spots down from Loretta, Aaron on the left and Jerry on the right. Loretta ran quickly to catch the door in case it might lock. She was almost too close to him.

He threw the door open and hurried in. She grabbed it just as it was about to close. She was in. She kept her distance and watched where he went. He entered an elevator and she saw that it indicated the third floor. Loretta found the stairs and ran as fast as she could. The two agents did not make the door, so she was on her own.

Loretta was winded when she reached the third floor, but she had almost beaten the elevator. She saw him walk down the hall and turn right. She followed. He took another right and entered a room—321. Loretta again ran as fast as she could and let in the two agents. They all bolted up the stairs to Room 321. It was going to be a long evening.

CHAPTER 84

The Bunker, May 30

Bates was all smiles because he had the second-to-last semi ready to go. He sat at his computer and contacted the boss to give him the update. He would speak to the old boss because of his loyalty to the man. He sent an encrypted message.

Boss,

We have the semi ready to go. All the preparations are completed. We'll have one more to send the last group out, and then we'll load the military trucks and empty the base. When should we send the last group? How do you want us to leave the bunker? Let me know and I'll get on it.

The old boss read the message and was happy, but he knew that they could not pull this off until January 2024, but preferably January 2025. He was concerned because the new boss wanted it to happen soon. They had discussed a few dates, but getting everything coordinated was going to take time. He knew that, but the new boss did not, and he did not understand logistics or timelines. Somehow, he had to slow the new boss down. He replied to Bates.

Bates,

Keep everything going as planned. We can get troops in place and have them get ready for the event, but it is going to take some time. It may be a year or more out as I see it. We have two helicopters that will land there. They are to be delivered to places in Michigan and Wisconsin, so get ready for that. I'll give you more information at a later date. The bunker is to be destroyed when we no longer need it. You will move on to your next location helping to coordinate the event. It should be around January 2024 at the earliest, but my plan has it happening later. When you are given the word, make sure you destroy all buildings at the site and get rid of any evidence that we were there. You know the drill!

Bates was not happy. He thought that he would be out of the bunker much sooner, and that the event was imminent. That's what he had heard from the other boss, but he knew the old boss was best for the takeover, and he was not going to complain. He'd put in his time and do what he had to do.

He thought that he could make it for another winter or two since they would definitely be his last, but he'd just have to take some time off and leave the place more often. This past year he had been in the bunker almost every day, 24/7. He was bored with it, but he had amassed a pile of cash, which he would use to set himself up someplace warm. He could buy a mansion now, and he could have anything he wanted.

He also thought about his old buddy, Wyatt, who was killed by the cops. *Wyatt wasn't really smooth. He made too many mistakes, and he was kind of crazy, but we got along great. Hope I can find people like him to hang with when this is over, but then who cares?*

Bates got another beer, burped, settled back into his comfy chair, turned back to the screen, and started searching for how to make more money. He was having a great time.

CHAPTER 85

Lansing, May 30, early evening

Loretta was smart. She knew how to trick this young guy into opening his door so they could get in the apartment without having to break it down. She had already gotten herself and the agents masks for cover. She also had them wear all black, just in case. She had one of the agents run down and check the name on room 321. It was Tyler something. The last name wasn't clear, but it began with a J. She was glad there was no peephole on the door.

When the two agents were hidden—one on each side of the door, she walked right to the front of it and knocked. "Hey, Tyler, this is Marsha. Open up. I don't have all day."

Tyler heard the knock and wondered who it could be. When he heard the name Marsha, he was confused. "Marsha? Who the hell is Marsha?" He walked to the door and asked, "Who's this?"

"Marsha. You know. Come on. Don't play dumb."

Now Tyler was really confused. He murmured, "Marsha? Was she at the party the other night? No way. I don't remember anyone with that name."

"Say, I got the exact liquid refreshments you mentioned. We can have a party." She thought, *nothing like a young girl who wants to party, and a boy with an imagination!*

Now that sounded like something Tyler would get into. "Sounds like fun even if I don't know you."

The door opened and Loretta pushed it into Tyler's head.

He had time to say, "What the hell?" before Aaron and Jerry had him on the ground, hands and legs zip-tied, and mouth taped. Loretta walked in. All three were masked. The apartment was small and messy. There wasn't much furniture, and dirty dishes were all over the counter. Blankets on the couch made Loretta think that he must sleep there.

"Mmphf," was all they heard as she turned her gaze to the young man.

Loretta said, "We need some information and we need it quickly, otherwise this will not end well for you." The two agents picked him up and tied him to a chair in his kitchen.

Loretta spoke. Her partners were not to say anything. "OK, lover boy, tell us about the meeting you had today." When she roughly ripped the tape off of his mouth, it tore off some of his skin.

"Ow! I'm bleeding! Shit! What is this?"

"The meeting. What was it about?"

"What meeting?"

"Don't get cute on us again. The one at the old building down on East Michigan. There were four of you—and one was an FBI agent."

"Hey, no worries if that's what this is about. He's with us. I mean that he's part of the plan to take down the Michigan government…and the country."

"He is, huh? And where is the woman who was being kept there?"

"What woman?"

"You know. The other FBI agent."

"Her? Like all those people, she's been eliminated. Had to get rid of her because she was in the way too much."

Loretta almost fainted when she heard that, but she knew he must be lying. They would not kill an FBI agent.

"So, you're part of this, right? Just checking up on me? Well, I'm good. I'm all in. I heard about people being checked to be sure they're in. I'm one hundred percent in, and so is my dad and my uncle. You probably know them. They were there too."

"Yeah, we know them. Where is this female agent again?"

"Like I said, she was eliminated."

"Meaning?"

"Say, if you don't know that, then how are you part of this group?"

"Good question. What happened to her?"

"No longer with us."

"No chance." Loretta was all choked up. If what he was saying was true, then this has gone farther than she ever imagined. She was sick to her stomach and tears were running down her face. The two agents had slumped over and were also very upset, knowing that they had brought her back to Lansing.

Loretta pulled herself together. "Where's the body?"

"No body. She was taken to Cheboygan to the warehouse to be disposed of. I'm not saying anymore until you call my father and uncle. I need to talk to them about this."

This was almost too much for the three agents. They had all they could do to keep it together, so they huddled and decided to get out of this place and see what they could do.

Loretta was convinced they needed to take him somewhere safe, so they waited until dark and the two agents slipped him down the back stairs into the trunk of Loretta's car. Loretta, in the meantime, left the place all neat and clean like nothing had happened there, wiped down any fingerprints, locked the door, and left.

CHAPTER 86

Colewin, Paul and Sarah's Place, Monday, May 31

It was late afternoon when Joe and Ron had completed the plan and had everyone assigned. By 8:30 p.m., they were all there—all twenty-four. They had come in groups to keep the number of vehicles down, and they hid their vehicles around the woods as best they could.

"We've arranged to have you all in the living room," Paul said. "Some of you will have to sit on the floor if that's okay."

Everyone agreed that would be fine. Most of the older ones sat on the couch and the chairs while the young people took the floor. Paul and Sarah had drawn all the shades and kept the house as dark as they could. Everyone needed to be in on the plan, so there were no sentries. Joe had transferred his plan to a transparency. He used an old overhead projector and projected it on the wall between two windows. Then he and Ron began to lay out the plan.

Joe started by saying, "Everyone, this is a risky plan. We have only twenty-four of us, and they have about 175 of them. We do have one person on the inside, but our only other advantage is that we have the element of surprise, so if anyone wants out, now is the time."

He paused…. No one said a word. Joe continued, "All right, here's the plan. Take a look. Everyone, focus on the map on the wall. It's not great, but it is accurate—thanks to the two young people who took the drone pictures. By the way, Carly is in the hospital in Marquette. We received word today that she is in critical condition, but they said she is going to make it. Sheriff Daryl was nosing around wondering how it happened. We didn't give him much, and he left."

Ron added, "And she has company. Her parents are there and so are a few of her friends. If nothing else, let's do this for her and for Wayne, who is also in Marquette doing rehab. He is doing much better, but he and Cathy have chosen to do all of his rehab there. He told Tommy that he could not wait to get back to help us destroy these insurgents."

There was a lot of talking all at once, and everyone wanted to say something, so Joe asked for quiet. "Let's move ahead and deal with the questions about those two people later. We should keep this meeting as short as possible and then we'll have people leave a few at a time—just in case."

Everyone quieted down and Joe began. "Look at the map."

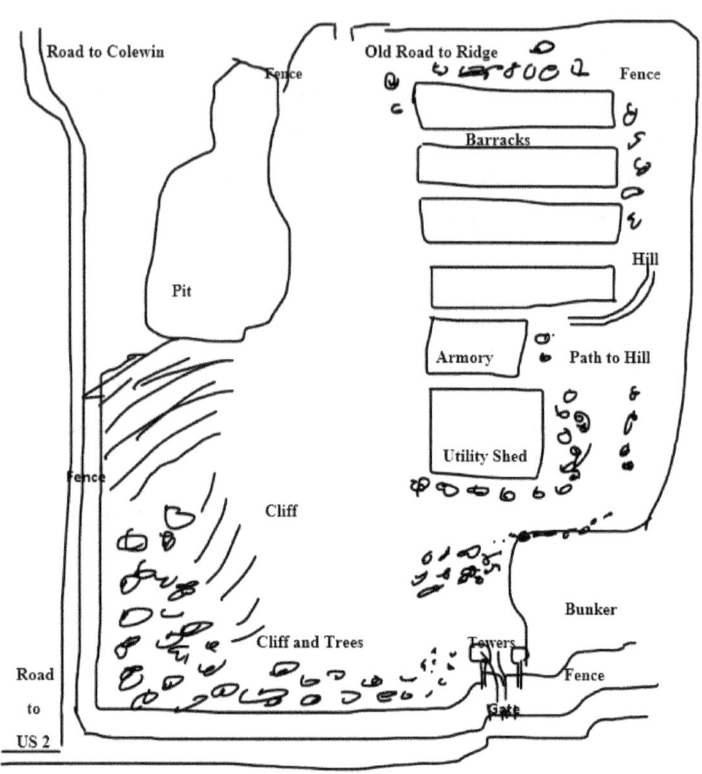

"Notice that the fence goes almost all the way around except where the bunker area is unapproachable." Everyone's eyes were on the projected map on the wall.

Joe continued, "First, I want to give you your positions. Notice that the hill has a fence separating the grounds from the forest. We'll need eight people up there. Unfortunately, we have only nine silencers, well ten, Shanice has one, and Joette has a compound bow that she can use."

A hand went up and someone spoke up. It was one of the sentries. "Joe, we have more silencers. We had three at the tunnel, and you only accounted for two, so that makes eleven."

"Great news. That'll help." Joe was happy to have one more silencer which would make the job a bit easier. "Okay, let me explain the rest. They have four guards up on the hill, spread out along the fence, and if we need to take them out, that will be Paul's crew."

Ron added, "Remember though. We only take out guards if necessary."

"Right," Joe said. "They no longer watch the tunnel area, so you could enter there, but be wary. We'll all need to be in place very early to observe each area and to report if anything changes. We text for the most part, but keep your phones on silent mode in case we need to talk. Remember, it's going to get very dark in the woods on the hill."

Joe looked up while he thought about the plan; then he continued. "There are some weak lights on the fence in spots, but not many. The old road has a spotlight as do the gates. The gates have floodlights there. We also have knowledge that the guards don't wear night vision goggles in the towers since there is so much light already. Those who are at the gate will have to stay back and hidden until given the word. The lights face the road. They won't be directly in their eyes, but they could be a problem. We might have to pick our spots in the woods carefully, so as not to be blinded by light."

Joe took a deep breath. "We'll need three people on the old road, two drivers for the military trucks that Charlie has, and two drivers for the armored vehicle, another vehicle that we can thank Charlie for acquiring. This is the vehicle that we will use to ram the doors. We'll need the rest of the force to attack the gates."

One of the sentries spoke up, "How are we going to attack the gates? They have six sentries, lights, and machine guns. I've been stationed there for a while, and they have a lot of fire power."

Joe and Ron both said, "We have a plan."

Then Joe said, "Here it is. We'll have nine people at the gate. We'll all enter through the trees and wait until dark. When we feel ready and everyone checks in—my guess it'll be somewhere between 2:00 and 3:00 a.m. When everyone checks in, that means we have eyes on the guards and could take them out. Remember it's going to be dark, but at the gates, we'll have those spotlights, so we won't be able to use night-vision goggles. We are limited in the number we have, so the hill people and the road people get the goggles."

"How many do we have?" Matt asked.

"Right now, we have enough for four people on the hill and two on the old road, however there is a light on the old road too, so they may not need them. I think that will be good."

Ron spoke up. "We'll make an effort to get a few more by Sunday, but we haven't had much luck recently, so don't get your hopes up."

"Paul, you, Matt, and Charlie have the most experience in this area, so you will spearhead the hill area. We'll need eight people all together. You and the three diggers, Jean, Francis, and Lucas, and the two younger sentries, Randy and Buck, are assigned there. You will ride in Paul's truck, so you will need only one vehicle. Any questions?"

Paul spoke up, "I think that's good. Eight of us should be able to handle the area. Matt and I have walked these woods for years, and we know every square inch. This area is a little out of the ordinary because the last few years, we have not been there as much with the bunker and all. Our tribe has always held this area as sacred until these clowns came here, so we'll be glad to get rid of them."

"I know you will do a great job. Let me know if you need anything when we're finished here."

"We'll probably need at least two silencers—in case."

"Got it. You will have three."

Ron added. "Tommy, you and Wendy and Frank will guard the old road. That work? You'll take two of the silencers. Your best approach will be from the ridge area."

"Sure. We got it. No problem."

Frank said, "Can't wait!"

Joe added. "Jack, you and your wife will drive us out there and stay with the trucks. Good?"

"Sounds good. We can do that."

"Everyone else is at the gates, that includes the four sharpshooters; our sons too, except that they will be in the armored vehicle," Ron said.

"That'll include Ron, Shanice, Joette, Sarah, as well as the four sharpshooters that we've been training, and me. So, that's where everyone will be. Questions?"

No one spoke or raised a hand.

Joe continued, "Our sharpshooters—Simon, Jacob, Seth, and Ted—will have silencers, so they can quietly take out the four guards in the towers. Ron and Shanice will be responsible for taking out the two on the ground, so they'll need just one silencer, since Shanice has her own. Joette will be the backup with her compound bow, and will help with the two on the ground. We'll be really close, so distance will not be a problem. If we're not successful, and someone from the gates fires a rifle or machine gun, we're going to call it off right there, and everyone will move out and head back to the hideout."

Joe stopped and took another deep breath. In the room, the only light was from the overhead projector, but he could see all the faces. They seemed determined. No one was showing any signs of backing out or being nervous. He had a very sound group of people. He was nervous, too, for Ron and he had come up with the plan, but they were both determined.

"When everyone has checked in, we'll begin."

Ron spoke up. "We'll contact you in two phases, so be alert to the signals."

"Yes, and once the first signal READY is given that means we are moving forward. The three people on the road, Tommy, Wendy, and Frank, will keep an eye on the two guards, and will only, if necessary, take out the two guards with their silencers. If they have to take them out, then they will move along the fence line to help the eight in the woods. If all the guards are taken out, we will continue only if this is done quietly and successfully. Otherwise, if there is a problem, we withdraw everyone."

Joe looked out at his team and continued. "If all is quiet, we'll give the signal, "BEGIN," which will start the order to take out the guards in the tower and on the ground. The sharpshooters and Ron and Shanice will have Sarah and Joette next to them to give them the signal as soon as they see "BEGIN," so all will be synchronized. No other guards should have to be taken out at this point."

Ron reiterated. "Remember that. We take out only those we have to."

"When the guards at the gate are taken out, Ron and I will cut the chain on the gate, and the others will double-check the guards we took out to be sure they are not a problem. Sarah and Joette will man the guns in the towers. The rest will set up a line facing the barracks in case their people are warned in some way."

Ron said, "If this is successful, you'll see the word: SUCCESS."

"This will begin the second phase that is the armored vehicle breaching the doors, and this is when you'll have to be alert to anyone who might hear any noise from the breaching. Take them out if necessary. Once inside the gate, the armored vehicle will take just a short run to keep out of sight and will break through the doors. It should be able to just push them in without a lot of noise."

Ron added. "If there are no problems, and this is successful, you'll see one word: BREACHED."

"Ron and I and four of the sharpshooters will move in and take Bates. My son and Ron's son will move the armored vehicle to the road, and Shanice will get it ready to drive down the hill. If we get Bates without incident, and no one is alerted by the noise, our sons will come back and get on the computer to see what they can find. If there is no time for that, they'll just load all the electronics, and take Bates gagged and blindfolded into the vehicle, and Shanice will drive it away. Everyone else will get the signal to leave. Ron and I will take to the road with the others and head to the waiting trucks."

Ron said, "If there is any trouble at any time, we'll call it off, we'll text WITHDRAW. Whenever you see that, move out right away."

"That's the plan," Joe said.

Seth, one of the sharpshooters, asked, "Will any of us have vests? You know when we storm into the bunker—if the guy is prepared and shoots?"

"We have a few vests, and they will go to the people storming the bunker, but I think we'll be a few short, so the people who will have to enter first will have the vests."

"Sounds good," Seth said.

Ron added, "There should be enough cover in the woods. The leaves are out enough, but make sure to wear camouflage. If you don't have any, see Charlie, and make sure if you take something to sit on that it's green."

"One other point. We have hats with mosquito nets. The mosquitos should not be too bad, but the black flies will be out. Everyone, grab a hat when you leave. Dress to cover all of your skin because we'll be in the woods for hours waiting for the right time. Sitting for a long time could get bad, and we don't want people slapping at flies or moving around. Make sure you have good shoes, nothing that would hamper getting around quickly, but no sneakers. You could step on something sharp or twist an ankle. It'll be wet in spots. We have some military boots if you don't have anything good for the woods."

Another hand went up, but at the same time, Joe's phone buzzed. He looked at the phone and knew he had to take it. "Ron, take this question. I need to take this call."

It was Loretta.

Joe immediately hoped they had found Ann. "Hello. This is Joe."

"Joe, Loretta here. I've got some bad news. Yesterday we followed one of the guys in that militia group that we now know our boss has joined, and he said Ann was sent to someplace in Cheboygan to be eliminated. We've been checking out everything we can, but can't come up with any leads. I can't force my hand by going to the boss because it seems like they have a huge network here that is trying to take down the Governor, and I believe in the same way as the last group that tried to do that. We've contacted the Governor and some people we can trust, and they're looking into that, but we want to find Ann."

"I hear you. You said, Cheboygan, right?"

"According to the militia guy we apprehended, that's what he said. He did not know anything else."

"I know the place. Ron and I were taken there last year to be eliminated, but we were able to escape. Let me tell you where it is, and you need to hurry. She could still be alive. They send many people there who are forced into some form of slavery or human trafficking. I can get you close. What in the world is going on when they can take out FBI agents and get away with it?"

Loretta agreed. "Something very evil is going on."

Joe then told Loretta how to get to the warehouse in Cheboygan, as well as all he knew about it. "Keep me posted. We have a situation here we're trying to deal with. Hope Ann is all right."

"Me too. Talk to you later. The Governor has given me some people to help, and we'll be headed to Cheboygan right away."

"Be careful."

Joe returned to the meeting, but now he was distracted, with Ann on his mind. They answered questions, and then had a few people at a time leave until everyone was gone. Joe, Joette, Ron, and Shanice were the last to leave. Tommy and Wendy stayed with Paul and Sarah.

CHAPTER 87

The Hideout, June 6, Late Afternoon

Joe was concerned about what Ann had found.

It had been almost a week, and Loretta had no word on Ann. She and a group of security people had gone to Cheboygan and found the warehouse. They were able to get help from the Governor's office, and had been given a force of twenty to deal with anything, but no one was there. What they found shocked them, however. Many large drums filled with acid. Why would anyone have gallons of acid lined up outside the building?

Loretta ordered the barrels to be picked up, and she had a large truck take and deliver them to a special plant for processing. It looked bad. She figured that someone had been dissolving something on the property, probably bodies. They found clothes and some identification. They were running the information to find out who the people might be.

After Joe heard all that Loretta reported, he was not surprised. He only hoped that Ann was somehow safe.

It was the night before the plan against the bunker would unfold. There were a lot of nerves and final preparations, but Joe was confident. Joe relayed what he had heard about Ann to Ron, Joette, and Shanice. They were all upset because they had all known Ann, and considered her a great friend, but they knew the type of people they were against right now, and they did not doubt anything. "Pure evil," Joe said.

"No conscience," Ron added.

"If we didn't have this plan ready to go, I'd go down and help Loretta. She sounds like she can handle whatever is going on, but who knows who's next? We were almost toast a couple of times ourselves."

Ron agreed, but he added, "Joe, we really need to focus on the task at hand right now. We'll have to help Loretta after tonight if all goes well."

Both Joette and Shanice agreed.

It was getting close to the time that they had to go. The word went out to all groups through a text, and everyone headed to the trucks at Charlie's place. Paul took his group to the tunnel area, and Tommy took Wendy and Frank to the old road. Once everyone was accounted for, the rest left for the bunker area, all except Joe's and Ron's sons who did not want to drive the armored vehicle during daylight. They were to leave just after dark. The two trucks carrying the people who would be at the gate were not going to drive all the way up the hill, but would drive part way up and be hidden in the woods, facing town, so they could exit quickly and be ready to move at a moment's notice.

They decided that the barber's son, Peter, would take shelter in the woods opposite the armory, but he would not give himself away because he would later stay with the bunker group to find out what he could about their plans and the event.

It was still light, and Paul and his crew were already in place close to the fence on the hill. They had located all four of the guards. Tommy and his group were stationed near the road and could see the guards there.

The individuals near the gate were deep in the woods and ready to move close when it got dark. As the light slowly gave way to nightfall, the people near the gate had to adjust to the light from the towers and move slowly and quietly into positions where they had clear sight lines to the towers, yet were not in view by the guards. At the adjusted angle from the tower, they could see the four guards who stood out behind a low wall and the two on the ground.

At the last light, the armored vehicle roared out of the woods and headed to the bunker. At 10:39 p.m., it was in place.

The group near the gate was in position. All was ready. Now everyone had to wait until the signal would be given. They were to watch and report on any out-of-the-ordinary movements. Joe thought they had several hours to wait. He wanted to make sure that Bates would retire for the evening. They knew from several reports that he worked late into the night, but he would often take a break for several hours. Joe counted on this, and figured they had some wait time.

Most of the crew knew they had to wait, so many brought portable foldable chairs with them. They could rest and even nap as others watched. By 2:00 a.m. Joe looked at Ron. They were both getting the same vibe. Were they ready?

They waited a while longer and at 2:45 a.m., they wanted to send the initial warning. The only problem was that only one guard in the left tower was visible. Where was the other one? Was he sleeping? They could clearly see the two guards on the ground and the two in the right tower. They had to wait. Joe was certain that Bates was asleep by now, so he was ready if the guard showed. Then, there he was. The second guard popped up. Joe sent this message:

Phase One: READY!

Then a few minutes later, Joe felt the time was right, and he texted—

BEGIN!

The two guards in each tower were taken down at the same time. Ron and Shanice got the guards on the ground. Joette was ready to send an arrow wherever needed, but none of the guards moved. Phase one was complete. Joe texted:

SUCCESS.

That was the signal for the armored vehicle to move as quietly as it could up the hill. Joe and Ron sprinted to the gate and cut the chain with huge bolt cutters. The gates swung open. The others checked on the six bodies of the guards. Joette and Sarah and two of the sentries climbed the two towers and turned the machine guns toward the barracks. Then the rest of the group made a firing line facing the barracks, and the vehicle swung into the gates, backed up a bit toward the woods, and moved forward.

The doors were breached in an instant. It made a loud noise, but it was far enough from the barracks so that it probably did not create much concern. Four men sprinted into the bunker. Bates was shocked and standing next to the computers. He ran for his weapon, but they had him on the ground and tied and gagged in no time.

Joe sent...

BREACHED!

On the hill, Paul heard the noise. It was quite muffled, but he noticed two of the guards inside the gate nearest the bunker turn and look. They had heard the ramming of the doors. They quickly huddled, and then one moved toward the path to the bunker. Paul did not want to take him out where the other guard could see, so he moved down the fence close to where he was headed. When the guard was out of sight of the other guard, Paul let him have it.

Tommy knew what was happening and was ready for when the bunker was breached. He thought the sound might alert the guards. Yet, as he and his companions waited, they heard very little. There was a muffled sound, but nothing more. The two guards turned their heads, but they did nothing.

The sentries threw Bates into the armored vehicle. Ron's and Joe's sons grabbed as much tech equipment as they could and put it inside the vehicle, too. Charlie wanted Joe to check the bunker for his military equipment. Joe opened the large door. It was completely empty except for one jeep, several trucks, a few assault rifles, some military clothes, and a few boxes of ammo. That was it. Charlie would not be happy. Joe figured the rest of Charlie's equipment must be in the armory—or gone.

Peter came out of the darkness and met with Joe and Ron. "You should get out quickly, I heard some rumblings from the barracks—not sure what it was. Get your people out."

Joe said, "Got it. We're out of here." He texted.

WITHDRAW.

Shanice drove off and the others moved to the trucks. On the hill, Paul had his group hold their ground until he heard that all were safely gone. Tommy did the same. Then some firing started. It came from the barracks near the armory. Someone was shooting. Peter ran for cover and waited, hoping all would escape. The person shooting had awakened the troops in the barracks, and they began to file out quickly. Peter saw someone with an assault rifle. It was Bill. Peter fired a few shots near the ground to scare him off. Bill bit the dust and lay there quietly. Peter bolted through the woods to the back of the barracks where he hid.

On the hill the two guards on the road and the three that were left on the hill headed for the base once they heard shots.

Tommy could not see what was going on at the bunker, nor could Paul. They had waited for a message. Their phones buzzed. Joe told Tommy all were safe and to leave quietly and meet at the hideout. Ron gave the same message to Paul. At the order from Joe and Ron, those by the gate all headed quickly for the trucks and were loaded and moving in no time, and Paul's and Tommy's groups headed out of their positions.

Peter snuck around the barracks and came up behind. Several men had acquired their weapons and were headed toward Bill and the gate. Peter joined in.

One of the trainers was there with several armed troops that moved close to the bunker. They saw the missing doors and entered. When they saw the mess and all the missing computers, they panicked. Then they noticed the dead troops. The head trainer exclaimed, "What the hell! We need to call the boss!"

The other trainer replied, "How? We don't know who he is, and we don't have any equipment."

The head trainer had come from a base in California. "I know someone out west who can help. I'll give him a call."

CHAPTER 88

The Hideout, June 7, that morning around 5:00 a.m.
Joe arrived at the hideout with everyone. He thought how often does a plan go so well? Not sure what we did right, but it worked. He did have to check with Paul and Tommy to make sure they had no trouble. They came flying into the hideout, wanting to know the results. They reported what they had heard and seen, and Paul mentioned that one guard was taken out. Joe could not be prouder of all of his people. They decided to count the people to make sure everyone was back. They were.

The only concern was Peter, and Ron walked to the barber and asked, "Any word from Peter?"

"None yet," he replied.

"Let us know as soon as you hear anything."

"For sure," the barber said.

"Now we need to get some information out of Bates and his computer system." Ron went out to help bring in the equipment they had taken.

As he turned to leave, Shanice walked in the door with a monitor, followed by Ron, Jr. with a computer and Joe's son with another one. A few others walked in with cords, monitors, printers, and everything else they had confiscated. Joe's and Ron's sons had the equipment together quite fast and were working to find out what they could.

Joe and Ron had Bates in the back room—hands and feet tied, blindfolded, and gagged. They also had him tied to an old, very heavy bed frame. Once they took off the gag, Bates went crazy.

"How can you two be alive? Vince killed you, or did that loser screw up again? He must have. I can't believe this!" Bates went on for some time. They tried to wait until he had calmed down, but he just kept ranting about Vince—and about how his boss is going to eliminate him now.

They began interrogating him. They needed his access code, and they were working on him when Ron, Jr. came in and said he had gained access, no problem.

Bates was visibly upset. He kicked and grunted and moaned, but to no avail.

"Find out what you can. We'll work on him to get some answers. Let me know if you find anything."

It was just after 8:00 a.m. when Joe was awakened. Ron was on watch with the captive. Bates had finally fallen asleep after fuming for hours.

Joe jumped up when he heard Ron's son call. Ron walked over to him. Joette and Shanice awoke too and were curious to know if he had found anything.

Ron, Jr. spoke, "We've got some really important stuff. I don't think we need him. Look what I found. I made some copies."

Joe scanned the information that was on the paper. It was a map of the White House and plans to take it, eliminate many members of congress, and take over the presidency. There was evidence of a huge number of troops in forty-nine of the fifty states. Each state had a list of people that would be taken, including all the state governors and many of the key people in each branch of the state governments.

Ron, Jr. added, "They have elite groups that will eventually shadow the governors in each state, and when given the signal, the governors would be taken, but some simply said—eliminate."

Ron and Joe had suspected nothing less. They always knew the event was a plan for something very big, but this was beyond the scope of anyone's thinking. Ron said, "Who was it that said great civilizations are not conquered from without, but they die from within?"

Ron, Jr. continued. "Not sure, but there's more. This is a main base, and they were preparing men to spread out throughout the Midwest: Michigan, Wisconsin, Minnesota, North Dakota, South Dakota, Iowa, Illinois, Nebraska, and Indiana. The other main bases are in California, Texas, Montana, Tennessee, Florida, and New York. All the states except Hawaii were divided among them.

Ron, Jr. took a deep breath. He was filled with emotion as he kept describing his findings. "Look at these dates. It says January 6, 2024 as a good day to complete the coup, but someone else has listed January 6, 2025 as a better time since they could slide their man right into the presidency and suppress the election results. They plan to have an organized takeover of the federal government, and they have trained hundreds of men to infiltrate and then storm the capitol."

Joe said, "This fits right in with what Loretta, Ann's friend, was saying earlier this week. I need to contact Loretta and see if she can get the Governor's and the President's ears for us."

Ron agreed. "We need to find out what she can do to facilitate us getting this information to the right people. In the wrong hands, this will go nowhere."

Joe pulled out his phone and called Loretta. It rang several times before she picked up. "Hello, Loretta?"

"This is Loretta. Is this Joe?"

"Yes. Got some key information for you, but first, have you found Ann?"

"Nothing yet, but the two agents who were helping me are with me, and we've gotten a couple of good leads. It seems that she wasn't taken to Cheboygan, but Ann was kept in Lansing for some reason, so we are trying to find her right now. Our boss had her kept here. We have a few leads and hope to have her soon. We also had our boss picked up. The Governor has been a big help. We also have a young guy we kidnapped who was part of the insurgence here. We're working on him to find out more about their plans. I'm trying to get to the Governor's place, but so far it has been tricky even with her help. What information do you have?"

"Let me tell you." Joe gave Loretta as much of the information as he could. They decided that Joe would have two of his trusted people take Bates to Lansing and deliver him to Loretta and the Governor.

Loretta said, "Getting him here should really help us. I'll get this information to the Governor as soon as I can. We need to inform the President too. We can take these people down if we can get his help."

"Make sure you tell them that there are seven of these bases around the country."

"Right."

"Great. That'll work. Time to destroy this organization!"

In Colewin at the hideout, everyone was excited that the raid had gone so well. They all felt they had succeeded. Matt was proud. "We've begun. We're definitely going to take these extremists down."

Joe agreed, "This is the first step. We put some hurt into the outfit here. We'll continue to fight until they're defeated. We have some help now too. Loretta says she has talked to the Governor, and the President will be informed."

Ron was happy to hear what Joe had to say. He said, "Well, we tried to destroy this organization from the top down—and that didn't work. This time we went from the bottom up. I hope this is the answer."

"We can only keep moving forward and doing what we can to end this insurgence."

As Joe and Ron discussed what Joe had just heard from Loretta, the barber and his wife walked in with Paul and Sarah. The barber had received a text from his son, Peter, who was still at the base, and he said the place was total chaos. No one really knew who was in charge now, although the one trainer from California was trying to step in and be the leader.

Joe was confident they had done something significant. He turned to Ron and Matt and said, "We've put a scare into the troops at the bunker. They should be toned down for a while. Hopefully, this puts a chink in the armor—at least here. Remember, there are six other bases."

Joe decided that everyone should be careful, so he set up sentries around the hideout. Everyone decided to stay in place at the hideout while they worked with Loretta in Lansing to find out what the next steps should be. Joe sat back and took a long breath. "What's next, Ron?"

"Not sure. We need to be vigilant though. If we can notify the right people, we'll have a good chance to end this mess. We also need to inform others of what they're trying to do. We need people on our side who can see the violence, lies, and deceit that these people are trying to spread in order to get complete power."

Joe said, "I agree. Unfortunately, look what we had to do to try to create a change. What have they turned all of us into? This Machiavellian world—all these cunning and unscrupulous actions—has got to end. They want to rule with fear and violence. I can't agree with that. Nobody can be indifferent any longer, and ignore what's going on here."

"Right. Their event will be fear-based, I'm sure."

Ron added, "Violence-based for sure. Vigilance is the only answer. That'll keep us safe. Let's stay on it."

Joe looked around the room. Several of the people had entered the cabin, along with Joette, Shanice, and Sarah who were already there, so Joe proposed a toast. "Well, everyone, I don't have anything other than some good wine, but I think we should have a toast."

Joette looked at Joe and said, "Really? We don't have enough glasses." She apologized, went to the cabinet, and pulled out several coffee cups, some glasses, and some paper cups. "These will have to do." She poured wine into each one, enough for everyone.

Joe took a glass and said, "Salute!" He raised it to the sky. "To all the others who came before us to call this country home."

They all repeated "Salute!" They looked at each other and quietly lifted their glasses and drank to victory, democracy, and the future.

www.ingramcontent.com/pod-product-compliance
Lightning Source LLC
Chambersburg PA
CBHW071939210726
48293CB00001BA/253